I0778719

I would like to dedicate this book to late aunt DD and Grandma Kathrine

Table of Contents

PROLOGUE

I strike down the creature with one swift motion, my blade cleaving through its thick, grotesque hide. The beast lets out a guttural scream before crumpling to the cold stone floor. Its body twitches once, twice, then goes still. I watch it for a moment, waiting, listening for any signs of movement. But there's nothing. The dark corridors of the Abyssal Dungeon are silent once more, the silence broken only by my shallow breaths and the faint hum of the dungeon itself. It always hums, the walls vibrating with an ancient energy wafting all through the corners of the dungeon.

My hand grips the hilt of the blade tightly, knuckles white against the steel. The blood of the creature pools beneath me, a dark stain against the cold gray stone. I watch it drip and bubble, becoming an even bigger puddle.

Red.

I step back, wiping the blade clean on my cloak before sheathing it. The flickering light from a distant, unseen source casts long, twisted shadows across the corridor, but I don't let it distract me. The walls are jagged and uneven here, slick with

moisture that catches the faint light in odd, unsettling ways. The dungeon seems alive—breathing, pulsing, shifting, evolving. I've learned to ignore the uncanny sensation, choosing to get used to it as there's nothing, I could do about it.

I turn away from the monster's body, my boots clicking against the stone floor. The path ahead is just as dark as the one behind me, the way forward as uncertain as every step I've taken before. There are always more monsters, more traps, more challenges. This place is infinite, and yet, I've wandered it for as long as I can remember. I know no other world, no other existence. The Abyssal Dungeon is everything to me, and in return, it has made me everything I am.

I pause and glance at my reflection in a patch of dark water, the surface still, like glass. My dark hair falls around my shoulders in tangled strands, long and unkempt. It's not something I concern myself with, though it has its uses in battle—shrouding my movements, hiding my face. My eyes are dark, murky pools of obsidian, without an ounce of humanity left in them. They're eyes that have seen the worst of the dungeon, that has witnessed its countless horrors and still kept going.

My hand moves up, tracing lightly at the jagged scar across my right eye. It's a permanent reminder of the price I've paid for this place. A deep cut, once caused by a monstrous claw, that I never bothered to heal. I wear it like a badge of honor, a symbol of survival. I had it at quite a young age, and it's what helped me push forward, despite it all, and get back my revenge by killing the Oglord. It doesn't hurt anymore—nothing in the dungeon hurts anymore, not in the way it used to. Over time, pain becomes something you ignore. You learn to forget it.

I don't remember a time when I didn't have this scar. I don't remember a time when I wasn't in the Abyssal Dungeon. The dungeon is my home, my world, my only reality. There was never a "before." It was just me and Sokh. Sokh, my mentor, my guide, the only other constant in this place. An entity older than I can even imagine, so wise, yet playful, holding a lot of wisdom and knowledge in him.

Sokh's voice echoes in the back of my mind, like a distant, haunting melody. I never question Sokh. I don't need to. I trust it, in the way that you trust the air to fill your lungs, the ground beneath your feet to support you. Sokh is as much a part of this place as the shadows themselves.

I pass a set of old, rusted bars on my left, an old prison cell long abandoned. I wonder who was once trapped there, and what kind of monster or person might have called this place home before it was left to rot. I can't say I'm curious, but the question still lingers.

I've killed monsters, creatures so twisted and terrifying that even their names would chill the bones of anyone who had the misfortune of hearing them. But I've also fought alongside the strange, half-forgotten remnants of the dungeon's past—beasts that have been twisted and changed by the same force that makes the dungeon what it is. Some are more animal than monster, their primal instincts driving them forward.

But I don't have time to think about that now. The dungeon is shifting again. The air feels thicker, and heavier now. Something is coming. I don't know what it is, but I feel it.

I pull my cloak tighter around me, adjusting the straps on my gear, adjusting the weight of the weapons at my sides. My hand instinctively reaches for the hilt of my sword, my fingers brushing against the worn leather grip. There's a flicker of movement ahead, something I can't quite make out in the dark.

I stop and listen. The air is still, but the silence feels heavier now. The dungeon is watching.

Then, a sound—a faint scraping, like claws on stone—comes from the shadows ahead. I tense. It's too quiet, too deliberate.

Something is coming.

My body moves without thinking, my senses honed from years of navigating this dark, unforgiving world. I draw my blade and step forward, ready for whatever emerges from the darkness.

***

I drag the creature's body into the chamber, the damp air of the dungeon growing heavier with each step. Its limbs scrape against the cold stone floor, the sound like a distant grinding noise in the endless stillness of the Dungeon. The beast's blood, thick and dark, stains the floor as I haul it toward the center of the chamber.

"Back again, I see," Sokh's voice calls out to me, echoing from the shadows. It's low and smooth, warm and friendly.

I stop in my tracks, letting the creature's body fall to the stone with a soft thud. There's no hurry in my movements as I stand up and glance around, letting my gaze settle on the figure that waits for me.

Sokh is a presence more than a figure, really. But if I had to describe him, it would be a tall silhouette with edges that flicker in and out of existence, almost like smoke. His form is ever-changing, always shifting. There's an unsettling quality to him— his power is ancient, and it thrums in the air like the hum of a distant storm. But despite the fact that he's far from human, there's something comforting in the way he speaks to me, in the way he guides me.

"Got another one, huh?" Sokh's voice sounds a little amused now, teasing like he's chuckling to himself. "You sure know how to pick 'em, Crilt."

I roll my eyes. "It's a monster, Sokh. It doesn't need to be picked. They attack, and I kill." I wipe my hands on my cloak, brushing off some of the grime that clings to them. My movements are slow, and deliberate, as I make my way toward Sokh.

"I know, I know," Sokh replies with a soft sigh, but his tone is affectionate. "Can't you take a joke, Crilt?"

I raise a brow. "No,"

"No fun. You could let loose for a bit, you know?"

I stand there, unmoving for a moment, watching the beast's body spill its blood onto the stone floor. I think about what Sokh said, but I just can't. The dungeon is about survival. It's always been about survival. You kill, you eat, you evolve. It's simple. The rules are simple.

"I'm fine," I reply, my voice low. "It's just another monster. Just another part of the cycle."

Sokh's voice softens. "You say that like it's nothing." His words puzzle me. It always sounds like he knows something regarding me coming ahead. And I don't know how to feel about that.

I glance over at the creature again, trying to ignore the nagging feeling in my chest. Sokh has a way of getting under my skin, of making me question even the slightest things. I worry about paranoia.

"Should we eat it?" I ask, dragging the monster closer to Sokh. "Or use it for something else?"

"Ah," Sokh exclaims. "You've got a good eye for these things, Crilt. It's a decent specimen, though a bit tougher than I'd like. I'd say we could get a good meal out of it, or maybe use its parts for medicine. You know, a little bit of both wouldn't hurt."

I nod, not really thinking much of it. Eating, making potions, or using body parts for weapons, is just the usual routine. Survival. Evolving. Enduring.

I crouch next to the creature's body and begin pulling at its hide, my fingers working with practiced ease. I don't look at Sokh, but I can feel his eyes on me, tracking my every movement.

"So, how far did you explore the dungeon today?" Sokh asks.

"Not too far," I answer, slicing through the creature's tough hide. "At least, not as far as I used to."

"Given up?"

I don't respond to that, focusing on the task at hand. What Sokh's referring to, is the goal I made several years ago, about trying to escape the dungeon. I had thought that perhaps, there's a secret exit somewhere, but after some time, I discovered that I was just being naïve and hopeful in such a bleak world.

The skin around my scar tingles. Never again.

"You know," Sokh continues, his tone shifting again, "Your idea is not as bad as you think it is,"

I pause mid-slice, my hand hovering over the creature's exposed flesh. I look up at Sokh, my brow furrowed. "What do you mean?"

Sokh doesn't answer immediately. Instead, I feel a shift in the air around us, a subtle change in the dungeon's hum. It's as if the walls themselves are reacting to Sokh's words.

"You're special, Crilt," Sokh says, his voice suddenly serious, more solemn than it's been. "That's a part of you that you've always known. But there's more to it than that. The dungeon—this dungeon—it's not just a place where you fight and survive. It's a place where you evolve. And I've been guiding you all these years to help you understand that."

I feel a faint twinge of unease in the pit of my stomach, but I don't let it show. I've heard Sokh speak of my demon blood before, but it's always been in passing. I never thought it was something I needed to worry about. "Yes, and I greatly appreciate your help, but what does that have to do with anything? Or my so-called plan?"

Sokh smiles sadly. "I've seen a lot of creatures, a lot of people like you down here with me, Crilt. It's just a shame,"

I glance up at Sokh, utterly floored by all his riddles. "What are you trying to say?"

"Never mind me, Crilt. Don't listen to an old man's ramblings," he says instead, snapping back to normal.

My hand tightens around the creature's flesh, my fingers sinking into its tough hide. I look at Sokh, studying him, but I don't speak. Why does this make me feel so uneasy like something bad is about to happen?

I stare at him for a long moment, the silence stretching between us. Sokh's words hang in the air, heavy with meaning, deep with tension and I can feel the weight of them pressing down on me. It's as if the dungeon itself is holding its breath, waiting for me to speak.

Finally, I speak. "I'll get a fire started,"

I stand up, setting the tough skin aside. Sokh's presence flickers, and for a moment, I almost think I see a smile form on the edges of his shadowy features.

His words echo in my head as I start the fire, over and over, refusing to settle, like whispers in the dark. What does he mean? What is he trying to tell me? Sokh doesn't speak without reasoning and meaning behind his words.

"Sokh, I—"

He suddenly yawns. "Oh, wow. This old man needs to get some rest," he says, interrupting me.

I close my mouth shut and purse my lips. "Okay. Good night, Sokh,"

"Good night, Crilt," I can hear the smile in his voice.

I sit on the edge of the stone slab, my back against the cold, damp wall. My hands are trembling, but I don't know if it's from the chilling atmosphere of this place or from the strange, unsettling feelings stirring inside me. My thoughts are swirling, a storm of confusion and uncertainty. For as long as I can remember, Sokh has been my guide. The only one who ever spoke to me with any real authority, the one who taught me the three rules of this labyrinth—survive, evolve, endure.

I lay down, staring at the ceiling. The stone above me feels cold, almost like it's pressing down on me. My mind refuses to quiet. I try to close my eyes and sleep, but the images of the outside world—the world I know nothing about—creep into my thoughts.

I don't know what to think anymore.

***

When I wake up, the weight of the previous night's confusion still presses on me. The darkness of the dungeon surrounds me as it always has. The dim, flickering lights from the torches along the walls do little to dispel the gloom, but I've long since stopped noticing. The air is thick with the scent of damp stone and ancient decay. Familiar. Comforting in a way. I push myself to my feet and stretch my limbs, working out the stiffness from sleeping in this cold, uncomfortable place. The shadows seem to shift as I move, as if the dungeon itself is alive, watching me.

I take a deep breath and remind myself of my purpose. I need to hunt.

I grab my sword and head out into the dungeon, stepping carefully over the jagged rocks and uneven terrain. The air is still, as it always is in the deeper parts of the dungeon. I'm used to this silence. It's both comforting and unnerving. There's always something lurking, always something waiting to strike, but I've learned how to move quietly, how to sense the presence of danger before it's too late.

I make my way toward my usual hunting ground, a labyrinthine section of the dungeon filled with monsters I've learned to track. The monsters here are tough, and dangerous, but not impossible to deal with. They're a challenge, and I've grown strong because of them. I know this place like the back of my hand, every twist and turn, every hidden crevice where creatures hide. It's my territory.

As I return back to the cave, the strange emptiness of the dungeon deepens. It feels colder, more oppressive. Something is off, but I can't place it. I quicken my pace, moving through the narrow passageways with practiced ease. But when I reach the spot where Sokh usually waits for me, I stop dead in my tracks.

There's nothing.

No sign of Sokh. No presence. Not even a faint whisper of his energy. Just the quiet, foreboding silence of the dungeon.

My heart skips a beat, and I instinctively reach for my blade, though I know there's no immediate danger. I scan the area, every corner, every shadow. I've never felt so exposed in this place before. I wait, listening. The faint sounds of the dungeon—footsteps in the distance, distant growls, the shifting of stone—are still there, but Sokh's presence is absent. Completely gone.

I can feel it in my bones, this strange unease. It's as though the dungeon itself is holding its breath, waiting. But there is no Sokh. He is always here. He never leaves without telling me.

I step forward, cautiously, as though any movement might provoke something. My breath feels shallow as I move deeper into the area, but I find nothing. The place is barren. The stone walls, the sharp edges, the creeping shadows—they all look the same, yet there is a sense of wrongness here that rattles me to the core.

My mind races, trying to piece together the puzzle. Sokh has never acted like this before. What does this mean? What does Sokh's disappearance mean for me? Is this some kind of test? Or is it something more? I can't afford to sit here and waste time. I need to find him.

My thoughts spiral, but they're broken by the faintest sound—a scraping, almost imperceptible, like something shifting just beyond my vision. I freeze, instinctively lowering myself into a crouch. My eyes dart around, scanning the darkness for any sign of movement, any hint of danger. But the silence is deafening. The scrape comes again, but this time, it's closer.

I narrow my eyes, readying my weapon. My breath is shallow now, each inhale feeling heavy. There's something in the shadows. Something moving, just out of sight.

And then it stops.

For a moment, I think I've imagined it. But the tension in the air is unmistakable. I start moving through the twisting corridors, my footsteps echoing in the otherwise still air. The deeper I go, the more oppressive the atmosphere becomes. The walls feel closer, and the darkness seems thicker, suffocating.

Hours pass, but I don't stop. I can't. I have to keep going. My legs ache, my chest tightens with each breath, but I push on. There's no time to rest, no time to hesitate. I need to find Sokh.

I follow the familiar path, down twisting passages, through chambers filled with remnants of past battles. The monsters are fewer here, but that only makes the silence more unsettling. I don't encounter anything alive in these depths, not a single growl or rustle of fur.

Then, finally, after what feels like an eternity, I see something. A narrow passageway I don't recognize, one that seems to pulse with an energy I can't explain. It's faint at first, a subtle shift in the air, but it draws me in as if the dungeon is beckoning me forward.

I don't hesitate. I step into the passage, my hand gripping the hilt of my weapon. The walls here are different, covered in strange carvings, and markings that I've never seen before. They seem to pulse with an odd, almost sentient energy, but they're unfamiliar. No part of this dungeon has looked like this. I've spent years memorizing every inch, but this...this is something entirely new.

I walk deeper, my senses heightened. I can feel the energy in the air, almost like a hum beneath my skin. The deeper I go, the stronger it becomes, and I can feel, without a doubt, that Sokh is close. This part of the dungeon is unfamiliar, but it's not a random place. He's been here before, and I know that if I keep going, I will find him.

And then, I do.

I round a final corner, and there he is. Sokh.

He stands in front of a large stone wall, his back turned to me, as always, his posture as imposing as ever. The wall itself is covered in hundreds of symbols, none of which I recognize. They twist and curl in complex patterns, some overlapping, others isolated in small clusters. The air is thick around them, as though they carry weight—real, palpable weight. They seem alive, moving, shifting under my gaze.

I stop a few paces away, unsure of what to do. Sokh hasn't noticed me yet. He remains focused, studying the wall as if he's in a trance. I swallow hard, trying to steady myself. The sight of him here, in this unfamiliar place, is both awe-inspiring and terrifying. I've never seen him like this before. He is so deeply absorbed in whatever it is that he's doing that he doesn't even seem to notice me.

I take a cautious step forward. "Sokh?" My voice is hoarse, quieter than I intended, but it seems to break the silence in the air.

He doesn't respond immediately. Instead, he tilts his head slightly, as if he's aware of my presence but chooses not to acknowledge it right away. Then, with deliberate slowness, he turns toward me. His eyes gleam in the dim light, an expression I can't quite read on his face.

For a long moment, neither of us speaks. The tension between us is thick. I can feel the weight of his silence pressing down on me. His eyes lock onto mine, studying me with that same inscrutable gaze that has always made me feel so small, without him meaning to. But today, it's different. There's something distant in his eyes, something far away. It's as if he's looking at me, but not really seeing me. Like he's seeing something else entirely.

I can't take it any longer. "Where have you been?" The words slip out, a desperate need for answers clawing at my throat. I hate acting so attached and whiny, but Sokh has been such a constant in my life, that I can't help it. "Why...why are you here?"

Sokh's lips curl into the faintest of smiles. There's a flicker of something in his eyes, something almost amused, but it's gone before I can analyze it.

He doesn't answer, his gaze drifting back to the wall. The symbols shift, glowing faintly in the dim light, as though they are reacting to him. His fingers brush lightly against the surface, tracing one of the patterns with slow, deliberate movements.

I feel a surge of frustration. "Sokh, please, stop with all this…shenanigans and just answer me. Why are you here? Is this a joke?"

The silence stretches between us, thick and suffocating. Sokh doesn't move, and doesn't respond. His smile deepens, but there's no warmth in it. It's like he's hiding something—something I'm not meant to understand, something I'm not meant to know.

Finally, after what feels like an eternity, he speaks, his voice low and deliberate. "I can't give you all the answers, Crilt,"

I feel my chest tighten at his words. "What do you mean? What are you talking about? You always have answers."

He turns his head back toward me, his eyes narrowing slightly. "For guidance, yes. But there are some things... some things that I cannot explain. Not yet."

I don't understand. My mind is racing, trying to piece together his riddles. My frustration grows, but I suppress it, clenching my fists at my sides.

Sokh looks at the wall again, almost absently. "You have to find those answers yourself, Crilt."

"Excuse me?" My voice cracks with disbelief. "What does that mean? I don't understand. Why are you leaving me in the dark? I need to know what's going on."

Sokh's gaze shifts back to me, the amusement in his eyes now tinged with something else—something akin to remorse, something I can't place. "The dungeon has its own plans, Crilt. And you have your own path to follow. This," he gestures vaguely at the wall, the symbols, "is not for you. Not yet. You will understand when the time comes."

I take a step closer, desperation overtaking my calm. "Sokh, let's just go back, okay? You're acting strange,"

Sokh remains silent for a long moment, his eyes never leaving mine. And then, finally, he speaks again, but his words are soft, almost like a whisper. "Because the time for guidance is over, Crilt. It's time for you to find your own way."

The words hit me like a blow. I had a feeling that he was leading to that, but hearing it aloud makes my heart shatter. The world feels like it's shifting beneath my feet, and I can't quite grasp the truth of it. "What do you mean, the time for guidance is over? Sokh?"

Sokh's smile deepens. "You've learned the rules of survival, Crilt. Now you must learn the rules of the world."

I take a step back, my mind racing, my heart pounding. His words make no sense. None of this makes sense. My hands tremble, my breath shallow, suffocatingly so.

I glance at the symbols on the wall above him, the mysterious markings that I cannot comprehend. They seem to pulse with a strange energy, as though they are somehow alive, yet there is no understanding behind them.

Sokh, the one constant in my existence, has been here all along, guiding me through it all since I was a child. He has always been my protector, and my teacher. And now…now, he is telling me that it's time for me to find my own way?

I can't bear it. The thought of losing him, of being left to navigate this vast, hostile dungeon on my own, is too much. I have no answers. I have no knowledge of the world beyond this place.

I can't do this without him.

"Sokh!" I call, my voice cracking with desperation. "You can't just leave me here. I… I don't understand! I need you!"

His smile falters for a brief moment, but he says nothing. He doesn't even look at me. Instead, he reaches out and brushes a hand over the markings on the wall, his touch sending a ripple through the air. The symbols flare with an ethereal glow, brighter than before, and the air becomes charged with an unsettling energy.

For a moment, I feel as though the world around me is shifting, pulling away from me, and I stagger back, feeling like the ground beneath my feet is no longer stable. A wave of panic surges through me, and I move forward instinctively, desperate to get him back, to return to some semblance of normalcy. I've never felt so alone in all my life.

"Sokh!" I try again, my voice rising in urgency. "Please! What is happening? Where are you going?"

Sokh remains silent, his focus still entirely on the wall before him. It's as if I don't even exist. My heart races in my chest, and I feel the panic building within me. I take another step forward, reaching out, my fingers trembling as I get closer to him. I need to pull him back. I need him here. Without him, I'll be lost forever.

But as I move to grab him, something happens that I can't comprehend.

Sokh's form shimmers, and flickers—like a mirage in the desert. My hand passes right through him as if he's made of smoke or shadow. For an instant, I feel the coldness of his presence, a fleeting sensation that vanishes before I can grasp it. He disappears before my eyes, just like that.

One moment, he's standing before me, and the next, there's nothing.

The shock hits me like a blow to the chest. My breath catches in my throat as I stagger backward, my knees shaking. "No! Sokh!" I shout, my voice a mix of panic and disbelief.

But there's no answer.

The empty silence presses down on me, heavier than before. My heart is hammering in my chest, my mind reeling. This is impossible. Sokh can't just vanish like that. He's… he's always been here, always been my guide, my anchor in this dungeon. How can he be gone? Where did he go? Why would he leave me alone, like this, in the depths of this labyrinth?

I stand there for what feels like an eternity, my mind spinning in circles, trying to make sense of what just happened. It's like the world itself is shifting, moving beyond my control. I don't know what to do. The panic rises in my chest, threatening to overwhelm me. My hands are trembling, and I feel like I'm going to collapse, but I can't—no, I won't—let myself break. Not now.

Get a hold of yourself, Crilt.

I try to steady my breath and force myself to think. This isn't like before. Sokh has never left me without a word. His disappearance is like a door slamming shut, leaving me in the dark, alone.

Just as the grief and sorrow threaten to swallow me whole, a sound cuts through the silence—a low, rhythmic thud.

My head snaps up, and instinctively, I reach for my weapon, my fingers closing around the cold bone hilt. I know that sound. The unmistakable sound of a creature's footfall. Something is moving, approaching, and the air grows heavy with the scent of danger.

My mind is still reeling, still trying to process Sokh's disappearance, but the noise shakes me out of my reverie. I can't afford to lose focus or else I'll get killed. The dungeon has never stopped being dangerous, and if I'm going to survive, I need to be alert.

The dungeon feels different now. Its walls seem to pulse with a new kind of energy, an unfamiliar energy that sets my nerves on edge. Every footstep echoes, and every creaking stone feels amplified. The sound of the creature's footsteps grows louder, and closer.

I don't have to turn around to know it's too late to run.

A hydra emerges from the darkness with a terrifying slowness, its massive form unfolding like a nightmare given flesh. The first head hisses, a deep, guttural growl vibrating in its throat, as its many eyes focus on me. The other heads follow suit, their mouths opening, revealing rows of gleaming, sharp teeth.

I swallow, my throat dry, and my hand grips the hilt of my weapon tighter. It feels small in my hand, insignificant against such a creature.

The hydra's heads begin to hiss, each one slithering independently but in harmony, like snakes on the hunt. Its body, thick and impossibly long, coils, and stretches, creating an intimidating wave of scale and muscle. I don't even know where to start. There are too many heads, too many dangers.

It roars, the sound deafening. The cavern seems to vibrate, and for a second, I almost forget to breathe. The force of it rattles my teeth, and the ground beneath my feet trembles.

The first head lunges toward me—its fangs wide and dripping venom. The speed is unbelievable. I dive to the side, just barely avoiding the snap of its jaws, but the wind from its strike sends me stumbling. The second head follows almost instantly, its mouth snapping inches from my face, but I manage to dodge again, adrenaline pushing me beyond my limits. I'm not sure how much longer I can keep this up.

I get to my feet, and before I even think about attacking, the hydra moves again. This time, its claws swipe down toward me, raking through the air with a terrible hiss. I barely dodge, the tips of its claws grazing my arm. A sharp pain shoots through my shoulder, and I stagger back, my footing unsure. Blood spills from the shallow gash, but I don't have time to register it. I'm already on the defensive.

The hydra's heads are relentless, each one moving at a speed that defies logic. The next head darts in from my left, and I swing my blade with all the force I can muster, hoping to land a strike. The edge of my sword catches the hydra's scales, but it doesn't pierce. The creature's hide is thick—impenetrable. It barely slows down, its mouth snapping at me again, forcing me to step back, heart hammering in my chest.

I can feel my fatigue building. I've fought before—survived before—but this…I've never encountered a creature this powerful. The hydra doesn't stop. Its jaws keep coming, and it's too fast, too powerful. The cavern seems to close in around me with each failed dodge.

The hydra's roar shakes me to the core, and I'm losing myself in the chaos of it all. It doesn't matter how many heads I dodge or cut down—they always grow back, faster than I can deal with them. And I know, if I don't do something soon, I'm going to be overwhelmed.

I'm not sure if I can survive this fight.

I take a breath, focusing on survival. My blade feels heavier, but my grip is unwavering. I've come this far. I won't die in this dungeon, not like this.

Then, an opening.

The hydra lunges toward me once again, its mouth open and wide, but one of its heads, the one to my right, swings too far. Its maw snaps shut just inches from my shoulder, and in that brief moment, I see it: a weakness. Its side is exposed. The scales there aren't as thick as they should be.

I act without thinking.

I dive forward, aiming straight for that exposed spot, and my sword sinks deep into the hydra's side. There's a sickening sound—flesh splitting under the force of my strike—and the hydra lets out a deafening hiss, its body jerking back as it roars in pain.

The blow didn't kill it, but it staggered the beast. I'm not sure how long it will take before it recovers, but I can't stop now.

I push forward, slashing again, aiming for the other side. My body screams in protest, but I ignore it. I need to finish this. I can't stop. Not yet. The hydra recoils again, its heads pulling back for a moment as if to reassess me, and I take that chance.

The pain in my side is unbearable, but my vision clears with sheer determination. I swing my sword one more time, this time aiming for the nearest head. It strikes true, cutting through one of the hydra's many necks. The head falls, the body convulsing with a violent shudder as it crashes to the ground.

The hydra screeches, its body flailing in every direction. I've wounded it. I've actually wounded it.

But the beast isn't done.

Before I can even take another breath, the other heads snap toward me with renewed fury. The hydra, in its madness, thrashes harder than before, and one of its claws swings down like a battering ram. I barely manage to duck, but the claws catch the edge of my shoulder, tearing through my skin, the force of it nearly sending me to the ground. Blood pours from the wound, and I stagger, my legs barely holding me up.

The hydra is relentless, its many heads now coming at me in a frenzy, jaws snapping and claws swiping. I can't keep up. I'm exhausted. I'm bleeding. My vision is blurring at the edges. The dungeon seems to spin, the sounds of the hydra's roars muffling in my ears as I struggle to stay on my feet.

I stumble, my back slamming into the wall behind me, the rough stone scraping against my skin. There's no escape. The hydra is coming for me, and there's nothing left. My weapon feels heavier, and my arms are like lead. I don't know how much longer I can last.

I can't die here.

A scream rises in my throat, and with the last of my strength, I push off the wall, charging toward the hydra. It's not strategy anymore. It's desperation. It's rage. It's everything I've fought for. I bring my sword down with everything I have, and this time, it strikes true.

The blade sinks deep into the beast's heart.

The hydra howls, its many heads thrashing in agony, but the body falters. The heads start to slow, their venomous hisses turning into desperate screeches. The beast stumbles. It falls. And then, with a final shudder, it collapses to the ground, its massive body coming to a halt.

It's over.

I stand there for a moment, panting, blood pouring from my many wounds. The hydra's body twitches for a moment before it finally goes still. My legs feel like they're about to give out, and I don't know how much longer I can stay conscious. Blood pools at my feet, mixing with the dirt and grime of the dungeon floor.

I've killed it.

But I'm not sure if I can survive much longer.

I stumble back, leaning heavily against the wall, my vision swimming, the world fading. But before the darkness takes me, I can see an overwhelming light emanate from the marked wall behind me. The symbols all over begin to glow white, surrounding me. But the darkness is stronger.

I finally succumb to the sweet embrace of death, and everything goes black.

CHAPTER 1

The cold mud is the first thing I feel when my senses slowly begin to stir. It's thick and wet, sticking to my skin, and it pulls me back into the world in a way that is almost painful. My whole body is stiff, my wounds throb, and my limbs feel like they're made of stone. Every breath is a struggle—shallow and ragged like something inside me is breaking with each inhale. The warmth of blood and sweat clings to me, and I can barely keep my eyes open.

I try to move, but the world tilts and spins like a chaotic storm of confusion. My head is pounding, each throb sending another jolt of pain through my skull. There's a strange, unfamiliar smell in the air—a mix of wet earth and something else, something sharp.

I force my eyes open, but everything is blurry. I see shapes and vague outlines of what I think are people, but they're all distorted. For a moment, I wonder if I'm still in the dungeon if maybe this is just another twisted trick, another part of the labyrinth designed to break me. But the walls around me aren't made of stone. There are no torches lining the hallways. The air

doesn't feel like the suffocating weight of the dungeon. It's…
different.

I blink rapidly, trying to clear my vision, but it doesn't help.
The sounds around me don't help either. There are voices—too
many voices, shouting, yelling, panic in the air. I hear the sound of
feet hitting the ground, running, scattering. And then a sharp,
terrified shout slices through the air.

"Demon!"

I wince at the word, though I don't understand it
completely. Demon? My head is swimming, and I feel like I've
been pulled out of one reality and thrust into another. But I can't
think too clearly. The throbbing pain in my chest is blurring my
thoughts. The world around me starts to sharpen as I force myself
to focus. Slowly, I lift my head, struggling to keep it steady as I try
to make sense of what's happening.

When my gaze clears enough, I realize with growing horror
that I'm not in the dungeon anymore.

I'm outside.

Like, in the outside world. I can see open skies and everything. It's way too bright, way too colorful.

The realization hits me like a blow to the gut. I'm in some kind of open space, muddy ground beneath me, and scattered in every direction are *people*. They look…terrified. Their eyes are wide, staring at me like I'm something monstrous, their expressions twisted with fear and repulsion.

"Demon!" One of them screams again, pointing at me with trembling hands. And then, with a collective gasp, the group of people takes off in all directions. Some sprint, others stumble, their voices rising in a cacophony of panic.

I blink again, trying to make sense of it. I'm not in the dungeon. I'm not in Sokh's domain. I don't know where I am. The people keep screaming, and I don't know why.

I try to move, to push myself up, but my body protests. The pain in my side is unbearable, and I can feel the blood trickling down my leg. I can barely hold myself up, let alone stand. I pull my hands out of the muck and push them against the cold, wet ground beneath me, but they slip. The mud is thick, and my arms are too weak to support my body.

But then I hear a shout from someone braver than the rest. A voice calls out from the edge of the crowd, a gruff tone.

"Get away from it!"

And then, a rock comes flying through the air. It's small, but it strikes me square in the chest with a force that makes me wince. I stumble backward, shocked by the impact. Another rock follows, and then another. Each one strikes with painful precision.

"Demon!" someone shouts again, and I realize that they aren't just frightened—they just hate me. They fear me so much that they'll throw whatever they can to make me leave. My heart beats faster, confusion coursing through my veins. I don't understand why. If not injured, I'm bigger and far stronger than them. I have my sword strapped to my waist. I can easily kill them, so why?

I barely have time to react before more rocks come flying, one of them grazing my cheek and cutting into my skin. The sting of it is sharp, but it's nothing compared to the terror that fills me. My vision begins to blur again as the blood loss starts to catch up with me, but I fight it, struggling to make sense of everything around me.

The pain is overwhelming. Every muscle in my body feels like it's been torn apart. My vision wavers again, and I feel the horror pressing in on me, threatening to drown me.

I stagger to my feet, my legs unsteady, my head spinning, and as I do, the people scatter further. They scream, pointing at me as they flee, their eyes wide with terror. I don't know why they're making such a commotion over my appearance, but all I know is that I can't stay here.

With no other choice, I stumble forward, every movement bringing a fresh wave of agony. I move toward a nearby building, a large structure with walls that look like they're made of rough-hewn wood. It's the only thing that looks solid, and stable, in this world that is so strange to me. With one final effort, I make my way to the side of the building, feeling the rough texture of the wood under my fingers as I reach out to steady myself. I press my back against the wall, and for a moment, I just stand there, barely able to keep my eyes open.

Everything feels like it's slipping away.

The pain. The confusion. The fear. It's too much.

I slide down the wall, my legs no longer able to hold me up. I collapse into a sitting position, my back still resting against the cold, uneven surface. The world around me is a blur of color and sound, but it's fading fast. The people are still shouting from a distance, but their voices are muffled like I'm underwater. The mud beneath me is cold, and the blood that stains my clothes feels thick and sticky.

I try to breathe, but it's getting harder. The world around me feels like it's closing in, narrowing, and my body is giving out. I can feel the darkness creeping at the edges of my vision. It's a sensation I know too well. It's what happens when my body is too far gone, too broken to keep fighting.

I hear distant voices, but they don't make sense. The air around me is heavy, suffocating. I blink slowly, but everything's slipping. The darkness is just too much, and I'm too tired to fight it.

I can't stay awake.

I don't know how long I've been here, or how long I'll stay, but I know that I can't keep going. Not like this.

My eyes close, and the world goes silent.

I wake up slowly, my body aching from wounds that feel too fresh to be forgotten. My mind is sluggish, struggling to piece together the fragments of what happened. The pain isn't as sharp anymore, though I can still feel it—the dull throb of my cuts and bruises, the burning sting of blood drying on my skin.

I sit up, my head spinning as I do, and immediately regret the decision. A wave of dizziness crashes over me, and for a moment, I think I might pass out again. But I force myself to steady my breathing, gripping the edge of the bed to keep myself from falling back into the abyss. When the spinning fades, I take in my surroundings, trying to make sense of where I am.

The room is dimly lit. The only source of light comes from a small lantern on a wooden table across the room. Shadows cling to the walls, twisting in unnatural ways, making the place feel even more unfamiliar. The air smells faintly of herbs, medicine, and something else I can't quite place. I try to make sense of the smell, but my senses are still dull. The walls are made of rough, unfinished stone, the kind that suggests an older, less polished structure. The bed I'm lying on is simple—a thin soft bed atop a wooden frame, covered in some kind of soft cloth.

I feel the bandages wrapped around my chest, my arms, and my legs. There's a heaviness to them, a tightness that is both comforting and confining. I reach up and touch my face—my jaw is still sore, but it's clean. The blood that had been caked there earlier is gone. I pull the cloth away from my legs to inspect my wounds, and I wince when I see the extent of the injuries I've sustained. The cuts and gashes are deep, but they've been carefully wrapped. The thought of someone taking care of me—someone who must have brought me here— makes my stomach tighten in confusion.

How did I even get here in the first place?

I close my eyes for a moment, trying to piece together what happened. The last thing I remember is the hydra—the monster's savage strike, the pain of its claws raking through my flesh, and the final blow that ended the fight. The memory is hazy, but I recall the moment. The relief washed over me as the hydra's massive form crumpled to the ground. That's the last moment I can hold onto before everything blurs into nothing.

I don't remember leaving the dungeon. I don't remember how I ended up outside. The only thing that's clear is the terror of those people—their fear, their hatred. They thought I was a demon. They screamed at me and threw rocks at me. But then… nothing.

I think of Sokh. My heart sinks as I remember the words he said to me. His riddles, his disappearing act. Did he leave me behind? Did something happen to him? The thought of Sokh, my master, being taken from me, thrown into the chaos of this world—if this even *is* the same world—fills me with dread.

But there's no time for that right now. I need answers.

I try to push myself up again, this time more carefully, testing my strength. The bandages creak under the weight of my movement, but I can't even move more than that. I lie back down, giving up.

Where am I?

Before I can think any further, the door creaks open.

I freeze instinctively, my muscles tensing. Two figures step into the room, tall and imposing. My heart skips a beat. I go on alert, wary, my instincts sharpening despite my exhaustion.

The first man is broad and rugged, with auburn hair that looks like it's been tousled by the wind. His skin is tanned and rough, and his gold eyes flash with a sharpness that tells me he's seen more than his fair share of battle. His grin is easygoing and kind. But the moment his gaze lands on me, I feel something like a low growl form in my throat, my body instinctively taking a defensive stance, ready to spring.

The second man is entirely different. He's pale, his skin almost translucent beneath the dim light, and his hair is white, flowing down his back like a strange curtain. His icy blue eyes seem to glow, but there's no warmth to them. Instead, his gaze is calculating, and assessing, and the way he stares at me sends an uncomfortable shiver down my spine.

They don't say anything immediately. They simply stand in the doorway, studying me. I stay still, my senses hyper-aware, every muscle in my body coiled. I'm not sure if I should attack if I should flee, or if I should do nothing and wait for whatever comes next. But I can't afford to act without understanding. I don't know who these men are, and I don't know where I am.

Finally, the auburn-haired man breaks the silence. His voice is rich and deep, and when he speaks, it almost sounds like he's laughing. "Easy there," he says, his smile widening. "We're not here to hurt you."

I don't respond. I just stare at them, eyes narrowed, the silence heavy in the air between us. My gaze flickers to the door behind them, wondering if there's any chance of escape if things go wrong, but I don't make a move. They're waiting. Watching. But I don't know what for.

The man chuckles softly at my lack of reaction, his voice still calm, though there's a hint of impatience in it now. "Look, we saved you, alright? You're safe. Just calm down." He steps forward, but not too quickly, as though he knows not to provoke me too much. "Name's Imran," he continues, "and this here is Kamea." He gestures toward the white-haired man, who doesn't make a sound or even shift his stance. Kamea's eyes stay on me, as cold as his name.

Imran's voice continues, and despite myself, I find my attention drawn back to him. "We saw you lying out there, all bruised and battered. Thought you'd be dead before long. We took care of you. Figured it was the least we could do." His tone is casual, but there's an edge to it. I don't know what they expect from me, but it's clear that they're trying to break the silence, trying to get some kind of response.

But I don't answer.

Imran's expression falters for a brief moment as he waits for me to speak. But when I don't, he glances at Kamea, who simply raises an eyebrow in response, his gaze never wavering from mine. Kamea's silence is almost unnerving. He's not like Imran. He doesn't seem concerned, or at least, he doesn't show it.

They both stand there for a long time, the quiet stretching between us. The air feels thick with unspoken questions. Finally, Imran lets out a sigh, running a hand through his hair. "Alright then," he mutters, more to himself than to me. "Guess you're not in the mood for conversation."

I keep my gaze locked on them, my body still tense and poised for action, but I make no move. The world outside this room feels like a distant memory, and the quiet oppressive nature of this place makes my skin crawl. I don't know who they are, what they want, or why they helped me, and every instinct tells me to be cautious. Trusting them feels wrong. Trusting anyone right now feels like a mistake.

But I still don't speak. Not a word. I can't bring myself to do it.

Imran seems to realize that he's not going to get anything from me anytime soon, and he exhales, his easy smile returning though it's tinged with frustration now. "You don't talk much, do you?" His tone is light, but there's a sharpness beneath it.

The silence stretches again, thick and suffocating, and Kamea speaks at last, his voice like ice scraping across stone. "Where are you from?" he asks, his tone flat and dispassionate. His eyes narrow slightly, as though he's waiting for a response.

I don't answer. I can't answer. Because I don't even know. The words are there, swirling in my mind, but they don't reach my tongue. I can't even make sense of where I'm from, let alone where I am now. And so I remain silent, eyes steady on Kamea and Imran, unwilling to reveal any more than I already have.

Another few moments pass in heavy silence before Imran sighs again, shaking his head as though he's giving up on me. "Alright then, have it your way," he mutters under his breath. "We'll leave you to it for now. Rest up. We'll talk later."

Imran glances at Kamea, who simply nods once, his expression unchanged. Without another word, the two of them turn and exit the room, their footsteps echoing down the hall.

The door clicks shut behind them, and I'm left alone once again. The silence is almost suffocating, and the weight of it presses down on me as I stare at the door, still locked in place. I don't move for a long time, my mind spinning with questions that have no answers.

I sit up, the pain in my body is relentless, but it doesn't stop me. I'm not staying here. Not after what I've just experienced. The air in the room feels suffocating, like I can't breathe like it's all closing in on me. These men—Imran and Kamea—I can't trust them.

The window. I focus on it. It's small, just enough for me to squeeze through. My mind is clouded, but the instincts drilled into me during my life in the Abyssal Dungeon are still sharp. I push myself up despite the dizzying pain in my chest, the bruises that still ache from the hydra's claws, and the weakness pulling at my limbs. But I can't stay here. Not when I don't know what they want.

I stagger toward the window, gripping the frame with bloodied hands, the bandages feeling tight and uncomfortable around my wounds. I don't care. I don't think. I climb up, my vision blurring with the effort and the blood loss, but somehow, I make it. My legs tremble beneath me as I stretch one foot out, then the other. It feels like every inch of movement is a fight against the burning ache in my body, but I don't stop. I can't.

When my foot hits the ledge, I feel my body sway dangerously. I almost lose my balance, but I grip the stone with both hands and steady myself. The night air is cold, and sharp, and for a moment, I let myself breathe it in. There's a sense of freedom in it. A sense of something beyond this place, beyond the cage I've been trapped in.

I try to take another step, but my legs give way under me, and I nearly fall. My heart skips a beat, the panic rising in my chest. I catch myself on the edge of the building, my fingers scraping against the rough stone, but I don't fall.

I'm not going back.

I pull myself up, summoning all the strength I have left. My muscles scream in protest, but I keep going, my feet finally hitting solid ground. I stumble, almost falling forward, but I manage to stay on my feet. The world spins around me, but I focus on one thing: escape.

I start running. My legs feel like they're made of stone, but the adrenaline surging through my veins pushes me forward. The sounds of the night—the rustling of the leaves, the creaking of distant trees—blend with the pounding of my own heartbeat. I'm moving too fast to think clearly, but it doesn't matter. I just need to get away.

I push myself harder, faster, ignoring the searing pain in my side, the sting of blood seeping through the bandages. I hear footsteps behind me, but I don't stop. My mind races, my body moving instinctively as I cut through the night, darting around corners, and weaving through alleyways.

But the footsteps keep getting closer.

I try to pick up the pace, but I'm slowing down. I can feel the weight of my injuries, the toll they've taken on me. Every breath is harder to draw, and every step feels heavier. The realization hits me like a cold slap: I'm not going to outrun them.

I need to fight.

I glance around, desperate for anything that can help me. That's when I spot it—a long, sharp stick, half-hidden in the brush beside the path. Without thinking, I grab it, clutching it in both hands like a weapon. It's not much, but it's better than nothing.

The footsteps are closer now, and I hear their voices. Imran. Kamea.

I turn to face them, my grip tightening around the stick. Imran is the first to come into view, his massive form silhouetted against the dim moonlight. He doesn't look winded at all. My heart hammers in my chest as I take a step back, but I stand my ground.

Imran smiles, slow and dangerous, as he approaches. "You really think you can escape, huh?" His voice is filled with amusement. "You're not going anywhere, kid."

I raise the stick, pointing it at him like a spear. It feels fragile in my hands, useless compared to his strength, but it's all I have. I take a shallow breath and charge.

Imran barely moves. When I strike, he blocks the attack with ease, parrying the stick with just his arm. The force of my strike bounces off him, and I stumble back, nearly losing my footing. His arm doesn't even flinch.

He grins at me, and I realize just how outmatched I am.

"You're not bad," he says, his voice casual, as if I'm nothing more than a passing distraction. "But it's gonna take more than that."

I don't have time to react before Imran unsheathes his sword, the glint of steel catching the light as he spins it in his hand. My breath hitches. A sword. I have nothing but this damned stick. I didn't even bring my sword.

I'm out of my depth.

But he doesn't strike. He stands there, watching me, waiting for something. My heart is racing, panic rising in my chest, and I wonder if he's just toying with me, enjoying my desperation. My grip tightens around the stick, but I know I can't win. Not like this.

Then, to my shock, Imran grins, tossing me something. It lands at my feet with a soft thud, and I look down to see a spare sword—gleaming, perfectly balanced. My fingers tremble as I bend down and pick it up. The weight of it feels strange in my hand, foreign, but I don't hesitate. I rise, leveling the blade, facing Imran.

He chuckles, clearly entertained. "I'll give you a chance," he says, "If you can beat me, you're free to go. But if you can't…" He shrugs nonchalantly. "You'll come back with us."

My eyes widen at his words, the implications sinking in. A fight. A chance to be free. I would escape regardless, but at least I won't have these two on my neck.

But even as I grip the sword, doubt gnaws at the edges of my mind. I'm still too weak, too injured. This isn't a fair fight. But what choice do I have?

Imran takes a step forward, his grin never leaving his face. "Don't make it too easy for me, alright?"

I swallow hard, trying to steady my breathing. I know I have no choice but to fight. If I don't, I'll end up back with them.

With that thought burning in my chest, I raise the sword.

And I charge.

The air is thick with the sound of clashing steel as I face Imran, my breath coming in ragged gasps. Sweat drips from my forehead, mixing with the blood that still oozes from my many wounds opening. My legs feel like they're made of stone, my body barely able to hold the weight of the sword, but I refuse to back down. Every instinct in my body tells me to keep fighting, to keep pushing, even as exhaustion claws at my limbs.

Imran is grinning, his laughter echoing through the night as we circle each other. His movements are fluid, and effortless, like he's toying with me. It infuriates me. This man—this human—who isn't even sweating, who doesn't even seem to be trying. How can he be so calm, so… casual?

I grit my teeth, tightening my grip on the sword, ignoring the stinging in my hands. I've fought creatures far more terrifying than him, far more deadly than anything he can throw at me. In the Abyssal Dungeon, I've faced countless monsters, all of them stronger, faster, and more vicious than any human. Yet here I am, struggling against this one man, this one pathetic human.

Imran strikes first, his sword a flash of silver in the dim light. I barely manage to block it, the impact of his blow reverberating through my arm. My legs shake from the force, but I hold my ground, refusing to fall back.

"You're not bad," Imran says with that damnable grin of his, his voice rich with amusement. "I didn't expect you to be this much of a challenge."

He moves in again, his sword swinging in a wide arc toward my chest. I step back just in time, the blade missing me by mere inches, but the force of the swing pushes me off balance. I stumble, trying to recover, but my body is already betraying me. The injuries from the hydra fight, the blood loss, the exhaustion—it's all taking its toll.

I fight through the pain, gritting my teeth as I lunge forward, trying to catch him off guard. But Imran easily sidesteps, his movements too quick, too precise. He's been trained for this, I realize. He's not just some random fighter—he's a seasoned warrior, and I'm just a broken, battered monster from a dungeon.

I can feel the weight of my inadequacies pressing down on me, but I refuse to let it show. I can't afford to falter. Not now. Not when I'm so close to freedom.

The fight rages on, the sound of our swords clashing echoing through the night. My body feels so weak and heavy, every swing of my sword sending jolts of pain through my muscles. But still, I persist. I refuse to give in.

Imran's smirk never fades, his eyes gleaming with that same amusement as he toys with me. He's not just trying to defeat me. He's enjoying this. He's enjoying watching me struggle, watching me fight with everything I have, knowing that I can't win.

The frustration builds in me like a storm, boiling over into rage.

I make my move, desperate, fueled by the rage that's coursing through me. I swing the sword with all my strength, aiming for Imran's midsection. He easily blocks it, but in that brief moment of distraction, I use the momentum to twist my body and swipe at his cheek.

The blade cuts through his skin with a sickening hiss, drawing blood.

Imran's eyes widen for just a moment, his smirk faltering before he throws his head back in a hearty laugh. "Well, well," he chuckles, his hand wiping at the blood on his cheek. "I didn't think you had it in you. Not bad, kid."

The sight of his blood, the momentary victory, feels like a distant, fleeting thing. I'm too tired to savor it. The sword in my hand feels heavier by the second, the weight of my exhaustion almost too much to bear. But I don't stop. I can't.

Imran steps back, twirling his sword lazily in his hand. "You've got guts, kid. I'll give you that." His voice is full of admiration, his grin wide and full of respect now, but there's something else in his gaze. Something calculating.

I pant heavily, my chest heaving with each breath, the exhaustion settling in like a lead weight. Every movement feels like it's taking a part of me with it, but still, I stand my ground. I glare at him, unwilling to let him see the weakness that's creeping into my body.

But Imran doesn't strike. Instead, he simply watches me, his sword lowered at his side. The silence stretches, and for the first time, I wonder what he's thinking.

"You know," he says, breaking the silence with a voice far more serious than before. "You've got potential. More than I thought. You've got the spirit of an adventurer."

I blink, confused. What is he talking about? I don't know this world, don't understand it. I just want to leave.

But Imran isn't done. He steps closer, his eyes studying me carefully. "I've seen a lot of fighters in my time, but you…you've got something different." He pauses, gauging my reaction. "You've got the heart of an adventurer. And if you'd let me, I could help you tap into that potential."

I'm too tired to understand. I can barely keep my eyes open as I try to process his words. My sword is slipping from my hand, the weight of it too much for me to carry. My legs are shaking, my breath ragged in my chest.

"You're not like the others we've met," Imran continues, his voice calm and sincere now. "You've got fire. You've got the drive to push through the pain, to fight even when you're at your limit. That's what makes a great adventurer. And I'm offering you a chance to join us."

The words don't sink in at first. I'm too exhausted, too hurt, to understand what he's offering. But when they do, when the weight of what he's saying hits me, I'm frozen. Then a scowl appears on my face. I've heard of that term from Sokh before. He wants me to fight for them? I don't even know who they are. I barely know this world, and he wants me to fight for them?

"If you can fight like this while barely holding yourself together, imagine what you could do with proper training," Imran says, his tone laced with genuine interest now. "You've got the potential to be something great. If you join us, I can help you unlock that. What do you say?"

I want to say no, but I hesitate. I can feel my body trembling, my mind spinning as I try to process his words. A part of me wants to refuse, to turn away from the offer. I don't know these people, don't trust them. But another part of me—the part that has always fought to survive, that has always wanted more than the dungeon—sees the opportunity he's offering.

"What do you say, kid?" Imran asks. From the corner of my eye, I can see Kamea standing behind Imran with his arms crossed and a bored look on his face.

"Crilt," I grumble, unable to stand the word, "kid". I'm a grown man.

Imran's smile grows wide. Freakishly so, that it disturbs me. "What do you say, Crilt?" Imran asks again, his smile is still wide, his voice softer now, more inviting.

I don't speak. I don't know what to choose. But I know I can't leave just yet, so I'm going to take whatever chance I get at survival. That's all that matters.

***

The room feels different when I wake up, quieter, almost suffocating in its stillness. I blink, trying to adjust my eyes to the dim morning light filtering through the small, grimy window. My muscles ache, still sore from the fight, but the exhaustion that had weighed me down the night before has eased, leaving only the dull throb of bruises and cuts. The bed beneath me is soft, too soft, and I feel strangely disoriented. I'm used to the hard stone floors of the dungeon, the constant crunch of rock beneath my feet, and the flickering, barely-there light from the dungeon's torches.

Here, it's warm. Too warm. And quiet. I don't mind the latter, it's just that I'm not used to it.

I sit up slowly, letting the weight of my body adjust. I can feel the bandages that cover my chest and limbs, the tightness of them as they press against my skin, but I'm in no mood to care. What matters now is finding out more—about these two humans, about where I am, and why I'm here.

The smell of food drifts into the room, faint but unmistakable. My stomach growls involuntarily, and for the first time in what feels like a lifetime, I realize how empty I am inside. I haven't eaten much since the battle with the hydra, just bits and pieces of what I could scrounge up in the dungeon, and whatever I could catch.

I get to my feet slowly, testing my balance, then push open the door, my eyes immediately falling on the two men from last night. They're at a table, looking like they've been awake for much longer than I have. Imran is grinning, his arms crossed over his broad chest, while Kamea is moving around a sleek black item that brings out a fire, the faint scent of something cooking thick in the air.

I approach cautiously, staying as far from them as I can while still being within reach of the food. Kamea notices me immediately, his sharp, pale eyes gleaming with quiet amusement as he adds a few more things to the pot on the stove.

"Sleep well?" Kamea asks, his voice smooth but full of quiet curiosity.

I don't answer. I don't want to engage with them. I just want to leave, to get back to the dungeon, to the only place I've ever known. But the thought of food—real food—gives me pause.

Without a word, Kamea sets a plate down in front of me. The food is steaming hot, and it smells rich, savory, and foreign. My mouth waters despite myself. In the dungeon, it's all raw meat, sometimes barely cooked at all. Carcasses of beasts, the occasional strange fungus, and some plants that were as bitter as they were inedible. This...this is something else entirely.

I hesitate for a moment, staring at the pile of food on my plate. There are some kind of eggs, cooked and yellow, the whites firm, the yolks slightly runny. Next to them, a piece of meat—juicy and tender, glistening with some kind of glaze. I don't know what it is, but the smell is enough to make my stomach growl again, more insistent this time.

Still, I don't eat. I simply stare at it, my mind whirring with suspicion. Why would they be feeding me? Why are they being so kind to me? There's something wrong with this whole situation.

Kamea chuckles, clearly seeing the suspicion in my eyes, and sits down opposite me, watching me intently. "Go on, then," he says, nodding toward the food. "I know it's unfamiliar, but trust me, you'll enjoy it."

I don't trust them. I can't. But my stomach is louder than my mind. Reluctantly, I pick up the metal object with prongs, the strange utensil feeling awkward in my hand. It's different from the sharp, jagged tools I've used before. But I can manage this. I stab a piece of the meat and bring it to my mouth.

The moment the meat touches my tongue, I nearly gasp in surprise. The flavors explode in my mouth, rich and savory, warm and comforting in a way I've never experienced before. The tenderness of the meat, the slight sweetness of whatever glaze is on it—it's almost overwhelming. For a moment, I'm so lost in the taste that I almost forget where I am. I chew slowly, savoring the unfamiliar burst of flavor. It's unlike anything I've ever had in the dungeon. It's soft and delicate, and it melts in my mouth.

The eggs are just as surprising. The texture is unlike anything I've ever experienced, too. The yolks are creamy and smooth, and they blend perfectly with the softness of the whites, unlike the monster eggs I've had in the dungeon, all green and inedible. I can feel the warmth spreading through me with every bite and the full, satisfying sensation of being fed.

I can't help the small, involuntary hum of appreciation that escapes my lips. It's a sound I haven't made in years, and it feels strange to acknowledge just how good this meal is. But I don't let it show. I don't let them see that this simple meal is giving me a pleasure I've never known.

Kamea watches me, his pale eyes glimmering with something like amusement, and he chuckles softly to himself. "You like it then?" he asks, the question almost playful.

I don't answer him. I'm still too wary of their intentions, of their kindness. It feels like a trap. Why would they feed me? Why would they care?

Imran, sitting across the room with his arms still crossed, grins widely. "It's pork and eggs," he says, his tone casual as if he's explaining something obvious.

I blink, confused. "Pork and eggs?" I repeat, the words are foreign in my mouth. I don't understand. I know what meat is— how could I not?—but I've never heard of these terms before. Pork. Eggs. What are they?

Kamea gives a small chuckle at my confusion, and Imran shrugs. "You don't know what pork is?" he asks, his voice teasing but not unkind. "It's the meat from a pig. A domesticated animal we raise for food. And the eggs come from chickens. You know, the little birds?"

I frown, unsure of how to respond. I've never seen such creatures. I've never been outside the dungeon. Everything I know, everything I've ever learned, has come from the trials of survival in that endless, dark maze. The idea of raising animals for food, of having animals that you don't even eat raw, is completely alien to me.

I glance at Kamea, hoping for some sort of confirmation, but he merely nods with a knowing smile, as if he's not surprised by my confusion. He's seen enough of the world to understand that I'm not from it.

Imran, still grinning, shakes his head, clearly amused by my ignorance. "Well, I suppose it's not surprising you don't know about it. You've been living in that dungeon your whole life, right? No pigs or chickens down there." His grin fades a little, and he takes a deep breath, his expression growing more serious. "It's hard to believe, really, that someone like you could be stuck in a place like that."

I don't respond. I explained very briefly and vaguely about my life last night since they kept bothering me about it. They looked so in disbelief that I didn't know if they believed me or not. But I don't seem to care. I don't even want to think about the dungeon. Not now. Not when everything feels so strange and new.

Instead, I return to my food, focusing on each bite as I try to ignore the questions swirling in my head. I have so many questions, but I don't know where to start. How did I get here? Why am I here? What do they want from me?

Imran seems content to let me eat in silence, and Kamea's gaze never leaves me. It's like they're studying me, watching me carefully, as if they know something I don't.

Finally, after what feels like an eternity of silence, Imran speaks again. "You've still got a lot to learn, Crilt. And a long way to go if you want to be an adventurer. But you've got potential. I can see that."

I don't say anything. I don't trust their words, but part of me can't help but wonder what it would be like—what it would be like to leave the dungeon, to live in a world where there's more than just survival.

But I'm not ready to trust them yet.

I eat my meal slowly, savoring the strange newness of it, and try to ignore the unease that still gnaws at me.

***

The day drags on, the heavy silence stretching in the small, dimly lit room. I can't stop thinking about everything. The dungeon seems like a distant memory, now, although its weight is still lodged in the back of my mind like a wound that hasn't healed. The truth is, I don't know what to do here. There's so much to this world—so much noise, so many people, so many unfamiliar things. None of it makes sense, and I feel out of place. The moment my feet left the dungeon, everything changed, and I haven't been able to find my footing.

Imran and Kamea move about the room as if they've been here a thousand times as if this world is as natural to them as the dungeon was to me. I can't help but watch them, my gaze flickering back and forth between them, trying to figure them out.

Imran is easy to read. He's loud, boisterous, full of energy. His actions are as exaggerated as his voice. He's sharpening his sword now, the rhythmic scrape of the blade against the whetstone filling the room as he hums a random tune. His grin is wide, his posture relaxed, even when he's working with the blade. It's almost as though he enjoys everything as if he finds joy in even the mundane tasks of the day.

Kamea, on the other hand, is the opposite. He's calm, quiet, even a little distant. He sits cross-legged on the floor, filing his arrows with precise, methodical movements. His pale eyes flicker up every now and then, taking in the room, and scanning everything with an unnerving level of focus. He doesn't speak unless he has to, and when he does, it's sharp, direct, and often laced with sarcasm. I can tell he's the kind of person who thinks more than he speaks.

I wonder how they've managed to work together for so long. They're such polar opposites. But despite their differences, there's something between them—some understanding, some silent bond that exists without words. I don't understand it, but I notice it. It makes me feel even more out of place.

I try to ignore the discomfort gnawing at me.

Imran looks up at me suddenly, noticing my stare, and grins even wider. "You're gonna wear a hole in the floor if you keep looking at us like that, Crilt." He chuckles, not waiting for an answer before going back to his sword.

I don't say anything. What could I say?

It's been hours since I first woke up, and I'm still stuck in this place. I feel weak, my body exhausted from the injuries, and my mind, though clouded with confusion and frustration, is still alert enough to notice every detail.

Kamea raises an eyebrow at me but says nothing. He's focused on the arrows in front of him, his fingers moving deftly over the shafts, adjusting the nocks with precision.

I've had enough. I've been patient long enough.

I sit up straighter, my frustration finally bubbling over. I can't stay here. I don't want to be here. I have no business being in this world. My mind is filled with the need to leave, to find my way back to the dungeon, to find Sokh. I can't be here with them, not when I have no idea what's going on, not when I don't even know what they want from me.

"I want to leave," I say, the words coming out more harshly than I intended.

The words echo in the small room and both Imran and Kamea freeze.

Imran looks up, his grin fading for a moment as he meets my eyes. "What?" he asks, his voice low with a hint of surprise.

"I want to leave," I repeat, more forcefully now. "I don't belong here. I need to go."

Kamea raises an eyebrow, his gaze sharp as he looks at me, his fingers stilling on the arrows. He doesn't speak at first, just studies me, like he's trying to figure out whether I'm serious or just confused. Then he shakes his head.

"You're injured," he says, his voice cold but matter-of-fact. "You can't go anywhere like this."

I scowl, my hands curling into fists at my sides. "That's none of your business," I snap.

Imran laughs a deep, boisterous sound that fills the room. "Ha! Now that sounds like something Kamea would say. You're a stubborn one, Crilt. You remind me of him back in the day." He chuckles again, clearly amused by my response.

Kamea curses under his breath, and I see the edge of a smile twitch at the corner of his lips. "Shut up, Imran," he mutters, but there's no real anger in his voice. It's a habitual irritation, the kind that comes from years of hearing the same nonsense.

I groan, rolling my eyes and slumping back against the wall. "I don't care about your comparisons," I mutter under my breath. "I just want to leave."

Imran leans back in his chair, his sword now clean and sharp, his hands resting on his knee. "And you will," he says, "just not today. Not like this."

"You're in no condition to go anywhere," Kamea adds, his voice flat. "We're not going to let you wander off when you can barely stand."

I grit my teeth, hating how they talk to me like I'm some helpless child. My body might be weak from the injuries, but my mind is still sharp, and I'm not about to let these two dictate what I do. I don't belong here. This world—these people—it's all wrong.

"I don't need your help," I say, my voice low but fierce. "I've survived alone my whole life. I don't need anyone to take care of me."

Imran chuckles, his grin never wavering. "I can tell. You're tough, Crilt. No doubt about that. But even the toughest need a hand sometimes. You're not going to get far on your own like this."

I clench my fists again, my knuckles white. The last thing I want is their pity, their help. I don't want to be stuck in this place, playing games with them, acting like some helpless creature.

"I'll leave when I'm ready," I say, my tone colder than I feel. I don't want to give them the satisfaction of seeing how much their words have affected me.

Imran doesn't respond to that. Instead, he leans back, stretching his long limbs and letting out a sigh of contentment. "Well, when you're ready," he says, "you can join us. We're adventurers, Crilt. You've got potential. You could do a lot more than just survive."

I don't say anything. What does he know about me? About survival? He doesn't understand what it's like in the dungeon. He doesn't understand what it means to be alone.

Kamea looks at me for a long time, his eyes narrow, before he sighs, shaking his head. "He's stubborn," he says, almost to himself. Then he stands up, pushing the arrows aside and moving towards the door. "You can leave when we say you're ready. Until then, you stay here and rest."

I open my mouth to argue again, but I choose not to. Kamea doesn't say another word as he leaves the room, and Imran follows shortly after, the two of them heading out into the hall.

I'm left alone, again. The silence presses in on me, suffocating, until all I can hear is the thudding of my own heartbeat. I clench my jaw, fighting back the frustration that's threatening to bubble over. I can't stay here. I can't let them keep me here.

I have to leave.

But I don't know how.

Not yet.

***

Over the next few days, I start to settle into a strange rhythm with Imran and Kamea. The routine is simple, and while I'm not used to it, I've begun to rely on it more than I'd like to admit. They've insisted on taking care of me, despite my protests. Every day, Imran insists on making sure my wounds are treated, while Kamea sits nearby, watching silently, filing his arrows or sharpening his bowstring. I'm still trying to understand why they're doing this, why they seem so intent on helping me, even when I don't ask for it.

Each morning, Imran wakes up before me, with a burst of energy as he stretches and starts to prepare breakfast. The smell of cooked meat and bread fills the air, and I can't help but feel hungry, despite my confusion. I don't know what they're cooking, but it tastes like nothing I've ever eaten in the dungeon. The food is rich and flavorful, and for the first time in my life, I feel full in a way I never have before. It's strange, the way it settles in my stomach. I almost feel human again after eating. Almost.

Imran talks a lot during breakfast. He's always cheerful, always full of stories, even though I barely understand half of what he says. He talks about the people in the town, about his adventures, and about the kingdom he and Kamea are part of. I catch snippets here and there: the Demon King's army, a kingdom struggling to defend itself, the need for strong warriors, and the growing desperation among the townspeople. But all of it is a blur. I'm still trying to grasp it all, and most of the time, I can't focus enough to make sense of it.

Kamea, on the other hand, is quieter. He sits across from me, eating his own breakfast with a small frown. Every so often, he catches me watching him, and his icy blue eyes flicker with something I can't name—perhaps amusement, perhaps irritation, I'm not sure. He doesn't speak much, but when he does, it's direct and to the point. He talks about the world outside of the dungeon, about the customs of humans, and the way people interact. He tries to explain the importance of things like personal space, the way people exchange greetings, and how to recognize someone's intentions by their posture or tone of voice. It's all overwhelming, too much to absorb at once, but I try. I have no choice.

After breakfast, the three of us usually go out to the town. Imran insists that I walk on my own, even though my body is still weak from the injuries. He tells me that I need to get used to being around people again, and I reluctantly agree. The people in the town stare at me, some with curiosity, a lot with fear. I've learned to ignore them, but I can't help the way their gazes feel like they're burning holes in my skin.

The streets of the town are bustling, and every day, I notice something new. There are children running around, playing games I don't understand. Women walk by with baskets of food, their conversations full of words I don't know. Men argue about weapons, about the war effort, about who is the better fighter. The sounds of the town—the chatter, the laughter, the occasional shout—are deafening compared to the silence of the dungeon.

Imran and Kamea always walk beside me, Imran talking loudly about whatever catches his attention, while Kamea follows with a more calculated step, his eyes scanning the crowd, always watching. There's an unspoken tension in the air, a nervous energy that I don't fully understand. People in the town are fearful of something—of the war, of the demon king's army, of something darker lurking beyond the walls. I hear whispers about the demons that have started to appear in the outskirts, attacking caravans, and burning villages. The kingdom is at war, and the people are on edge.

Imran and Kamea sometimes stop to talk to the townsfolk. Imran shakes hands, laughs loudly, and hands out coins to the children. Kamea, in contrast, speaks in short, clipped sentences, rarely making eye contact, and always keeping his distance. His interactions are more efficient, and professional, if you will. He talks about the kingdom's survival efforts, about the kingdom's need for recruits to fight in the war, and the resources being stretched thin because of the Demon King's constant attacks. It's all over my head, but I know that they're talking about a struggle for survival—one that I'm not a part of, but that is still threatening this entire world.

As the days pass, I start to learn about the kingdom's efforts to resist the demon king. There are constant raids and skirmishes between the kingdom's soldiers and the demon king's forces. The kingdom is holding on by a thread, relying on every able-bodied warrior to defend the towns and villages from the monsters that have begun to spread throughout the land.

Imran seems to take pride in the kingdom's resilience, in its ability to stand tall despite the constant threat of the demon king's army. He tells me that they've been fighting for years, and even though they're losing ground, they've never given up. He insists that the kingdom will prevail and that no matter how many demons the king sends, they'll always be ready to fight back.

Kamea, on the other hand, is more pragmatic. He doesn't sugarcoat things the way Imran does. He talks about how desperate the situation is, how the kingdom is barely holding together, and how they've lost so many soldiers already. The way he speaks about the war—the fatigue, the fear, the constant battle against the odds—makes my stomach twist. But he's right. They are losing, and there's no easy solution in sight.

It's hard to grasp the magnitude of it all. The war, the prophecy, the demons… it feels so far removed from my life in the dungeon. But every time I see the worried expressions on the townspeople's faces, every time I hear the fear in their voices, I realize that this world is just as dangerous, if not more so, than the dungeon I've spent my entire life in.

By the afternoon, Imran and Kamea take me back to the inn. It's a small, unassuming building in the center of the town, but it's comfortable enough. Imran and Kamea go over their weapons, repairing what's broken, and cleaning what's dirty, even when they hardly use it. I don't belong here. I'm not like them. I never will be.

In the evenings, Imran often talks about his past—about the adventures he's had, about the places he's been. He's had many battles, he tells me, and each one has made him stronger. He talks about the thrill of the fight, the rush of adrenaline, and the satisfaction of victory. But there's something else, too. Something he doesn't say out loud. A weariness that I can see in his eyes when he thinks no one is watching. It's there, beneath the surface, in the quiet moments when he's alone with his sword.

Kamea too doesn't share much about his past. He keeps things to himself, but I get the sense that he's seen his fair share of war, of loss. There's a sharpness to his movements, a precision that suggests he's always on alert. He's always watching, always calculating. I wonder what drives him. What keeps him going.

It's strange, being in this world. But as the days go by, I begin to realize that I'm not as alone as I thought. Imran and Kamea are my companions, whether I like it or not. They've taken me in and kept me alive, and while I can't trust them completely, I can't deny that they've shown me a side of the world I never knew existed. There's still so much I don't understand, but with each passing day, I start to see the cracks in this new world. The people here are just like the monsters in the dungeon—they're fighting for survival, but they're also capable of kindness, of compassion, of loyalty.

I guess that makes us all similar in a way.

A week passes, and the slow burn of healing begins to work its way through my body. Thanks to my demon blood, I'm recovering far faster than I should. The cuts, bruises, and gashes that once marred my skin are starting to fade, replaced by new, smooth skin. My muscles ache less with every passing day, though there's still a dull throb in my side where the hydra's claws tore through me. The fact that I'm even still alive at all seems like a miracle to me, given how close I came to death in the dungeon.

Imran and Kamea have been watching me closely during this time, checking on my condition, making sure I'm eating enough, making sure I'm not doing anything too strenuous. They're kind to me, in their own strange way, but their kindness is still too hard for me to grasp. I now understand that they have no malicious intent toward me, but I'm not used to being treated with care, not used to being looked after. My life in the dungeon was a constant struggle, with no one but Sokh guiding me. And now, here I am, in this strange world, surrounded by people who seem to genuinely care for my well-being.

It's unsettling, in a way, but not entirely unwelcome. I find myself appreciating Kamea's cooking more than I expected. His meals are simple but satisfying—he's been teaching me how to cook, explaining the different spices and techniques as he does. It's bizarre to think that a few weeks ago, I had no concept of food other than the raw meat and carcasses I scavenged in the dungeon. But now, I sit down at the table every morning, forced to enjoy the rich, earthy flavors of his meals.

Imran, on the other hand, keeps me entertained with his endless stories of war and the adventures he's had. He's loud and boisterous, always laughing and talking about the battles he's fought, the enemies he's defeated. Some of the tales he tells are exaggerated, no doubt, but I can see the glimmer of truth in his eyes when he speaks of the dangers he's faced. The man lives for the thrill of battle, and while I don't share his enthusiasm for it, there's something about the way he talks about his experiences that intrigues me.

Still, despite all their kindness, despite their attempts to integrate me into their world, I can't shake the feeling that I don't belong here. I don't belong with them. Every time they offer me a chance to become an adventurer like them, I can't bring myself to accept. I'm not one of them, not by a long shot. They are human. They fight to protect their kingdom, to defend their people. But I…

I don't even understand what a kingdom is, or why people fight for it. I only know the cold, dark walls of the Abyssal Dungeon and the monsters that lurk within it.

And so, I continue to try and escape. It's an instinct now. Every time Imran and Kamea leave for a mission, every time they step outside the inn, I take the opportunity to slip away. It's not that I want to run from them—it's that I can't help myself. The moment they leave, I feel the compulsion to flee, to find Sokh, to return to the only world I've ever known. But no matter how far I get, no matter how fast I run, they always catch up with me. Every time.

The first few times, they seemed surprised by my attempts to escape. They would chase me through the streets, capturing me with ease and dragging me back to the inn, where they'd scold me like a child. But now, after a week of this, it's almost become routine. They expect it, and when I make my break for freedom, they don't even seem to hurry. It's as if they're letting me go just to see how far I'll get before they reel me back in.

Today is no different. Imran and Kamea are getting ready for another mission. They've packed their things, checked their weapons, and are preparing to leave when I seize the opportunity. As soon as they step out the door, I slip into the shadows, moving quickly through the alleyways and side streets. I can feel the pulse of adrenaline in my veins as I sprint, my feet pounding against the cobblestone ground.

I don't know where I'm going—as usual, but I dash at the thought of escape. But my legs are already tiring, my injuries still nagging at me, and I can feel my body slowing down. Just as I'm rounding a corner, I hear a voice behind me.

"Crilt."

It's Imran. I don't even need to look back to know that he's there, a grin on his face, a casual swagger in his step. He's been watching me this entire time, I know it, just waiting for me to make my move.

I don't stop. I push myself harder, my heart pounding in my chest as I try to outrun him. But it's no use. In the distance, I hear the sound of footsteps quickening, and before I know it, Imran is at my side, grabbing my arm and yanking me to a halt.

"Where are you going?" he asks, still grinning, though I can hear a hint of amusement in his voice.

I don't answer him. I try to pull away, but he holds me firm, his grip unyielding. Kamea appears a few moments later, standing in the shadows, watching us with a brow raised.

"You know you can't get away," Kamea sighs, shaking his head. "We've been over this."

I glare at them, frustrated. The urge to escape burns in me, but I know it's pointless. I've been running for days, and they've always caught me. They'll always catch me.

Imran chuckles, slinging an arm around my shoulders. "You're relentless, Crilt. I'll give you that. But you're not getting rid of us that easily."

I don't respond. I just stare at the ground, my teeth gritted. I want to scream, to demand that they let me go, to return me to the dungeon, to Sokh. But I know it won't change anything.

Kamea steps forward, his eyes flicking over me with a faint hint of something—perhaps pity, or maybe just resignation. "You can't keep running forever, Crilt. Eventually, you'll have to accept that this is your life now."

I don't answer him. I can't. The words don't even make sense to me. This is my life now? What is that supposed to mean? I was never meant to have a life outside the dungeon. They can't just force me into one.

Imran grins again, clearly not deterred by my silence. "Come on, Crilt. It's not so bad here. I know you pretend to hate it, but it's okay. You can just stay here with us, join us."

I want to scoff. I want to tell him that I don't want to be an adventurer, that I just want to find Sokh, to return to the only place I've ever known. But the words are stuck in my throat. They sound childish even in my head.

So instead, I just shrug out of Imran's grip, turning away from both of them. "I don't want to be here," I mutter, the words bitter on my tongue.

Imran doesn't seem offended. He just shakes his head, as if he's heard this all before. "We're not letting you go, Crilt. You might as well get used to it."

Kamea is silent, watching me carefully. His icy blue eyes flicker with something unreadable before he nods, turning to walk back toward the inn. Imran follows, clapping me on the back as he does.

"Don't worry, Crilt. You'll do just fine here."

I don't answer. I don't know what to say. All I can do is follow them back to the inn, knowing deep down that I'm trapped in this strange world, with these strange people. And maybe… just maybe… that's not such a bad thing.

CHAPTER 2

The past few weeks have been a strange mixture of frustration, confusion, and something I can't quite define. The wounds from the hydra fight have healed, and my body is almost as good as new.

Imran and Kamea have become… familiar, more than I ever expected. The awkward silence between us has lessened over time, though the air still feels stiff whenever we're around each other for too long. They don't push me as much as they did in the beginning, but their kindness has somehow become more pronounced. It's not like Sokh's cold, calculating care—it's different. I don't even know if I'm ready to let it mean something. I don't know if I ever will.

Imran, as usual, is boisterous and persistent, the type of person who wears their feelings on their sleeve, never shy to tell you exactly what they think. Kamea, on the other hand, is quieter, more introspective, but no less perceptive.

Today, I sit at the table, watching Imran sharpen his sword with a lazy grin plastered across his face. He's talking about a recent skirmish with a band of marauders, telling the story in an exaggerated tone, making it sound like he single-handedly defeated them all. I try not to roll my eyes—he always embellishes his stories. But there's something about the way he speaks that's oddly captivating, a rawness to his words that makes even the most ridiculous details seem important.

Kamea is sitting across from me, his pale fingers absentmindedly tracing the rim of his mug, his eyes occasionally flicking toward Imran but mostly staying focused on something far-off. He's not as animated as Imran, and I know he's not interested in the tales of glory, but there's still a certain quiet tension between them, something that's been building over the last couple of days.

"Crilt," Imran says, his voice loud and upbeat as he finishes with his sword and leans back in his chair. "You ever thought about what you want to do next? I know you've been recovering, but you can't stay here forever, can you?"

I keep my gaze steady, not responding right away. The question lingers in the air, one I've heard a few times over the past week. I know what Imran wants. He wants me to become an adventurer like them, to join their little band of merry warriors and wander the world, seeking out monsters and treasure.

But I'm still not sure. I don't know anything about this kingdom, or the people, or the war with the demon king. I don't know what it means to be an adventurer, to fight for something greater than just survival. The idea makes me uneasy, and I can feel my chest tighten at the thought of it.

"I don't know," I mutter, finally speaking up. It's the most honest answer I can give, even if it's not much.

Imran grins, oblivious to my hesitations. "Well, you better start thinking about it. You've got potential, Crilt. You've got the skills—hell, you've got more skill than half the people I've seen fight. And that's not just because you're a demon."

Kamea's eyes flick toward Imran then, a subtle tightening of his jaw as he shifts in his chair. "Imran," he says quietly, his voice low, "You're pushing him too hard. He's not ready for that yet."

Imran shrugs, unconcerned. "He'll be ready when the time comes. Don't you think he's got it in him? He's been through hell already. If anyone's built for this kind of life, it's him."

"I don't think pushing him into something like this is going to help," Kamea replies, his tone almost detached. "We've all got our own reasons for doing what we do. But he doesn't need to be forced into the same path."

I can see the tension building between them. It's subtle, but it's there. Kamea's face is still calm, but his eyes hold a sharp edge. Imran smiles, but there's an underlying seriousness in his demeanor. It's almost as if they're testing each other, feeling out how far the other will go before something breaks.

I stay silent, watching the two of them go back and forth. I don't want to get involved in their argument—whatever…this is.

Finally, after a few moments of uncomfortable silence, Imran stands up, clapping his hands together with a decisive grin.

"Alright, alright, enough talk. We're heading to Ashroth soon, and I'm not letting you just sit around here any longer," he announces, his voice booming.

Kamea raises an eyebrow, looking at Imran with a mixture of skepticism and exasperation. "Now? With Crilt?" he asks, his voice cautious. "You're not even giving him a chance to choose."

Imran waves him off, unfazed. "Oh, come on, Kamea. We've been sitting around here for too long. We've both been dying for some action, and Crilt needs to get out of here. What better way to get him involved than taking him along?"

I sit up straighter at that. Ashroth. I've heard them mention it before, a large city that harbors a kingdom. Where Imran and Kamea come from. Apparently, they don't live in this town, they're just here for a brief stay. I've been told it has a massive castle there. Whatever that means.

The thought of going to Ashroth doesn't appeal to me, but it sparks something inside me—something that feels like hope. Because Ashroth might be the key to everything. It's a large city, with many people, and if I can just slip through the cracks, maybe I can find a lead on Sokh. Maybe there are other people who know about him, about the dungeon. Maybe…

I stand up suddenly, cutting through the conversation.

"I'll go," I say before I even have time to think it through.

Both Imran and Kamea stop talking and look at me, surprise written across their faces. Kamea's eyes narrow slightly as if trying to gauge whether I'm serious. Imran, on the other hand, grins widely, as if he's just won some victory.

"You'll go?" Imran asks, clearly thrilled. "Well, that settles it then! We'll be leaving first thing in the morning. No backing out now, Crilt."

Kamea's gaze flicks toward me, unreadable. "Are you sure about this?" he asks softly, his tone almost hesitant. "It's not a decision you should make lightly. The roads are dangerous. We don't even know what we're walking into."

I swallow, my throat tight as I meet Kamea's gaze. The uncertainty in his eyes is clear, and I can tell he's worried. Maybe it's not just about me. Maybe it's about what will happen to us all once we get there.

But I nod, firm in my decision. "I'm sure," I say quietly, my voice steady. "There's nothing I can't handle."

Imran slaps me on the back, his laughter filling the room. "Then it's settled! We'll head out in the morning, and we'll figure it out along the way. You'll be an adventurer in no time, Crilt!"

Kamea sighs, but his gaze softens. "Fine. Just don't do anything stupid, alright?"

I give him a brief nod, and for the first time since I've been here, I feel something stir in my chest—something almost like relief. For the first time in days, I feel like I might finally be on the right path.

***

The morning sun rises slowly, casting a soft glow over the town as I stand outside the inn, staring down at the items in my hands. The air is cool, the kind of freshness that I've never experienced in the dungeon, and the weight of the sword in my grip is almost too much to bear. I hold my trusty rusted blade in my hand, and adjust the leather armor Imran gave me. It's a two-piece outfit, snakeskin, with thick scales designed to offer some protection while still being flexible. It doesn't feel like armor, though. It feels like a costume, something I'm wearing just for show.

I look down at the sword again, my fingers brushing the jagged edge. It's the same one Sokh gave me. I remember that day—how he'd pulled it from the skeletal hand of a fallen adventurer, offering it to me with a quiet nod. That sword has been with me for as long as I can remember. It's the only weapon I've ever known. And yet, now, here, in this world, it feels wrong.

I sigh and look up at the sky. It's too bright here. I don't know how to explain it, but everything is too... open. In the dungeon, everything was tight and claustrophobic. The darkness surrounded me and comforted me. I could always count on the shadows, the oppressive silence that kept me company. But here, in this world, the air is too wide, the sun too harsh, the people too... loud.

I glance down at the sword again, trying to focus on something familiar. The rust, the jagged edge, it brings a little comfort, a tiny shred of something I can hold onto. Sokh had given me this sword, but it feels like I've left him behind with it. It's hard not to feel like I've abandoned my entire life in the dungeon. I can't shake the thought of Sokh, wherever he is, wherever I left him.

"Hey, Crilt!"

I look up, startled by the booming voice. Imran is strapping his sword to his back, his bag slung over his shoulder, already ready to go. I don't know how he's always so eager, so ready to move forward, but I guess that's the difference between him and me. He's never had to be afraid of where he's going. He doesn't know what it's like to live in a place where every step could be your last. He has no idea what it's like to live in constant fear.

"You ready?" Imran grins, his broad face lighting up with excitement.

I just nod. I can't find words right now. What's the point? He's excited. I'm... uncertain. But I've already decided that I'm going with them. I have to find Sokh. I don't know where I'm going, but Ashroth is a start, and I'm not about to waste this opportunity to get closer to finding answers. The only thing I'm sure of is that if I don't do something, I'll never know what happened to Sokh, to the dungeon, to everything I've left behind.

***

The sun is still low in the sky as Kamea drives the carriage along the dirt road. The rhythmic clop of the horses' hooves against the ground blends with the soft creak of the cart, and the world seems to move slowly around us. The wind has a cool bite to it, but it's nothing compared to the chill of the dungeon. I pull my cloak tighter around my shoulders, the leather armor creaking slightly under the movement. I'm not used to wearing it, but it's starting to feel less foreign, though it still feels like it doesn't belong on my body.

I sit across from Imran in the back of the carriage, leaning against the wooden side, my eyes fixed on the horizon, where the fields stretch endlessly into the distance. Kamea, as always, is silent. His eyes are focused on the road ahead, his posture rigid as he guides the horses with steady, practiced hands.

Imran, on the other hand, doesn't stop talking. I've come to expect it from him—his voice is a constant, like a river that never stops flowing. But today, his words carry weight, and for the first time, I'm actually listening.

"So, Crilt," Imran begins, his voice loud and booming, "you ever wonder what's out there? Beyond the monsters in the dungeon, I mean. The rest of the world?"

I glance at him and shrug, unsure of how to answer. I've never given much thought to the outside world. The dungeon was all I knew, all I cared about. But now...now things are different. I have to know what's going on in this world. I need to understand it, or I'll be lost.

"I never thought about it," I reply, keeping my voice neutral. "I've been busy." Sarcasm drops down my tongue.

Imran chuckles that loud, infectious laugh that makes the air feel lighter. "Yeah, I get that. But now you're here, right? I know you're curious about it."

He shifts in his seat, leaning forward, his eyes gleaming as if he's about to tell me something important. Kamea doesn't even acknowledge him; his hands are steady on the reins, his face unreadable, though there's a subtle tension in the way his jaw tightens.

Imran continues, his voice lowering slightly as if the story he's about to tell carries a sense of gravity that needs to be handled with care. "You see, Crilt, the world's been under siege for years now. The Demon King—he's the one behind it all. A monster of unimaginable power. He's got an army of demons, dark creatures, enslaved beasts, and worse. They've been slaughtering villages, wiping out whole towns. We've been fighting him for as long as anyone can remember."

"So I've heard. What about the Demon King anyway? What's the big deal with him?" I ask, despite myself.

"That's just the tip of the iceberg," Imran says, ever the one of dramatics. "He's not just some powerful monster, Crilt. He's a force of destruction. He has magic, dark magic that can tear through entire cities, and his armies... they just keep growing. The worst part? He controls people—and turns them into slaves. I've seen it myself. People are taken, and twisted into something else. It's like there's no escape from him."

I sit back, the words sinking in. I'm used to monsters, used to the dark, used to creatures that lurk in the shadows. But this? This is different. The thought of someone—something—controlling entire armies of these creatures, enslaving people, feels surreal.

Kamea finally speaks, his voice cutting through the silence like a knife. "Ashroth is the last kingdom standing. The only one left that hasn't been overrun. We've been holding the line, barely. But the Demon King's forces are always pushing. The battle isn't over. It's just...waiting for the final push. We're not sure how much longer we can hold out."

Imran's eyes flick to Kamea for a moment, his grin faltering. There's something in his expression that's different now—more serious. "Yeah, the last bastion," Imran mutters, his voice quieter, almost to himself. "And we're the ones who fight on the front lines. We've all lost something to the Demon King. And we'll keep fighting, no matter what."

I look at the two of them, really looking at them for the first time. Imran, always so full of life, so loud and boisterous, but now there's a shadow in his eyes. And Kamea—silent, distant, always watching—his expression unreadable, but his voice laced with something darker, something that says he's seen too much.

I hum, trying to process what I'm hearing. "So, you fight him? You fight the Demon King?"

Imran nods, leaning back in his seat with a smirk. "Of course we do. Not directly anyway, I don't think anyone has ever seen the demon king before, but we fight his legions. That's what we're good at. Adventurers. Swords for hire, monsters to kill, kingdoms to save. All in a day's work, right?"

His grin is so wide that for a second I almost forget that what he's talking about is serious. But the laughter in his tone is hollow, and I know he's not entirely joking. There's too much pain behind it. I can see that in the way he grips his sword hilt and the way his eyes harden when he talks about the Demon King.

"Don't let his jokes fool you," Kamea says quietly, his eyes still focused on the road. "The war is real. The Demon King is real. He's not something you can laugh off."

Imran's smirk fades slightly, and he nods in agreement. The silence hangs for a moment as Kamea's words sink in, and I find myself lost in thought. The Demon King. Hm. A force of destruction. Magic that could tear cities apart. It's hard to imagine that this world—this world of sunlight, of green fields, and wide-open spaces—could be in such a state of chaos. But I suppose I've only seen the surface of it. I haven't seen the true destruction, the fear that these two have lived with.

I glance at them, my mind racing. "You've lost a lot, thanks to him, huh?"

Kamea's face tightens, his jaw clenching for just a moment. His voice is hard when he answers like the words are something he's not used to saying. "We fight because if we don't, there won't be anything left to fight for."

Imran's eyes flick to Kamea, and for the first time, I see a flash of understanding between them. It's brief, but it's enough to make me realize how much history and trauma they share. This is their fight.

"We fight because it's the only thing we can do," Imran adds, his voice quieter now. "The Demon King... he doesn't care about who's left. He'll take everything, all of it, until there's nothing left. If we're going to have any hope, we have to keep him at bay. We have to hold the line. Ashroth is the last line of defense."

I feel the weight of those words, and I feel a strange connection to them. I don't know why, but the way they talk about this war, the way they've made it their purpose... it makes sense to me, somehow. I've never had a purpose. I've always just been surviving. But now, here, I see it—this war, this fight against something greater, something that threatens everything. And I feel a flicker of something inside me. Maybe it's anger, maybe it's fear, maybe it's just the idea that I finally have something to fight for.

"Do you think you can win?" I ask, my voice low.

Imran chuckles, but it's quieter, more thoughtful. "We can't afford not to. If we don't win, then what's left? Everything else falls apart. The Demon King doesn't leave survivors."

Kamea glances at him, his lips pressing into a thin line. "It's not about winning, Crilt. It's about survival. You of all people should know that. We keep the Demon King's forces from destroying everything else. That's the only reason we fight."

We fall into silence after that. The tension between them hangs in the air, but it's not uncomfortable. We're headed to Ashroth, and as much as I want to find Sokh, I can't deny that I'm curious about this battle. This war.

I look out the carriage window again, the wide-open landscape stretching ahead of us. The sky is clouded now, and the shadows are starting to grow longer. This world has consumed them all. And whether I like it or not, I'm part of it.

***

Night falls, and the world around us shifts. The sky darkens, and the stars twinkle faintly above. The air grows colder as the carriage rattles along the worn path. Kamea drives for most of the night, his face illuminated only by the dim glow of the lanterns inside the carriage. Imran sits across from me, his eyes scanning the horizon, his posture tense as though something more than fatigue is weighing on him.

I'm exhausted. I've never traveled before, and sitting in one place for hours and hours on end is quite tiring, to say the least.

There's a strange heaviness in the air like the sky itself is holding its breath. The further we go, the more I begin to see signs of it. The signs of war. I don't speak—Kamea and Imran have already spoken enough about the war, about the Demon King—but I watch, my gaze taking in everything around us.

It's not until the morning comes that the true scope of the damage reveals itself.

As the first light of dawn breaks across the horizon, we pass through what seems to be a former village. The houses are little more than charred ruins, smoldering remnants of what once stood. The trees are bent, and twisted, their trunks marked with burns, their leaves blackened and curling like brittle paper. There are no signs of life here—no children playing, no laughter, no movement at all. Just silence. Eerie silence.

I look away quickly, my stomach churning.

"This was once a bustling town," Imran mutters, his voice quiet. He's leaning forward in his seat, his eyes focused on the empty, blackened landscape. "Now look at it. Demon King's forces rolled through here a few months ago. Nothing's left."

Kamea doesn't speak, but his lips press into a thin line, and his knuckles are white as they grip the reins.

We don't stop in the village. There's nothing to see here, nothing to salvage. The people who once lived here are either dead or scattered, forced to wander the wastelands left behind by the demon army. I don't even see any survivors, and for a moment, I almost forget that there are humans who have been left behind in this hell.

The carriage moves on, and I try not to think about the destruction I just saw. But it's hard to forget. Everywhere I look, I see more devastation. Villages were reduced to smoldering ruins, fields torn up, and roads torn apart. And with each passing hour, I begin to notice something else—something darker. The people.

Human survivors are scattered across the landscape. Some travel in groups, huddling together for warmth, but others are alone, carrying only what they can fit in the tattered bags slung over their shoulders. I see men, women, and children, but they all share the same look—eyes haunted, faces gaunt with starvation, limbs thin and frail. They move like ghosts, with no purpose, no hope, no future.

In some of the towns we pass, there are soldiers, but not soldiers fighting for a cause. These men, these women, are slave traders, rounding up survivors and forcing them to march under the threat of violence. Some of the survivors try to resist, but they're quickly subdued. The soldiers are armed with cruel weapons, their expressions cold, and impassive, as though this is just another day of business.

"What's happening?" I mutter; my throat tight as I watch a group of people being herded into a small camp. They're shackled, their heads bowed, their faces empty. The soldiers stand around them, laughing, and making cruel jokes. It's a sight I thought I would never see. It reminds me of the monsters in the dungeon, but it's worse. So much worse.

Imran turns to look at me, his eyes dark with something I can't quite place. "This is what the Demon King has done to the world. He's destroyed everything. Whole towns, villages, families—he's turned people into slaves, treated them like animals. And anyone who resists, anyone who fights back... they're crushed."

"But why?" I ask, my voice rising in disbelief. "Why would they let this happen?"

Kamea speaks, his voice low and steady, but there's an edge to it. "The world is broken. The people have no choice but to bow to the Demon King's forces. We're all at his mercy. And what's left of the kingdoms—like Ashroth—are fighting just to hold on. To keep the last remnants of civilization from being swallowed up."

Imran scoffs. "It's not just that, Crilt. It's the fear. People are scared. They're afraid of losing what little they have left, and the Demon King knows that. He uses that fear to control them. It's not just the armies he commands; it's the fear he spreads, like a disease. Once he's in your head, once he breaks you, there's no going back."

I sit back in the carriage, stunned. I thought I understood what fear was. I thought I knew what survival meant. But this... this is a different kind of fear. A fear that surpasses even death itself.

We continue on. The next few hours blur together as we pass more destroyed towns, more enslaved people, and more reminders of the war that rages outside the walls of Ashroth. I try not to look at the faces of the survivors, but I can't help it. I can't turn away. Their hollow eyes meet mine, and I wonder—what happened to their families? To their homes? What did they lose, and why are they still fighting to survive? Isn't death a far more suitable option than living like this?

I feel a pang in my chest. I've been alone for so long, so used to the darkness of the dungeon, that I never thought about what others might have gone through. I never thought about the world outside. But now... now, I can't stop thinking about it.

The carriage creaks again, and I turn to see Imran watching me closely. His eyes are softer now, almost like he's studying me. "You look like you've seen a ghost."

"I've seen worse," I reply, though the words sound hollow even to me.

Imran chuckles, but there's no warmth to it. "Yeah. You'll see more, too. If you're going to be an adventurer, you'd better get used to it. The world isn't kind to anyone, and it sure as hell isn't kind to those who fight back."

Kamea doesn't say anything. He's focused on the road ahead, his hands steady on the reins. But there's a tension in his shoulders, something that tells me he's not unaffected by what we've seen. I don't think anyone could be.

And yet, despite everything—despite the horror, the destruction, the suffering—there's a part of me that feels something stir inside. A desire, a hunger. Maybe it's anger. Maybe it's a need for vengeance. Maybe it's the part of me that's still just a monster; still driven by the same primal instincts I've always had.

But it's also something more. I don't know what it is yet, but it's there, burning inside me.

"Ashroth's not far now," Imran says, pulling me from my thoughts. Right.

Ashroth.

It's all that's left. The last bastion of humanity. The last hope against the Demon King.

And I'm heading straight for it.

***

As the carriage lumbers along the desolate road, Kamea takes the reins again. His expression is calm and collected, a stark contrast to the grim reality unfolding around us. Imran, however, is more animated today, his deep voice echoing in the air as he leans forward, clearly enjoying the chance to impart knowledge to me. His hands, worn and calloused from years of battle, are resting on the hilt of his sword as he looks at me with a gleam in his eye.

"You're still quiet, Crilt," Imran says, breaking the silence. "I figured by now you'd have a hundred questions for us."

I don't answer. What's there to ask? The world is broken, the war is endless, and nothing makes sense anymore. My mind keeps returning to Sokh, the only person I ever cared about. But that feels so far away now, a distant memory in a world of carnage. My grip tightens on the rusted sword at my side, the only possession I have left from the dungeon.

Imran doesn't seem bothered by my silence. Instead, he continues, "Alright, since you're out of questions, I guess I should tell you about the Demon King's generals. You'll need to know about them if you want to survive in this war."

I shrug. There's nothing to do anyway, so I might as well.

Imran leans back in his seat, crossing his arms over his chest. "There are five generals, each one more terrifying than the last. They were human once, you know. At least, that's the rumor. They're monsters now—monstrous in both power and appearance. I've seen a couple of them myself, and let me tell you, they're not the kind of thing you want to run into in the middle of the night."

He lets the words sink in, then begins to speak again, his tone heavy.

"First is Zaroth. The General of War." Imran's face darkens. "Zaroth is ruthless. He's the Demon King's right hand and his primary strategist. He doesn't leave much to chance. When Zaroth sets a plan, you can bet your life that it's already been executed in his mind a thousand times. He's a master of battlefield tactics. His forces are always well-prepared, well-armed, and utterly merciless. Where Zaroth goes, there's war. Whole cities fall beneath his boots. And those that survive are left in ruins, broken."

Imran pauses, glancing at Kamea for a moment, as if weighing whether to continue. Kamea doesn't react, his face as unreadable as ever. So, Imran presses on.

"The second one is Isha, the General of the Dark Arts." Imran's voice drops lower as if the name itself demands a sense of reverence. "She's a sorceress and not just any sorceress. She's a nightmare, Crilt. You'll hear stories of her magic—curses that turn people to stone, plagues that wipe out whole villages. She controls the very essence of life and death. They say she can raise the dead, twist souls into monsters, and bend the elements to her will. Her magic isn't something you can just fight with a sword. It's... it's something far beyond what you can even imagine."

I try to picture such a being—someone who could control life and death so freely—but I can't. The idea is too foreign, too impossible.

"The third general is Draxus," Imran continues, not missing a beat. "The General of Deception and Trickery. He's a master of manipulation. Draxus can make you believe anything. He's the one who sends spies into our ranks, poisons minds with lies and plays both sides. His enemies never see him coming—because he's already in their heads. He'll convince you that your allies are enemies, that your own friends are traitors. His power isn't in brute strength but in the ability to break people's trust and create chaos from within. You can't fight him with steel—his weapon is the mind." Imran leans back in his seat, his eyes narrowing. "Draxus is the kind of enemy who will make you doubt your own reflection. He's poison to the soul."

I'm quiet, taking in all he's saying, still unable to comprehend that such creatures exist.

Imran notices the frown on my face and grins slightly, though it doesn't reach his eyes. "Yeah, it's a lot to take in. But don't worry, Crilt. We're getting to the fun ones now."

I don't share his enthusiasm, but I'm ready to listen.

"The fourth general is Mathael, the General of Chaos," Imran continues, his voice now tinged with bitterness. "You want to talk about destruction? That's Mathael. He doesn't care about strategy. He doesn't care about armies. All he wants is to tear things apart. Whole cities. Whole civilizations. He'll send his forces in, and all they'll do is destroy, burn, and spread fear. It's all about the chaos for him. The more destruction, the better. It doesn't matter who dies, who gets caught in the middle. He's pure anarchy, and nothing else."

"The last one," Imran says quietly, his voice dropping a notch, "is Arius. Now, Arius is a strange one. He's rumored to be the final general, but no one has ever confirmed it before. We don't even know how the rumors began to spread, but I might as well just mention him," he explains. "He was once a hero—a warrior who fought for the light, fought for what was good. Some even called him the Champion of Ashroth. But after a certain point, something... changed in him. No one knows why. Some say he was corrupted by the Demon King's power, others claim he was manipulated. All we know is that he joined the Demon King, and when he did, he brought with him an army of loyal followers."

A man who was once a hero, is now a traitor? It's a bitter thought—one that makes my stomach churn for some reason. Going against your roots? I can't even fathom it.

There's a heavy silence after that. Kamea doesn't speak, his hands still gripping the reins tightly as he guides the horses through the rough terrain.

***

The air smells different here. It's cleaner, fresher—like life itself. As the carriage rumbles to a halt in front of a massive, iron gate, I'm left staring, barely able to process everything. My eyes drink in the sight of Ashroth, this city I'd heard about, this place where humans still fight to survive against the Demon King's army.

Imran's grin is wide as he opens the carriage door, the sound of his boots hitting the dirt ringing in my ears as he steps out. "Welcome to Ashroth, Crilt," he says, his voice bright and almost playful as if we're not standing at the edge of a war-torn world.

I step out of the carriage behind him, and the ground feels softer underfoot, the cobblestones smooth. Kamea is already by the horses, guiding them to the side as he takes the reins from Imran.

The first thing I notice is the size of everything. The walls around the city are enormous, stretching high into the sky with sharp, jagged metal and stone. The gate itself is a testament to how much the people here are prepared for anything. It's thick, heavy, and covered in intricate engravings and symbols all over. The guards posted around the gate are alert, their weapons ready but not raised, their eyes darting around the area as if constantly expecting an attack.

The city is of stark contrasts, where beauty and danger mix in an uneasy balance. The architecture of the place is grand—tall, lavish buildings rise up in every direction, their marble exteriors gleaming under the midday sun. Ornate statues stand proudly at intersections, their faces weathered by time but still noble in appearance. Even the ground here seems more cared for than anything I've seen outside the dungeon. Everything is polished, pristine, untouched by the inevitable decay of war.

But even as I admire the elegance of it all, I can't help but feel out of place, even more than I did back in the smaller town. The people who walk along the cobblestone streets seem so…normal. They're not covered in dirt or blood like the survivors I've seen in other towns. Their clothes are clean, brightly colored, and well-maintained, their faces smooth and unmarked. They smile and laugh, seemingly carefree, their voices light and full of life as they walk with one another, oblivious to the reality that exists outside the walls.

It's a world so different from the dungeon. The soft and delicate sounds of civilization are overwhelming. I don't know what to make of it. How can they be so happy when the Demon King's forces are at their doorstep? How can they live without fear when the world is falling apart?

Then, I realize why they might seem so happy—why they look so pristine. They have something that's been stolen from everyone else: safety. These people are lucky, hidden away behind these grand walls, protected from the horrors outside. In my chest, something tightens. I'm not sure what it is, but it feels like bitterness.

The guards at the gate eye me suspiciously as we approach. Their eyes flick from Imran to me, lingering a little longer on my appearance. I don't blame them. I must look like a demon to them, my long, dark hair flowing behind me, my pale skin almost ghostly under the sunlight. My obsidian eyes no doubt stand out, sharp and unsettling. My fangs are visible every time I speak, though I don't let them show unless I have to. I look demonic through and through. I don't blame them for being on their guard.

"Who's this?" one of the guards asks, his voice gruff.

"Relax," Imran says with a shrug, waving his hand dismissively. "He's with us. Just a new recruit."

The guard doesn't seem entirely convinced, his gaze flicking over me once more, but after a moment, he nods curtly. "Let them through."

Imran smirks at me. "See? Nothing to worry about."

I say nothing. I don't let petty things like that get to me. After all, they do t know what I've had to go through, nor do they know me. They see a monster, not a person, and I can't change that, or even begin to try to. The people in this city will never understand what it's like to live in the dark, in a place where survival is a daily battle. To them, I'm just some kind of freak, something to be wary of. I can feel their eyes on me as we pass, but I refuse to let it bother me. I have no time for their judgment.

Once inside the gates, the city opens up before us. The streets are lined with rows of shops and market stalls, some selling food, others peddling weapons or clothing. There are children playing in the open areas, their laughter ringing in the air, but even they seem... different. They don't look like the children I've seen before—those who have known nothing but pain and fear. These children look clean, full of life, and sheltered from the ugliness of war.

The castle looms in the distance, towering over everything. I understand why Iran was so prideful about it; it's massive. I can't even begin to fathom how people could manage to build such a terribly huge structure, but I can at least admire it.

We pass through the streets, drawing some stares as we do. Imran and Kamea are clearly known here—people wave to them, and a few even stop to speak with them, though the moment they glance at me, their smiles falter, their voices quiet. I can hear whispers.

"What is that thing?" one woman murmurs to her friend.

"Is it a demon?" another asks.

"It looks like it. Maybe they captured a demon?"

"But there aren't any shackles, see?"

"They better not let that thing roam around free,"

I roll my eyes, but I say nothing.

Kamea leads us through the marketplace, and I follow closely behind him, glancing around at everything. The contrast between this place and the dungeon is staggering.

We stop in front of a modest building with a sign that reads "The Silver Blade Inn" hanging above the door. Kamea opens the door, and we step inside. The air smells of fresh bread, roasting

meats, and something else—something I can't place but smells
comforting.

Inside, the atmosphere is warm. The lighting is dim, with
candles flickering on tables. A few people are sitting at the tables,
eating, drinking, talking. A man is playing some kind of instrument
in the corner, and I can hear the hum of conversation all around.
The room seems alive with energy. But then, as I move deeper into
the room, it's like the energy is instantly sapped by my presence.
Every pair of eyes in the room falls on me, and the chatter dies
down. Some people look away quickly, others stare for a little
longer than they should.

Imran notices and his smile grows wider. "Don't mind
them," he says to me, clapping me on the back. "They're just not
used to new faces, especially not one as handsome as yours."

I don't respond. I don't need to. Imran is kind for trying to
cheer me up, but I don't have the strength in me to care. They can
look, they can judge, but none of it matters.

As we settle into a table, I feel my body relax a little,
despite the tension I still carry. Kamea walks to the bar,
exchanging a few quiet words with the innkeeper. He orders a few

drinks and some food for us, all without so much as glancing back at me. Imran, on the other hand, is already waving at people across the room. His laughter is loud, drawing a few glances, but no one seems to mind. I sit down at the table, my fingers running over the rusted sword at my side.

"You, okay?" Imran asks as he takes a seat across from me. His voice is casual, though there's an undertone of concern behind it. "You've been quiet."

I nod but don't say anything. I'm not sure how to respond. I'm still adjusting to this place, to everything.

Kamea comes back to the table, setting down three mugs of something dark and steaming. He doesn't look at me directly, his face set in a stiff, unreadable expression. I can tell something's wrong. He's not his usual self. He's tense like something's bothering him, but I don't press. I've learned by now that Kamea keeps his thoughts close.

The silence stretches between us, heavy and thick. The food is brought to our table, steaming bowls of meat, vegetables, and bread. The scent is enticing, and I realize just how hungry I am. But as I reach for my bowl, I overhear a conversation next to us.

"Goddamn Demi-human," the guy spits and I can see him throwing a glare at me.

His friend grips his arm tightly. "Shut up, mate. You're drunk. Don't let him hear you,"

"I don't understand," I say, turning to Kamea and Imran. "Demi-human?"

The words hang in the air, and I can feel Kamea stiffen. Imran's smile falters slightly, and he looks at Kamea, then back at me. The atmosphere shifts, something dark seeping into the air between us.

Imran is the first to break the silence. "It's a complicated story," he begins, scratching his neck nervously, his tone losing some of its usual warmth. "The Demon King's invasion didn't just destroy human societies. He tore apart families, villages, and entire cultures. After he conquered most of the world, he didn't just stop at enslaving humans. He began experimenting on them,"

I watch as Kamea's eyes flicker toward Imran, a barely perceptible nod of understanding passing between them.

"Demi-humans are… a result of that," Kamea continues, his voice quieter now, more serious. "The demons would either breed or mix their blood with that of humans—creating hybrids. They were treated as tools, as weapons, or worse—slaves."

I frown. Why would he do that? It doesn't make sense. I can barely wrap my mind around it. I knew the Demon King was ruthless, but this… this is something else.

Imran leans forward, his elbows on the table, his expression grave. "The Demon King wanted an army. He saw humans as weaklings. He didn't care about human life. He tried to create pure bloods, but it didn't work of course, but he saw potential in those hybrids. You see, they had powers—abilities that regular humans didn't have. And in his twisted mind, they were the perfect soldiers. Perfect slaves."

I sit back in my seat, trying to process what they're saying. I've heard of demons before, of course. But this is new to me.

"It doesn't make sense," I mutter, staring at the half-empty mug in front of me. "Why would they do that?"

"Power," Kamea answers quietly. "The Demon King wanted to build an army, an army with power beyond anything the world had seen. So, he used humans, mixed their blood with his own, and created hybrids—Demi-humans. Some of them are just like you, Crilt."

I freeze. The words hit me harder than I expect, like a physical blow. "What do you mean, just like me?" I ask, though I already know the answer.

Kamea looks at me then, his icy blue eyes holding mine for a long moment. "I mean that you're a Demi-human too," he says softly, his voice almost sad. "You're one of them. You've got human blood in you, just like the others."

The words settle over me like a cold blanket. I've always known I was different—hell, I've been told by Sokh countless times that I was unique—but to hear someone else confirm it, to hear it spoken so plainly, feels like a shock to my system. I'm part human? I have human blood flowing in my veins?

But I am, aren't I? I can feel it in my veins, the same fire that burns inside both the demons and humans. It's always been there, lurking just beneath the surface.

I can feel my chest tightening, my breath coming faster as I try to process this. How could I not have known? How could I have lived my whole life in the dungeon with this knowledge, this part of me, hidden away?

Imran watches me carefully, his expression unreadable. "We didn't mean to upset you," he says softly. "But the truth is… well, sometimes the truth is hard to swallow. Kamea and I have seen a lot of Demi-humans over the years—most of them slaves, others rebels trying to survive. But none of them are like you, Crilt. You don't seem…broken, like the others."

I can feel the sting of his words. "Broken?" I whisper, more to myself than anyone else.

"They were used. Trained. Forced to fight for the demons. But you…" Imran trails off, scratching the back of his neck. "You're different. You lived a far different life than they did. I don't know how or why you ended up in a dungeon, but apparently, it's for a good cause,"

I don't know what to say to that. Different? Sure. I've always known I was different, but that doesn't make it any easier to accept. I glance up at Kamea, who has his eyes fixed on me, his expression unreadable.

"You're not like the others," Kamea says, his voice soft. "You still have control over yourself. You haven't been completely consumed by the demon blood. That's something rare."

I don't know if I'm supposed to feel relieved or not. I've never thought of myself as special—just a survivor. But hearing it from them, hearing that I'm different, makes me question everything I've known. If I'm not like the others… then what am I? Who am I, really? What does that mean for me?

I look down at my hands, the skin pale and cold, the veins beneath almost glowing with an eerie light. Human and demon blood. *Hybrid.* I can feel it now, running through me, tainting every breath I take. How much of me is human? How much of me is a demon?

"I don't know what to do with all of this," I admit quietly, my voice breaking the silence that's settled between us.

I sit there for a long moment, absorbing it all. The world I knew was simple and easy to understand. Fight, survive, learn from Sokh, and repeat. But now, with the realization of what I am, everything feels fractured. I don't belong to either the demons or the humans. I'm in some kind of limbo, and it's suffocating.

I never thought about my past, my parents, or who I really am. All I had ever cared about was living, honing my skills, and learning from Sokh. But now… now the questions come flooding in. Who was I before Sokh found me in that dungeon? What happened to my parents, and why wasn't I with them? Was I abandoned, or did something else happen? All of these questions swirl around in my mind, gnawing at me, but no answers come. It's frustrating.

And yet, it feels strange that I never thought to ask these questions before. Why didn't I care before? Why is it only now, in this strange world, that I'm starting to question everything? Maybe it's because Sokh was the only thing I needed back then. Maybe it's because I always thought that as long as I had him, nothing else mattered.

But Sokh isn't here now, is he? He's gone, and I'm left in this strange city with people who are kind to me, but they're still strangers. They've taken me in, offered me shelter, even food. I don't understand it. They expect something from me. But what? To become an adventurer? To join their fight? To be like them?

I don't know. I don't know anything anymore. I don't belong here. I can't forget Sokh. And I can't forget what happened in the dungeon. Rinse and repeat. Why am I so adamant about going back to how it was? Is it because I'm groomed to that particular routine?

I can't breathe.

I stand up abruptly, my chair scraping against the wooden floor as I do. Both Imran and Kamea glance at me, their expressions a mixture of concern and curiosity. But I don't care. I can't stay here. Not like this. I need space. I need air. I need to think.

"I'm going out for some air," I say, my voice sounding strange in the room. A couple of heads turn my way, but I don't look at them, just turn and head toward the door.

Both of them hesitate for a moment. I can sense their unease, but they don't stop me. Kamea looks at me, eyes narrowing slightly, but then he just nods, his lips pressing into a thin line. Imran, ever the louder one, simply raises an eyebrow but follows suit, leaning back in his chair and letting out a heavy sigh.

"Don't be gone too long," Imran calls after me.

I nod without turning around, walking out of the inn and into the crisp afternoon air. I welcome the coolness against my skin, the way it sharpens my senses.

I walk aimlessly, my boots tapping on the cobblestone streets. The city of Ashroth is strange to me—beautiful in a way, but unsettling. I don't know why, but the pristine buildings, the well-dressed humans, and the orderly streets all make me feel uneasy.

My hand rests lightly on the hilt of my sword as I move through the crowd. The sound of conversation and laughter fills the air, and yet, I feel so disconnected from it all. My eyes catch glimpses of the people around me—men, women, children—all of them seem so… normal. So, content. They don't even notice me. The few that do glance my way, look away quickly, eyes wary, as though something about me unsettles them. I suppose it's hard to miss someone like me, even though I do share a percentage of blood with them.

Even the thought makes me want to curl into myself again.

Their disproving looks are the least of my problems now. What bothers me is the weight of the knowledge dropped on me earlier—the fact that Demi-humans like me are treated as second-class citizens, used as slaves by the demons and the Demon King's generals. I'm part of that group. A part of something so dark, so terrifying that the people here in Ashroth would sooner turn away than look at me for too long.

I feel a gnawing in my gut, an unease that refuses to go away. Before, I never really cared. I never thought much about the people around me, whether they were human or not. But now? Now, everything feels different. I can't ignore it anymore. I'm a Demi-human, an outcast, and the only place where I might as well be able to fit in is under the thumb of the Demon King. And that, I cannot accept.

I glance around again, my eyes narrowing slightly. The people here are smiling. Laughing. But it feels wrong. They don't know what's happening outside these walls. They don't know that their very existence is in danger. They don't know what it's like to survive by the skin of their teeth. How could they? They live in a safe haven, free from fear. Free from the daily fight for survival. They have no idea what the world outside of Ashroth is like. They have no idea what it means to be enslaved or slaughtered by demons.

But I don't know what it's like either, and it hurts. I can't even boldly say what I am, because I have never shared any of my people's struggles.

I feel a lump form in my throat. I never thought I would care about them. I never thought I would care about anyone but Sokh, but here I am, torn apart by feelings I can't even name.

I continue walking, lost in my thoughts. But the deeper I go into the city, the more I begin to feel like a stranger. Like I don't belong here. I don't belong anywhere.

I think back to the dungeon. The endless dark. The cold, brutal atmosphere. The monsters I fought. The survival of it all. There was simplicity in that life, wasn't there? It was hard. It was lonely. But it was simple. I And Sokh… Sokh was there. I never thought I needed anything else.

But now, I don't know. I'm not sure anymore.

Was I happy there? The question feels like an impossible one. Happy… what does that even mean? I never had the luxury of thinking about happiness. But in the dungeon, at least there was purpose. At least I knew what was expected of me. I knew what I was supposed to do. I had a goal, even if I didn't fully understand it at the time.

Now? I don't even know where to begin. The world outside the dungeon is so complicated. Full of emotions I don't know how to handle. People who are kind to me, when I've done nothing to deserve it. A place where I'm neither fully human nor demon, caught in between like some… mistake. It's too much. Too much to process at once. Too much to make sense of.

I pass by a group of children, laughing as they chase each other through the streets. They're carefree, their joy filling the air with an energy I can't even fathom. I watch them for a moment, the pure innocence of it, and it makes something twist painfully in my chest. It's not jealousy, not exactly. It's something darker. A feeling of loss, of being unable to touch that innocence. Of never being able to go back to a time when everything wasn't so complicated.

It's hard to explain.

I'm feeling too many things at a time.

I shake my head, trying to push the thoughts aside. I don't have time to feel sorry for myself. I have to focus. I have to keep moving forward. I have to find Sokh. I have to know what happened to him, why he's not here with me. He's the only thing that ever-made sense. If I can just find him, maybe everything will be okay again.

But even as I think it, a voice in the back of my mind tells me that it won't be. It can't be. Sokh was the only thing holding my world together, and without him, everything feels like it's crumbling around me. What if I don't find him? What if he's gone for good?

I push the thought aside, my chest tightening. I can't afford to think like that. I can't afford to let the uncertainty paralyze me. Even if it means facing things I'm not ready to face.

I feel a sudden pang of regret for wanting to leave Ashroth. For wanting to escape this place and run back to the dungeon where everything was simple. But the thought of staying here, being a slave to my own confusion, is worse. I can't stay in one place forever. I can't keep hiding from the truth, no matter how painful it is.

I stop in my tracks, suddenly overwhelmed by the noise and the crowds around me. I take a deep breath, trying to steady myself. But the emotions keep crashing over me, and I don't know how to stop them. I feel like I'm drowning in all of it.

I make my way down the winding streets, trying to put some distance between myself and the chaos of the city. The noise, the people, all of it—it's too much for me right now. I need a moment of peace, a place where I can be alone with my thoughts without feeling like I'm drowning in the noise.

Eventually, I reach the edge of town. It's quieter here, the sound of bustling city life fading into the background as I approach a small, serene fountain nestled near a cluster of trees. I've seen one of these in the last town. The soft trickle of water as it splashes into the stone basin is a welcome relief. I sit on a nearby bench, staring at the water, trying to clear my mind. I let my thoughts wander, thinking about everything I've learned since coming to Ashroth—the Demon King, the generals, the fact that I'm a Demi-human. It's a lot to process, and I'm struggling to come to terms with it. It all feels like a dream.

Suddenly, a voice cuts through the silence, startling me.

"Hey, you're new around here, aren't you?"

I blink, looking up to see a woman standing in front of me. She's a bit chubby, with tan skin, warm brown eyes, and a scattering of freckles across her face that give her a kind, approachable appearance. Her long brunette hair is tied up in a loose braid, and she's smiling at me with a look of genuine curiosity as if she's seen me for the first time and can't wait to talk.

I tense instinctively. I'm not used to this, people approaching me like this. I don't know what she wants, and I don't know how to respond. I've had enough of humans looking at me with either fear or curiosity, both of which I don't need right now. I stay silent, glancing away from her.

But she doesn't seem to care about my silence. Instead, she lowers herself onto the bench beside me, as though she's perfectly comfortable here with me—someone she doesn't know.

"I don't mean to intrude," she says, still smiling warmly, "but I haven't seen you around here before. You're a stranger, aren't you?"

I don't answer. I don't know what to say. Her presence is unfamiliar to me, and I'm not in the mood for conversation. I want to be alone. But she doesn't seem to mind my silence.

She continues, unbothered, "I've been living in Ashroth for years, and I don't often see people like you here. I'm just excited to meet someone new."

I stiffen at her words. People like me? I don't like the sound of that. The last thing I want is to be reminded of what I am, and what I've become. A Demi-human.

"I'm Kaze, by the way. Are you…" she continues, her voice a little quieter, "Are you a Demi-human too?"

That word catches my attention. Too? I look at her again, this time with more focus. I study her face, her skin, her eyes. She looks perfectly human. I don't see any obvious signs of her being different, and yet she asked me the question. She must know something.

I narrow my eyes slightly, still suspicious. "Are you?" I ask, my voice low.

She grins, clearly amused by my question. "Oh, now you're talking! I knew you'd speak eventually."

I shift uncomfortably, but she doesn't seem to be bothered by my lack of enthusiasm. Instead, she pulls her top lip up with her fingers, revealing two sharp fangs, very similar to my own. My eyes widen for a split second before I quickly mask my surprise.

"Surprised?" she teases, tilting her head slightly, her smile playful. "I'm Demi-human, too. Just a small percentage of demon blood in me, though. That's why I look mostly human. But I've got these little reminders of what I am."

I'm frozen for a moment, my mind racing to process what she's said. Just like me?

I study her more closely now, and I can see it. The faint shimmer in her eyes, the subtle but distinct way her body holds itself—there's something in her movements, a quiet power, that makes her seem a little more… than human.

But why hasn't she been treated like I have? Why is she so free, so casual about her heritage, when people like me are considered monsters?

"Wait," I finally ask, my voice uncertain, "You're a Demi-human, but you—" I can't finish my sentence, my mind swirling with the questions I don't know how to ask.

She laughs a soft, melodic sound that makes me feel a little less on edge. "Yeah, I get it. You're probably wondering why I'm not, you know, hiding my identity. Why I don't get the same treatment as you. Well," she leans back a little, eyes scanning the area around us, "it's because I'm not as… 'demonic' as you, I guess. I'm not covered in scars or fangs or anything that screams 'Demi-human.' People like me, we've got just enough demon blood to give us these little features. But to the average person, we blend in perfectly with humans."

My frown deepens. "So, you've never had to hide yourself? You're treated like… normal?"

Kaze gives a short, almost bitter laugh, shaking her head. "Not exactly. People still notice. They still judge. But it's not as bad. I don't have the same stigma attached to me as someone like you does. We're not all treated the same, you know."

I clench my hands into fists, trying to control the surge of anger and confusion that floods through me. Why is it like this? Why does it matter so much what I look like or where I come from? Why is being part demon such a damn curse?

Don't get me wrong, I completely understand the fear humans have, toward demons, after all, they've lived their lives being terrorized by them, but from all I've heard, Demi-humans are fairly harmless, and they've not caused any humans or anybody any trouble, so why the stigma?

"I don't understand," I mutter, my voice low. "I'm just like you. But everyone treats me like… I'm something wrong. Like I'm a monster."

Kaze's expression softens. She glances down at her hands, fidgeting with her fingers as though searching for the right words. "I know. It's not fair, but it's the way things are right now. You see, there's a big difference between what people like us have in our veins and what the full-blooded demons are. We're seen as a mix, a 'compromise,' if you will. And that makes us dangerous. To some people, that means they see us as a threat—like we might turn into demons at any given moment. I guess, for humans who don't understand what it means to be part demon, we're still something to be feared. We're not pure."

The words sting more than I expect them to. *Not pure.* I wonder if she can see the way I flinch, the way her words hit a nerve.

"So what? You just accept it?" I ask, bitterness creeping into my tone. "You just live with it?"

Her smile fades a little as she looks at me, eyes softening with a kind of sadness. "It's not easy. I don't *like* it. I don't like how people see me either. But… you get used to it. You learn to live with it because there's no other choice. You find a way to make peace with who you are."

I don't know how to respond. I've never thought about it like that. I stare at her for a long moment, taking in her words, feeling a little less alone in this strange, overwhelming city.

Kaze smirks, and I can't help but feel a pang of irritation in my chest. She's still looking at me like I'm some sort of oddity. "I'm surprised they even let you into Ashroth," she says, her eyes scanning me from head to toe, though her expression is more curious than judgmental. "With your looks, I figured they'd have turned you away. I guess you have Imran and Kamea to thank for that, huh? They're pretty high up in the kingdom's ranks—one of Ashroth's prized adventurers."

Her words feel heavy. The idea of Imran and Kamea being seen as some sort of asset to this kingdom doesn't quite sit well with me. They're just…normal. I'm pretty sure they don't want to be put on any pedestal. They're kind to me, sure, but they don't hold any more importance than I do. Still, I don't respond to her teasing. I just let her talk, the words swirling around me like the sound of the fountain nearby.

"They've probably vouched for you. Ashroth's supposed to be open-minded when it comes to Demi-humans," Kaze continues, shaking her head with a half-smile, "but there's still plenty of prejudice. I wouldn't expect the average townsperson to embrace you with open arms."

I frown, keeping my gaze on the rippling water in front of me. "I don't care about that," I mutter quietly, my voice low. I don't feel the need to justify myself to her. I don't want her pity, or anyone's. It's a strange thing, being looked at like some kind of specimen—half-human, half-demon. I never asked for any of this.

But neither did they.

Kaze sighs, breaking me from my thoughts. "I know. It's just… it's all a mess, isn't it?" Her voice takes on a more serious tone now, and her eyes lose their usual light. "The war, the Demon King… It all feels hopeless sometimes." She slumps slightly, resting her elbows on her knees. "I just want everything to be over. I want peace again. I want things to go back to normal."

The words linger between us, thick with the weight of them. I want to respond, but I'm not sure how to. I've never been a part of anything normal. Not in the dungeon, not now. Peace is a foreign concept to me. It feels like something for other people, people who aren't me, who aren't stuck in a world that's falling apart.

She turns her head to look at me, her eyes softer now, as though she's reading something in my expression. "What about you?" she asks quietly, her voice searching. "What do you wish for?"

Her question hangs in the air, pressing on me, and I realize I've never actually thought about it before. What do I wish for? The thought of having a desire for something other than living feels strange, and foreign.

"I don't know," I say after a long silence, my voice empty. "I don't know what I want."

Kaze's lips twitch into a small, understanding smile, though there's something more somber behind it now. "It's okay. I get it."

Her voice is soft, almost gentle. "I don't really know what I want either."

She falls silent for a moment, staring down at her hands. When she speaks again, it's in a quieter, more vulnerable tone. "I guess…I just want to be with my family again. I want them back… They were captured by the Demon King's forces. And I…" She trails off, swallowing hard. "I don't know if I can ever save them."

Her words make something cold settle deep in my chest. I don't know why, but I feel a sharp pang in my stomach—like I've been punched, but in a place I can't see. The idea of someone being torn away from their family, of being powerless to do anything, is a feeling I know all too well. I've never known my family, but I'm familiar with it.

I swallow hard, feeling the sickening nausea rising in my throat. The Demon King. The war. Everything feels so out of my control. And now Kaze—someone who seems so full of life—is trapped in this same hopeless cycle. When does it end?

"You'll save them," I say without thinking, my voice more to myself than to her. But I can see the doubt in her eyes when she looks at me, and I realize that my words probably sound empty. There's nothing I can say to make her feel better.

She shakes her head, smiling faintly. "I'm not sure how Crilt. But thanks. For saying that."

We fall into a quiet that lingers for several moments, the only sound between us the gentle trickle of the fountain's water. Kaze is staring ahead, lost in thought.

Finally, she sighs, breaking the silence again, this time with a lighter tone. "Sorry about all that depressing talk. I'm just getting a little worn down, you know? Anyway, I'm glad we finally talked. It's nice to meet you, though."

She stands up, brushing the dirt off of her pants, and for a moment, I think she's about to leave. I stand up too, ready to retreat back to the inn, but she pauses midway, glancing over her shoulder at me.

"Hey, if you ever want to stop by sometime, I own a little herb shop in the middle of town. It's not much, but I've got some good remedies if you need anything. You know, in case you're ever looking for something to take your mind off of things." Her smile is back, though it's a little more tired this time.

I nod, though the idea of visiting a shop doesn't really appeal to me. It feels more like a polite gesture than something I'd genuinely pursue, but I can't bring myself to turn it down. "Thanks," I mutter, unsure what else to say.

Kaze seems satisfied with that, and with a small wave, she starts to walk away. But then, halfway down the path, she stops and turns back to me, her expression curious.

"By the way," she calls, "what's your name? I never caught it."

I hesitate for a moment, and my mind flashes back to the way the others—Imran, and Kamea—looked at me when they first met me. The way they still look at me. I've never had a real name. I've never been anyone important, no one with a title or a label. But this, this is different.

"Crilt," I say, my voice quieter now. "Just Crilt."

She smiles, nodding as if that's all she needs to know. "Crilt. Alright. I'll see you around then, I guess."

She turns and walks away, leaving me standing by the fountain, still overwhelmed by everything.

I can't help but feel something shift inside me. This city, these people—they've got their own battles, their own struggles. Just like me. The Demon King has taken so much from everyone, and I'm no different.

I take a deep breath and turn back toward the inn. The streets are still bustling, but I feel a little more certain of myself now. A little less lost. Kaze's words echo in my head, and for the first time, perhaps I can be a little selfless.

***

With a newfound determination burning in my chest, I stomp back toward the inn, the streets of Ashroth seeming to blur around me. I'm not sure where I'm going, but I know where I need to be. I've learned new things today, and I've felt all kinds of emotions swirling in my chest, and it's all pushing me forward. There's a fire in me now that wasn't there before. I know what I have to do.

As I reach the inn, the door creaks open when I throw it open with more force than necessary, startling both Imran and Kamea inside. It's less full than before, only with a few men sitting scattered all over. They're sitting at the small table, talking quietly, and both their heads snap toward me in surprise.

"I'm in," I say, not bothering with any preamble. I don't have time to waste on hesitation. "I'll join you as an adventurer."

For a long moment, neither of them speaks, and I can see the surprise on their faces. Kamea raises a brow, his expression neutral but calculating.

"Why the sudden change of heart?" he asks, voice as cool as usual. His tone makes it clear he's not sure whether this is a good thing or a bad one.

I hesitate for just a moment, the words coming slowly like they're foreign to me. "I had an epiphany," I say simply, though it's not really a complete answer. It's the truth, in a way, but it feels like there's more I'm not saying. More I'm not ready to admit.

Kamea doesn't push me further, though I can see his sharp eyes tracking me carefully, gauging my sincerity. Imran, on the other hand, seems more than willing to accept my decision. His face lights up with that characteristic grin of his, wide and infectious.

"Hell yeah!" Imran claps me on the back, nearly knocking me off balance. "That's the spirit! You're officially part of the squad now!" He gives me a hearty, exaggerated salute like I've just joined some kind of grand cause. "Welcome aboard, Crilt! It's gonna be great having you with us!"

I can't help but feel a small flicker of something in my chest at his enthusiasm. I've never felt this way before. It's hard to ignore the warmth that creeps in at his welcoming words. They're like a balm to the rawness inside me, but it only lasts a second before I push it down again. This isn't about them. It's not about me getting all sentimental.

"Tomorrow," Imran continues, his tone dropping into something more business-like, "we'll be heading over to meet with the Ashroth council. We'll go over some basics, get you officially signed up as part of the team, and then we'll head out on our first mission. Sound good?"

I nod, already imagining the upcoming meeting with the council, and what this next chapter of my life might look like. It's strange to think about. A part of me feels like I'm betraying Sokh. I promised I would find him. I promised I wouldn't leave him behind.

But another part of me… it's telling me that this is what I need to do right now. I need to learn. I need to grow. I need to understand what it means to be alive in this world. I could be investing in a greater cause other than myself. Maybe, by doing that, I'll eventually be able to find Sokh. And maybe, just maybe, I'll be able to do something more than just survive.

Imran starts humming a tune, moving around the room, probably thinking of the next big adventure. Kamea just watches, seemingly content to let us talk about the details. But I feel the weight of the silence between us. It's like I'm being pulled in two different directions.

I glance at Kamea, and for a moment, I catch his eyes. He's still studying me, his usual coldness tempered with something more. He looks like he's waiting for me to say something else. Something deeper.

But I don't know what else to say.

I'm not sure what's going on inside of me anymore. I never expected to be standing here, having this conversation. A part of me still feels like I'm going to wake up back in the dungeon, surrounded by the cold stone walls and the scent of damp earth. A part of me still wants to run, to escape all of this.

But the other part, the part that listened to Kaze today, the part that saw how she talked about her family, how she wants to fight for something more than just survival, that part knows that this is where I need to be. I need to be with people who want to do more than just endure. I want to be with people who fight for something better.

Kamea finally breaks the silence, his voice smooth and calm, as always. "You know, Crilt, it's not going to be easy. Being an adventurer isn't all glory and fame. It's about risk, danger, and making choices you might regret." His eyes narrow slightly, assessing me. "Are you sure you're ready for that?"

I meet his gaze, holding it without flinching. I've been through more pain than I can count. I've fought and bled for survival every day in the dungeon, with no one to rely on but Sokh.

"I'm ready," I say, my voice firm. "I don't know what lies ahead, but I know I want to try."

Imran grins again, clearly satisfied with my answer. "That's the spirit! You'll fit right in. We'll show you the ropes. And who knows? Maybe you'll even become stronger than us." He laughs at the thought, though it's lighthearted.

Kamea, on the other hand, seems to contemplate my words for a long time. After a pause, he nods once, almost imperceptibly. "Fine. If it's truly what you want to do, then I won't stop you. We'll see how things go," he says, his tone unreadable.

I nod back, feeling a strange sense of finality in the air. There's no turning back now. I've made my decision.

But as I stand there, watching Imran eagerly start to gather up his things for tomorrow's meeting, I can't help but feel a pang of regret in my chest.

Sokh. I can almost hear his voice in my head. I can still picture his face so clearly—the way he would smile at me, the way he would talk to me when I was lost in my thoughts. He's been the only constant in my life. I don't know if he's still alive, but if he is, I promised I'd find him. I promised him I'd never give up on him.

I swallow hard, pushing the thought down. I'm not betraying him. I haven't given up my search for him. That would mean I've truly given up.

"I'll be ready for tomorrow," I say to them both, breaking the silence again.

Imran shoots me a grin and gives me a thumbs-up. "Good to hear! Get some rest, Crilt. Tomorrow's going to be a big day."

I nod, still lost in thought, as I walk to the back of the inn to prepare for the next day. It's a new chapter, and I'm quite excited about it. It's refreshing in a way. I have another purpose to keep me going, and that itself is enough.

I'm not sure where this path will lead me, but I know one thing for sure: I'm not going back to the dungeon. Not yet, anyway.

CHAPTER 3

The next morning arrives with a crispness more sharper than yesterday. I stand by the window of the inn, staring out at the bustling city, my thoughts swirling around the things I've learned in the past few days. I've made my decision, and there's no turning back now.

A vow has settled in my chest, heavy and unshakable. I'm going to fight against the Demon King. Not just for Sokh, but for the people of this world, especially the demi-humans like me. No more standing on the sidelines. No more hiding. If I'm going to make something of myself, now that I've been thrust into this world, I'm going to fight for something greater than survival. I'm going to protect the weak and uphold justice for everyone—no matter their bloodline or status.

I turn away from the window, my resolve firm, and glance over at Imran and Kamea. They're preparing their gear for the meeting with the Ashroth council, but I notice a subtle tension in the air. Even though they haven't directly spoken of it, I know they're both wondering if I'm truly ready for what's coming.

I meet Kamea's gaze, and he looks back at me with a calmness that's somehow reassuring. "You're sure about this?" he asks, again, still unable to believe that I'm willingly going through this, after my lack of enthusiasm to join.

"I'm sure," I reply without hesitation. "I've made my decision. I'm ready."

Kamea nods slowly, his expression unreadable. Imran, ever the optimist, claps me on the back with a grin. "That's the spirit! Let's go make history!"

We all pack up, preparing to leave the inn and head toward the castle. My heart beats a little faster as we make our way through the streets of Ashroth. The city is alive, bustling with people going about their daily lives, all carefree and alive.

As we approach the castle, the atmosphere grows even more tense. The massive stone walls loom over us, and the iron gates are guarded by heavily armed soldiers. It's clear that Ashroth is preparing for something, but the air feels thick with tension and a gloom that I didn't expect to be, in a place like this.

Inside the castle, things are even worse. The hallways are filled with murmurs of political discourse, voices arguing, shouting over one another. The rulers of Ashroth, those who remain, are desperately trying to figure out a way to save the kingdom. The air is thick with uncertainty and fear. Some of them suggest surrendering to the Demon King, offering up whatever the Demon King wants in exchange for survival. Others are advocating for one final war, to fight to the bitter end. The tension in the room is palpable, and it's clear that Ashroth's leaders are at a crossroads.

I stand beside Imran and Kamea, unsure of my place in all of this, but it's not like I'm able to walk away. Here, there's hope, but it's fragile, barely hanging on.

A man steps forward at the head of the council, his eyes tired but sharp. He's one of the kingdom's top generals, his armor polished and gleaming, but his face betrays the weight of the decisions he's had to make. "We cannot afford to fight the Demon King," he says, voice hoarse with desperation. "We're losing. Our resources are dwindling, and our forces are too thin. If we don't act soon, we'll be wiped out completely."

His words hang in the air, and I can feel a knot tightening in my chest. These people… they're talking about surrendering. I can see it in their eyes, the fear, the hopelessness. They're so close to giving up. But I refuse to believe that surrender is the only option.

"We cannot give in," another voice rises, this one a woman with fire in her eyes. "We must fight. If we give up now, then we've lost everything. What will become of Ashroth if we surrender? What happens to the people, to the rest of the world?"

She's right. She's saying what I've been thinking. The moment they give up, Ashroth will be nothing more than another casualty in this endless war. The demon forces will not stop until they've conquered every inch of this land. And the worst part is, no one seems willing to even try to fight back.

The room erupts into chaos as the general's words about surrender still linger in the air. Kamea's expression shifts from stoic calm to one of barely contained fury. His jaw clenches, and I can see the tension in his shoulders, the way his hands tighten into fists at his sides.

"Unbelievable," Kamea growls, his voice laced with venom. "You would just *give up*—after everything we've fought for? After everything *we* have sacrificed?" He takes a step forward, but Imran places a firm hand on his shoulder.

"Kamea now's not the time," Imran says quietly, though his voice is strained. He knows his friend's temper well. Kamea shakes off his hand, his gaze still fixed on the council members.

"They're cowards," Kamea spits, his voice dripping with disdain. "You would lay down your swords and surrender? Let them take everything from us without even *fighting* back?" He scoffs. "I don't blame you. You don't have to risk your lives on the frontlines. You just sit here in your precious little tower, waiting for others to get their hands dirty for you. Are you really Ashroth's leaders, or just puppets of the Demon King?"

Before anyone can respond, the sound of hurried footsteps echoes from the hall, and a guard bursts into the chamber, breathless, his face pale and drenched in sweat.

"*Siege! Siege! We're under attack!*" the guard cries, his voice frantic.

I freeze, every muscle in my body locking up as the words hit me like a slap. The entire room goes silent for a heartbeat before pandemonium ensues.

"Demon army, coming from the south gate!" The guard's voice cracks as he continues, panic evident in his every word. "They're here! They've breached the outer defenses!"

Imran's face immediately shifts, morphing into stone-cold seriousness. Kamea's already moving, his hand going to his arrows with practiced ease.

"We're not waiting for orders," Imran barks, already grabbing his sword from its resting place beside him. "Everyone, get ready to fight!"

The council members are in a frenzy, some shouting orders, some scrambling in panic. I stand there, frozen for a moment, my mind reeling. I'm baffled. We just came into the city yesterday, and now we're under attack? This early? But I don't have time to dwell on it. This is it. This is what I've been training for. I've been thrust into this world, and now I'm thrust into a battle I didn't expect to face so soon.

Kamea looks at me, his eyes dark with both fury and something else—determination, perhaps. "Get ready," he commands, his voice sharp. "We're fighting."

I snap out of my reverie, my body moving on instinct as adrenaline surges through me. I race to the door, my heart hammering in my chest. Guards run past me, some carrying swords, others with shields, heading toward the southern gate. I follow their movements, feeling the rush of urgency.

One of the guard's hands me a piece of equipment—just a simple leather tunic, a shield, and a sword that looks like it hasn't seen battle in decades. I look at the sword, feeling the weight of it in my hand, and the rust on the blade makes my stomach churn. It's not as efficient as my sword, but I don't have time to complain. This is it.

The sounds of battle reach us even before we're outside—clanging steel, guttural roars, the screams of the dying.

As I step out into the chaos, I feel my nerves snap into place. Imran and Kamea are already ahead of me, charging toward the frontlines, Imran's sword drawn and ready and Kamea's arrows cocked, firing shots as he runs. A dozen adventurers are with them, and as we race forward, I see the carnage for myself. The streets are lined with the fallen. Ashroth's soldiers and adventurers are already engaged in combat with the demon horde. And the demons—they're relentless.

They're monstrous, twisted forms of every size and shape, some humanoid with horns and claws, others beasts with scales and fangs. Their eyes glow with malicious intent, their shrieks echoing in the air. The stench of sulfur and blood hangs thick in the air, suffocating, choking.

I'm barely able to process the scale of it all. The air hums with tension. The ground beneath my boots shakes with every step as demons charge at the defenders with terrifying ferocity. I grip my rusty sword tighter, steeling myself.

Imran's voice rings out above the chaos. "Move, Crilt!" He's already cutting down demons with his sword, his strength unmatched. "We've got no time to waste!"

I run forward, my heart pounding. The first demon I encounter is a hulking beast, its skin covered in dark scales that glisten in the blood-soaked sunlight. It roars, swinging a massive club toward me, and I barely dodge out of the way in time. The ground shakes as the club slams into the cobblestones where I was just standing.

Without thinking, I thrust my sword into its side. The blade meets its tough scales, and I feel the jarring resistance, but somehow, the demon stumbles back, snarling in pain. I twist the sword, pulling it free, and then slash again, finding its weak spot beneath its arm. The demon lets out a howl of agony, and it stumbles, crumpling to the ground in a heap.

I don't have time to celebrate my small victory. More demons are charging at us, and the battle continues to rage around me. There are adventurers fighting beside me, but we're all vastly outnumbered. Every time I look around, I see more demons swarming toward us, their bloodlust in their eyes.

Kamea is a whirlwind of movement. He's fighting with lethal precision, dropping demon after demon. I see him take on two at once, his agility and skill unmatched as he dodges their attacks and shoots with deadly accuracy. His face is grim, but there's a fire in his eyes, a fierce and unwavering determination.

Imran, ever the brawler, is taking on demons twice his size. His sword moves like lightning, cleaving through enemies with ease, though even he can't help but show the strain as the demons continue to press forward. Blood splatters his face, but he doesn't slow down.

I'm fighting alongside them, but the pressure is overwhelming. It's all I can do to keep up. My sword feels clumsy in my hands, but I fight through the awkwardness, each swing feeling heavier than the last. The demons aren't letting up, and neither can I.

One demon—a massive creature with four arms—swings at me with a terrifying roar. I barely manage to block one of its blows with my shield, but the force of it sends me crashing backward. My feet slip on the slick cobblestones, and I hit the ground hard. Before I can even react, the demon's foot comes crashing down toward me.

Instinctively, I roll to the side, narrowly avoiding its crushing weight. My heart is racing, and I can hear my pulse pounding in my ears. I scramble to my feet, my sword trembling in my grip.

Just as the demon lunges toward me again, I see Kamea's figure flash past. With a swift, graceful jump, he grabs an arrow, piercing it through the demon's arm by hand, ripping it through the muscles in a brutal form, and the beast stumbles back, shrieking in pain. I don't hesitate. I charge forward and drive my sword into the demon's chest, the blade finally finding purchase as it lets out one final, agonized roar before collapsing to the ground.

I pant heavily, the weight of the battle pressing down on me. The ground is slick with blood, the air thick with the smell of death. But I can't stop now. Not when we're so close to the end.

By the time the final demons are slain, the street is littered with the bodies of the fallen—both human and demon alike. The heat of the battle lingers in the air, and my arms ache with exhaustion. My clothes are soaked through with blood, the remnants of the demons we've killed clinging to my skin.

I stand there, breathing heavily, surveying the aftermath. The sounds of the battle fade into silence, the air thick with smoke and the scent of blood. The city is eerily quiet now, the streets littered with the broken bodies of both adventurers and demons.

The victory feels hollow. We've won this battle, but the war is far from over.

I turn to see Kamea and Imran, both covered in blood but standing tall, their expressions grim.

"We're not done yet," Kamea mutters, looking out at the horizon. "But we've made it through this one."

Imran claps me on the back, smiling. "Good job, Crilt. You did good."

I don't respond. I can't. My mind is still processing what just happened—the violence, the bloodshed. The demons. I've never experienced it before. I don't know how to feel, but I feel a surge of overwhelming confidence consume me. If this is what the Demon King got, then I'm ready for it.

***

The aftermath of the demon siege is both overwhelming and sobering. The streets of Ashroth are littered with the remnants of battle—broken weapons, shredded armor, and the bodies of the fallen. The once-bustling town square now stands eerily still, marked by the stench of blood and the silence of a battle that raged just hours ago. I stand amidst the carnage, my chest heaving with each breath, my body sore and stained with the blood of demons and comrades alike. The adrenaline from the battle is starting to fade, and in its place, a sharp sense of reality sets in.

I look around at the injured guards and adventurers, their wounds severe yet somehow still alive, some tending to each other, others limping along with help. They are bruised and battered, but there's something about them that makes me pause—a determination that echoes in the air. They didn't stop fighting when the demons came. They fought until the end until the last demon was slain. The same determination that I see in Imran and Kamea, who are both still standing tall despite the exhaustion evident on their faces.

"That was more trouble than it needed to be," Kamea mutters, looking over the battlefield. His voice is low, but I can hear the weight behind it—the disbelief mixed with relief. But even as he speaks, I know that this victory is temporary. The fight isn't over, not by a long shot.

As I scan the destruction around us, something shifts inside me. For the first time since I came to Ashroth, I fully grasp the severity of the situation. This is just a glimpse of what's at stake. The kingdom's forces are stretched thin, and the demons seem to be multiplying. Every battle we fight brings us closer to the inevitable—more bloodshed, more death.

I think about the people here—the humans and the demi-humans. Kaze's face flashes in my mind, the sadness in her eyes as she spoke of her family, and how she couldn't save them from the clutches of the Demon King. And even more, I think about the demi-humans, like me, who are enslaved by demons, their freedom stripped away. They're hunted, used, and abused—just as much a target of the Demon King's cruelty as humans.

As much as I've resented being pulled into this world, something inside me shifts. My thoughts turn to Sokh, to the one person I've ever trusted. If I truly want to find Sokh—if I want to change anything—I have to help stop the Demon King's reign of terror.

I grip the rusty sword in my hand. This is about freedom. This is about fighting for those who can't fight for themselves. Whether they're human or demi-human, we all deserve a life free from tyranny.

I walk toward Imran and Kamea, who are talking with other adventurers, giving orders to help the injured and ensure the city is secure. When they notice me approaching, Kamea raises an eyebrow, his arms crossed. "You alright?" he asks, his voice still serious but tinged with concern. He looks me over as if assessing whether the battle has affected me.

I don't answer right away. My thoughts are too tangled, too full of the emotions and realizations from the past few hours. Finally, I speak, my voice firm. "I want to do it now."

Imran raises a brow, confused. "Oh? What?"

"To officially join your party. I want to do it now,"

Both of them stare at me for a moment, and for a heartbeat, I wonder if they'll question my decision.

Kamea's expression softens. "Sure," he mutters, almost to himself, though there's no judgment in his words. Just acceptance. "Did the battle speed your resolve?"

I take a breath, feeling the weight of my decision sink in. "I've seen and heard enough." I gesture toward the battlefield, where injured adventurers are being tended to by medics, where the fallen soldiers are being carried away. "This war... it's not going to end if we just keep hiding behind our walls. We're all affected or going to be affected by the demon king anyway, so I don't see why I shouldn't help."

Imran slaps me on the back, a hearty grin breaking across his face. "Aww, you softie," he ruffles my hair. I scowl at him. They both laugh. "Glad to see you finally getting on board, Crilt. Welcome to the team." His voice is warm and sincere. There's no hesitation in his words, no second-guessing. Just acceptance.

I nod in response. The decision is made. I will fight. I will stand side by side with Imran, Kamea, and everyone else who believes in something worth fighting for.

The sounds of the battle outside the castle walls slowly fade as we turn our attention back to the present. The next step is clear: We need to regroup, heal, and prepare for whatever comes next. But I know one thing for sure—I will not run. I will not hide. Not from the war, not from my past, and certainly not from the future.

As the day fades into night, and we return to the inn to rest, the weight of everything finally settles into place. I've been thrust into this war against my will, but now, it's my choice.

This is where I belong now.

CHAPTER 4

The days after my decision to join the Kingdom's forces are filled with a grueling series of training sessions with Imran and Kamea. I'd always been a fighter, having survived the depths of the dungeon and battled countless monsters by Sokh's side, but this was different. Adventuring wasn't just about strength or survival. It was about strategy, teamwork, and understanding the nuances of combat in a way I hadn't been taught before.

Each morning, after a quick breakfast prepared by Kamea, we'd head out into the wilds surrounding Ashroth for our training. The thick woods on the outskirts of the city were perfect for learning how to survive in the wild—how to track, how to hide, and most importantly, how to fight and kill efficiently without being caught off guard.

Imran starts by teaching me the basics of combat in a way that's distinctly different from Sokh's style. Sokh taught me to rely on instinct, using whatever weapons or tools were at my disposal, in whatever way I could make them work. However, Imran's approach is more structured and more controlled. He's a master of the sword, and his style is graceful but deadly, calculated but fluid.

He shows me how to hold my blade, how to balance my weight, and the importance of maintaining a firm stance.

We spar, and at first, I'm all instinct. I swing wildly, trying to land a hit, using brute force to my advantage. But Imran easily dodges, his movements almost a dance as he sidesteps my blows and counters with swift strikes to my side. His laughter echoes through the trees, and I grow frustrated with each failed attempt to land a blow. "You're too rigid," Imran says between smirks. "Relax. Let the sword become an extension of you like it's just another part of your body. Don't force it."

Kamea, on the other hand, watches from a distance, his arms folded, a stern expression on his face. Surprisingly, he's quite good with a sword, but he prefers to use his arrows instead. "Don't get too caught up in the strength of your strikes. The enemy won't wait for you to land a perfect hit. It's about quick decisions, fast counters, and recognizing when to strike. Control. Precision."

I don't respond. I just grit my teeth and keep going. After all, if I'm going to be a part of this, if I'm going to fight the Demon King's forces, I need to be better than I was before. Every failure, every bruise I earned during our sparring sessions, only fuels the fire inside me to grow stronger.

Over time, I begin to feel the rhythm of the fight, the ebb and flow of combat. I stop forcing my attacks, learning to use my agility and speed to my advantage. Imran's sword strikes are swift and precise, and though I still can't match him in terms of raw skill, I begin to land some hits. Not clean ones, but enough to prove that I'm improving.

Kamea occasionally steps in, his style of combat starkly different from Imran's. Kamea prefers to use his longbow and his daggers, a more stealth-oriented approach. I'm amazed at how silent and precise he is, how he moves like a shadow through the trees. "Combat isn't just about direct confrontation," Kamea tells me one day as he walks me through some basic stealth techniques. "The key to surviving in the wild is knowing when to engage and when to fade into the background. A good warrior doesn't just fight; he knows when to hide when to track, and when to strike with deadly precision."

We practice for hours on end, running through various techniques—striking from the shadows, silently moving through the underbrush, and retreating without leaving a trace. Kamea's expertise in stealth becomes invaluable. He teaches me to use the environment to my advantage, to camouflage myself against trees and rocks, and how to strike without warning.

One afternoon, Kamea hands me his bow, his usual expression unreadable as he watches me. "Try it," he says simply.

I've never used a bow before. The idea of shooting a projectile feels strange to me, but I don't let my hesitation show. The string feels unfamiliar in my hand, and the bow's weight throws me off balance at first, but Kamea stands behind me, offering quiet guidance. Slowly, I find my rhythm. My first shot misses entirely, the arrow sticking into the dirt far beyond the target. Kamea doesn't say anything, but I can see the subtle shake of his head in my peripheral vision.

"Focus," he murmurs. "Relax. Let the bow become part of you."

I nock another arrow and try again, this time remembering the lessons I've learned from swordplay—don't force it. My second shot lands much closer to the target. I can feel a shift in the air as I nock another arrow, and this time, when I release it, the arrow flies straight and true, striking the target with a satisfying *thwack.*

Kamea nods once, acknowledging the improvement, though his expression remains as neutral as ever. "Good. Now, do it again."

As the days pass, I train with both Imran and Kamea, not only focusing on individual combat skills but also learning the importance of teamwork. We go through mock battles, where one of us plays the role of the enemy, and the others must work together to defeat them. It's hard at first—Kamea moves with the silent precision of a shadow, while Imran relies on his brute strength and quick reflexes to overwhelm the enemy. And me? I'm still learning to find my place.

But over time, I start to anticipate their movements, to understand their strategies. I learn to communicate without words, to recognize when Imran is going to draw the enemy's attention so that I can flank them from the side. I learn to position myself so that Kamea's arrows find their mark. Slowly, I become part of the team—my movements were fluid, and my strikes coordinated with theirs. I begin to see that the fight isn't just about individual skill; it's about trusting the people around you and working in tandem to take down a much larger force.

One of the most difficult training exercises comes when we simulate an ambush. Imran leads the charge, and Kamea takes cover in the trees to provide support. I'm left in the middle of the "battlefield," acting as a decoy to draw out the mock enemy. At first, I'm skeptical. I'm used to fighting alone, used to relying on my own instincts. But when the battle begins, I quickly realize how important it is to play my part. I draw the enemy's focus with a few well-placed strikes and allow Imran to take advantage of their distraction. Kamea picks them off from the shadows, his arrows hitting their marks without hesitation. It's all over quickly, and the mock enemy—another adventurer from Ashroth—lies in the dirt, defeated.

"You did well," Imran says, clapping me on the back. "You've got the instincts. Just remember: don't let your pride get in the way of the team. It's about the group, not the individual."

Kamea doesn't say much, but I catch the faintest nod of approval from him.

***

Training isn't just about fighting, so I've learned. It's also about surviving in the harsh wilderness that surrounds Ashroth.

Kamea takes me on long treks through the forest, teaching me to track animals and gather herbs, to make shelter out of whatever materials we can find, and to create fire with just the most basic of tools. He's an expert in survival, and I'm amazed at how easily he adapts to his environment.

On one of our trips, he shows me how to find food in the wild. "The forest gives us everything we need," he says, pointing to a patch of mushrooms growing on the side of a tree. "These will help with energy. That over there?" He points to a stream nearby. "Fish. And if you're lucky, you can find small game, like rabbits."

I'm still a little skeptical, but as Kamea demonstrates how to catch fish using just a simple spear, I realize that there's more to survival than just brute strength. It's about knowledge, about knowing the land and using it to your advantage.

By the time we return to Ashroth, several weeks have passed, and I'm no longer the same fighter I was when I first arrived. I'm stronger, more confident in my abilities, and more in tune with the people I fight alongside. I've learned to trust Imran and Kamea, and they've learned to trust me.

I'm no longer just an outsider. I'm part of their team, part of the fight. And with every training session, with every battle, I grow more determined to see this war through to the end, to free the people who have suffered under the Demon King's reign, and to find the answers I've been searching for.

The journey has only just begun. But I'm ready.

***

The more time I spend with Imran and Kamea, the more I realize how little I truly know about their pasts and their motivations. In the beginning, I saw them only as allies, partners in this endless battle. But as the days pass, I start to see them as people, with their own stories, their own pain and struggles. It's hard not to, especially when we're fighting side by side, day in and day out, each of us pushing the other to become stronger.

Imran is the first to open up to me, though it doesn't happen all at once. It's one evening, after a particularly brutal training session, when he's sitting by the fire, his sword resting across his lap. His voice is quieter than usual, almost a murmur, as he speaks.

"You know," Imran starts, glancing at me from across the fire, "there's a reason I fight. A reason I keep pushing forward."

I don't say anything at first, unsure of how to respond. I'm still trying to understand his personality—his boisterous energy, his constant jokes, his almost reckless fighting style. But when I look at him now, I can see something darker beneath the surface. Something painful. So, I wait for him to continue.

"My wife," Imran says, his voice low and steady, "her name was Sara. She was... the light of my life. We had a child, a son. His name was Elias. He was just a baby when the Demon King's army attacked our village. I—I was away at the time, on a mission. When I came back... everything was gone."

I'm stunned by the news. I never thought that Imran would be married—or had been married with a child, and I can only imagine how painful that would have been for him.

He pauses, his hand gripping the hilt of his sword so tightly that his knuckles turn white. His eyes are distant, and unfocused, as if he's lost in a memory that's both painful and vivid. "I found them in the ruins. My wife. My son." His voice cracks, just for a moment, before he pulls himself together. "I couldn't save them. And that's why I fight. I fight because I couldn't protect the ones I loved. I won't let that happen again."

I'm silent, processing his words. There's so much pain in his voice, so much loss. It's hard to imagine that kind of grief, especially when I've never truly had anyone to lose in the way he has. Sure, I've lost Sokh, but I never had the kind of love he describes, and I still have a little hope that he's coming back, something Imran doesn't have the luxury of having.

"I don't know what to say," I say, my voice softer than usual. "I can't say that I know what you've been through, but I'm truly sorry about your loss. I'm sure they were lovely."

Imran looks at me, his eyes softening for just a second. "They were," his voice trails off, wistfully. Then, with a shrug, he picks up his sword again, flashing me a grin. "Anyway, don't feel sorry for me, Crilt. You being sappy doesn't fit you. It's my cross to bear. But thanks for listening."

We sit in silence for a while, the fire crackling between us, the weight of his words hanging in the air.

***

The next day, I get a chance to learn more about Kamea. We've been practicing archery, and Kamea's precision is—well, it's inhuman, I wonder if he's a Demi-human too. The way his arrows fly, hitting their mark every time, with deadly accuracy. It's almost like he's one with the bow, the arrow, and the target.

But after training, we take a break near a stream, and Kamea seems... off. He's sitting on a large rock, absently tossing stones into the water, his usual quiet self but somehow more withdrawn today. I sit next to him, unsure of what to say. He's never been the type to offer much about himself, but I figure now is as good a time as any.

"You don't talk much about your past," I say, keeping my voice low, "What's your story, Kamea?"

He doesn't look at me right away. For a moment, I wonder if he's even going to respond, but then he sighs deeply, tossing another stone into the stream.

"I lost everything," he says quietly, his voice tinged with bitterness. "My family. My home. My entire bloodline. The Demon King's forces slaughtered us. I wasn't there when they came. I was away, out on a mission. When I came back..." He trails off, and I can hear the unspoken pain in his words. "There was nothing left. No one. Just the bodies of the ones I loved, burned and desecrated."

Again. Another loss, thanks to the Demon King. It makes my blood boil. It's almost funny. Look for far I've come to care for Kamea now, in my own way.

I turn my head slightly, watching Kamea closely as he speaks. His words are so detached, so cold, that it's hard to imagine the kind of destruction he's talking about. And then, something shifts in him, and he finally looks at me, his expression hardening.

"I've spent years trying to piece myself back together," he continues. "I let rage overtake me for far too long. I met Imran, I try to be calm and live in peace, trying to find peace within myself, but the truth is, Crilt, I don't know who I am anymore. I don't even know if I'm doing this for the right reasons. The lines are so blurred now, that I don't even know who I'm doing this for anymore. Sometimes, I wonder if it's worth it. But then I see people like you, people who've been through hell and still fight to survive. And I think maybe... maybe this war is worth fighting for. Ashroth is the last bastion of humanity. If we lose it, then everything else is for nothing."

His words hit me harder than I expected. Kamea's not just fighting for revenge like Imran; he's fighting for peace. For a better world. I can see the weight of his past in his eyes, and I feel a flicker of respect for him that I didn't have before. He's not just a stoic warrior; he's a man who has lost everything, yet still pushes forward because he believes in something bigger than his own pain.

"I didn't realize..." I start, but Kamea cuts me off, shaking his head.

"Most people don't," he says, his voice soft but resolute. "But that's the reality of this world now. You either fight, or you die. And I'll be damned if I let this kingdom fall. Even if I die in the process, I'll make sure it's a fight worth remembering."

I don't know how to respond to that. It's not what I expected. But I think I understand him a little better now. Kamea isn't the type to show his emotions, but underneath that calm exterior, there's a man who carries the scars of a lifetime of loss. He's a protector, a survivor, and he'll do whatever it takes to make sure Ashroth—and the people he's come to care about—thrive.

***

Later that night, we sit together around the fire, the three of us. It's one of those rare moments where there's silence between us and peace. Imran is cleaning his sword, Kamea sharpening his bow, and I'm simply staring into the fire, my mind swirling with everything they've told me.

I enjoy moments like this. And it makes me wonder if the world would be like this if the demon king was defeated. I prop my hands under my head and close my eyes, falling into a dreamless sleep.

***

As the days pass and I continue my training, I hear whispers among the adventurers, rumors that stir a new, unsettling curiosity in me. The name "Arius" begins to pop up more frequently in conversations, spoken with reverence, awe, and sometimes, hushed tones of fear. Every time I overhear a conversation, I find myself drawn in, trying to piece together the fragments of his story.

Arius. The former hero. The one who had led the charge against the Demon King's forces, the man who was said to have single-handedly turned the tides of battle on countless occasions. His name carries weight, and yet, no one speaks it openly without a certain caution, as if the very mention of him could bring doom.

The more I hear, the more fascinated I become. They say he was the kingdom's greatest warrior, a beacon of hope to the people of Ashroth. He was known for his tactical brilliance, his unwavering courage, and his overwhelming strength. He fought with a sword in hand and a heart filled with an unshakable resolve. His victories against the Demon King's forces were legendary. No one had fought like him, no one had inspired like him.

But then, something happened. The stories begin to change.

Arius had disappeared during a pivotal battle. Some say he was slain by the Demon King himself, and his body never recovered. The kingdom held a grand funeral, his loss mourned by all, and the hope of Ashroth seemed to dim in the wake of his death. The world moved on, but the shadow of Arius's absence lingered.

Or did it?

As I listen to more rumors, I begin to hear whispers of something darker. A few say that Arius is not dead at all. They say that he was taken by the Demon King's forces and, through some dark magic or twisted fate, turned into one of the Demon King's generals. The rumors are fragmented, and none of them are solid.

Some adventurers laugh it off, dismissing it as paranoia. But there are others who speak of it with conviction, their eyes filled with uncertainty.

"Arius, alive?" one of them murmurs one evening around the campfire. "Impossible. The kingdom would have found out by now. He was a hero. How could he join the demons?"

But then another adventurer, a grizzled old man with a scar across his face, shakes his head, his voice low and secretive. "You don't know what they're capable of. The Demon King is powerful, and he has ways of twisting even the most noble of men. They say Arius was... changed. Not just in body, but in spirit. He was betrayed by his own people, left to die, and now he serves the very thing he once fought against."

I can feel the weight of the words as they hang in the air. The idea is unsettling, almost unbelievable, yet there's something that gnaws at me. The truth is, no one knows for sure what happened to Arius. No one except the Demon King himself, and maybe—just maybe—Arius.

I don't want to believe it. How could I? How could someone like Arius, a hero who inspired so many, possibly fall so far? It doesn't make sense. The stories, the glory he once brought to the kingdom, it's all too powerful. Arius was the embodiment of what I want to be.

A model. A role model. A true hero. Someone who people could look up to. An example of being better is to do great things. Several months ago, I would have been highly opposed to being such a public figure, a hero, even. But the more I spent here, the more the idea looked enticing. He was everything I ever thought a warrior should be—strong, unyielding, and unafraid. Without all the unnecessary attention, I would love to be like him. And now, to think that he might have been corrupted, twisted into a general of the Demon King's army… It sounds too depressing to think about.

What would be so horribly displeasing that would turn a loved hero into an enemy? Nothing! Which means that the rumors are all a sham.

Yet the more I think about it, the more I realize I'm drawn to him, in a way that isn't healthy. The idea of Arius, this legendary warrior, being turned into something so... wrong, it twists something inside me, as the thought of it offends me in a way. It just sounds too crude to me. I want to understand what happened. I want to know if it's true because if it is, it means that even the strongest of us can fall. Even the greatest heroes can be broken.

In some strange, unhealthy way, I begin to idolize Arius. Not just because of his achievements, but because of the idea that he might still be out there, somewhere. What if he's alive? What if he's still fighting, still leading the charge, but on the wrong side? What if, just maybe, I could find him?

I find myself asking these questions more and more. I can't stop thinking about it. Arius—once a hero, now a symbol of the ultimate fall from grace. I can't shake the thought.

***

Training with Imran and Kamea becomes even more intense as the days go on. Imran continues to push me harder, drilling into me the finer points of combat, while Kamea focuses on teaching me how to be more aware of my surroundings, how to read people, and how to strategize. But as I'm training, my mind keeps wandering to Arius. I wonder what kind of man he really was. Was he truly the hero they said he was? Or was there more to the story that they left out?

I mean, the story sounds glorious in itself, the fact that a mere, fragile human could stand its ground against the Demon king, whom I've come to truly hate, fills me with such excitement that I can't contain. He's the first of his kind to achieve such a feat. It's so inspiring because it pushes me to become better and stronger. I could become the first of my kind to achieve great feats too.

I talk to Imran one evening as we sit by the fire, the sounds of the forest around us. "Imran," I begin hesitantly, "what do you know about Arius?"

Imran raises an eyebrow, clearly surprised by the question. He leans back against a tree, his expression thoughtful. "Arius? Well, he was the best of us, Crilt. There was no one who fought like him. He led the charge against the Demon King's army, and the kingdom trusted him with everything. He was the one who inspired hope when all seemed lost."

"And you don't think it's possible that... he could have turned?" I ask, my voice quiet, unsure of how to phrase the question. I'm not sure if I'm asking for validation or if I'm just hoping to hear something different.

Imran's eyes harden at the suggestion. He chuckles bitterly. "I don't know. With how strong the demon king is, who knows what is what anymore. But I choose to believe that he didn't betray mankind, that it's all just a rumor, if not, it would be terrible for us. After all, they have powerful demon generals on their side. Imagine having the world's most skilled and powerful human on their side? That would be catastrophic."

But even as he says it, there's a hint of doubt in his voice, like he's trying to convince himself more than me. I don't press him further, but the seed of doubt is planted in my mind. What if Imran's right? What if Arius really is one of the Demon King's generals now?

***

The next morning, I wake with another determination in my heart. I want to know more about Arius. I want to know the truth. I *have* to know, even if it destroys the image of the hero I've built in my mind.

I find Kamea at the training grounds, adjusting his bow. "Kamea," I say, a sense of urgency in my voice. "Do you know where I can find more information about Arius? About what happened to him?"

He looks at me, sensing the seriousness in my tone. "Why do you care about Arius all of a sudden?" he asks, his eyes narrowing slightly. "That's a name from the past, Crilt. It's better to leave things buried."

I shake my head, determined. "No. I need to know. I need to understand what happened. If he's still alive, I want to find him."

"Are you crazy? Don't you know how dangerous that can be? Stop fixating over him for your own good. You'll thank me later," Kamea scolds.

I huff. "Fine then. If you don't want me to go searching for him, then tell me what you know about him. That's the least you can do for me, right?"

Kamea hesitates, and for a moment, I think he's going to deny me, but then he sighs, shaking his head. "Alright. If you're set on it, I'll give you what I know. But don't expect an easy answer. Arius was too important to be just another casualty of war. He's a symbol. A story. Some truths, Crilt, are buried for a reason."

"I'll take my chances," I reply, my voice steady, though my heart races with anticipation.

Kamea looks me over, his expression unreadable. Then, with a final nod, he begins to speak, "Arius disappeared after the Battle of Dawn's Peak. That was the last time anyone saw him. After that, there were rumors. Some say he was captured, others say he died on the battlefield. But the truth is... no one knows for sure."

I feel a tightness in my chest. The mystery deepens. "And the rumors?" I ask.

"Rumors are dangerous," Kamea replies. "But there's one thing I'll tell you—Arius didn't just disappear. Something happened to him, I don't know what, but it was the turning point that changed everything."

CHAPTER 5

The summons to Ashroth's castle came quickly. We were to be sent on a mission: protect the village of Hurin from a demon raid.

I, Kamea, and Imran are joined by five other adventurers. The group's dynamic is tense from the start—no one's particularly eager to bond. We're all in this together, but no one is ready to share their stories yet. Still, we can't help but exchange introductions as we make our way out of Ashroth's gates and head for Hurin.

Risa, an archer like Kamea, is the first to speak as we ride out of the city. She has short red hair and a strong, muscular build, a testament to her many battles. She's also the most vocal of the group, which is both a blessing and a curse.

"So, you two are the famous ones, huh?" she asks, glancing at Kamea and Imran. "The elite squad?"

Kamea doesn't answer her, instead staring straight ahead, his expression as unreadable as ever. I stay silent too. I'm not interested in small talk right now. Imran, the ever-friendly one, just grins.

Risa doesn't seem put off by our lack of response. She presses on, clearly trying to get a reaction. "I've heard about you too," she says, referring to me. "You three are supposed to be pretty strong. Let's see if it's true, shall we?"

I glance sideways at her but don't respond. She doesn't seem to mind, laughing lightly as if it's all just a joke. Maybe it is for her.

"I've been with the kingdom's forces for a while," she continues, talking more to herself now. "But nothing like this. Ashroth's elite? I guess I'm lucky to be riding with you."

"That's enough, Risa," Bran says, stepping in. He's a massive man, broad-shouldered with a shaved head and an imposing presence. "Save your stories for when the demons show up."

Risa shrugs nonchalantly, and there's a small moment of silence. It's clear that Bran prefers action over conversation, and I can respect that.

Killian, the swordsman, stands a little apart from the group. His long blonde hair is tied back, and he's quieter than the rest of us. He doesn't seem interested in speaking either, but I catch him watching Kamea and me. His blue eyes narrow slightly as if assessing us.

Seni, the elderly mage, is the least talkative of the group. He's quiet, slow, and calm. His long white beard brushes against his chest as he rides, and he doesn't speak unless necessary. I notice him looking at the surroundings often, but he doesn't offer much in terms of conversation.

Falin, also a mage, with pastel green hair and blue eyes, is silent, a shy type, it seems. I catch her glancing at us from time to time, and when I catch her looking, she blushes red and turns away instantly. I can tell that she wants to talk, but is too shy to bring herself to do it. I'm a bit grateful for that because I'm honestly not in the mood for any conversations.

The journey itself is long and quiet. For most of the day, we ride in silence, the only sounds being the rhythm of hooves on the dirt path and the occasional rustling of trees around us. The landscape we pass is a mixture of beauty and devastation. Ashroth may be the last bastion of civilization, but the land surrounding it is scarred, marked by the wars that have raged for years. Burned villages, abandoned farms, fields of charred earth.

As the day stretches on, we stop occasionally to rest, but no one speaks much. We're all too lost in our thoughts. I still find myself thinking about Arius. Where could he have gone? It's naive thinking, but I hope to stumble upon him one day.

I shake the thoughts away, focusing instead on the journey ahead. There's no room for distractions now. My mission is to protect Hurin. But even so, I can't ignore the feeling of unease that lingers in the pit of my stomach.

When the sun begins to set, we find a place to make camp. Kamea insists on setting up watch, as usual, while the rest of us begin to prepare for the night. Risa seems to want to keep talking, and as she sets up her bedroll, she glances at me again.

"Don't mind me, but I'm curious," she starts. "What's your story?"

I glance over at her. "There's nothing to tell."

Risa laughs. "You're one of those, huh? Mysterious. All right, all right, I won't push." She turns to Bran. "What about you, then? Any juicy stories from the front lines?"

Bran gives her a grunt and shakes his head. "Ain't got time for stories. Just focus on the job."

"Fair enough," Risa mutters, though she doesn't sound entirely convinced. "How about you, gorgeous? Not much of a talker too, huh?" She winks at Falin.

As expected, Falin squeaks and turns a bright red. She shakes her head and Risa grins, pouncing on the smaller girl. "Cute," she begins to tease Falin, tickling and touching the poor girl, and two roll around on her bedroll.

Seni, who has been quietly studying a map by the fire, finally speaks up, ignoring the two. "The journey will be long. We must remain vigilant. The demons won't stop."

"Right," Imran says, his voice low but steady. "The farther we go, the more dangerous it will be. Hurin's close to the front lines."

I stay silent, but I feel a sense of camaraderie among the group. Even though we're all strangers, we're bound by a common purpose. We're going to protect Hurin. At least, that's the goal.

***

The night is quiet, and we take turns standing watch. Kamea takes the first shift, and I settle into my bedroll, staring up at the stars. The sounds of the night are a strange comfort. I try to block out my thoughts of Arius and focus on the task ahead.

When my turn comes to stand watch, I sit by the fire, listening to the crackling wood. The others are asleep, and for the first time in a while, the silence feels peaceful. I let my mind wander to thoughts of the future. What will it be like when we reach Hurin? Will we be able to defend the village, or will it fall like so many others?

The silence is broken when Kamea speaks. "You're quiet."

I look over at him. He's standing nearby, his eyes scanning the horizon, always alert. "I'm always quiet."

"Not like this," he says, his voice barely above a whisper. "You're tense. Is it because of the raid?"

I don't respond. Kamea doesn't push it, and we sit in silence for a while longer, the weight of the journey settling on us.

The fire crackles, its warmth creeping into my bones, but it's not enough to settle the restlessness inside me. The night stretched on, and I'm still unable to sleep. Kamea is already worn out, tucked in his bedroll and I listen to his soft breaths, the occasional rustling of leaves, and the low, steady breathing of the rest of them as they sleep. I continue staring up at the stars, but even their beauty can't quiet the buzzing in my mind. It's like my body and my mind are two separate entities, one wanting rest and the other wide awake, pacing in circles. I can't shake the feeling that something is coming—something terrible.

Demons. They're not the worst I've faced. Far from it. But their agility… that's what gets to me. They don't fight like other monsters. They move fast, too fast, almost impossible to track. And they're relentless. Once they get a taste of blood, they don't stop until they've spilled more. I remember my last encounter with them, how I nearly lost my footing just trying to keep up. My stamina isn't infinite, and demons can run me dry quicker than any other monster I've fought.

I close my eyes, trying to force my mind into silence, but the thoughts keep flooding back in. What if we're not ready? What if we fail to protect Hurin? What will happen then?

"You're still awake?"

I open one eye, meeting the gaze of Killian, who's sitting a few feet away, his sword resting across his lap. I hadn't noticed him getting up, but there he is, looking at me like he's waiting for something. I don't respond at first, thinking if I ignore him, maybe he'll go away.

But he doesn't.

"I get it," he continues, his voice light, almost casual. "Not much sleep when you've got demons on the mind."

I glance over at him again, narrowing my eyes slightly. He doesn't seem to mind that I'm not responding. In fact, he looks almost… relaxed. Like he's used to this. To talk when people don't answer.

"You know," he goes on, "when I first started out, I thought I'd be done in a week. I mean, really. The stories they tell about adventurers, the ones who come back after fighting monsters and demons, it all sounded so easy. But let me tell you, it's a lot different when you're out here."

I stay silent, but I can't help but listen. There's something about his voice—it's oddly comforting. I don't know how to feel about that.

"You ever faced anything like the demon horde before?" he asks, now looking at me more closely. "They're a bit of a pain, aren't they? Fast, agile... they can wear you down pretty quick if you're not careful."

I shift slightly, a grunt escaping my throat. "I've fought demons before," I finally say, my voice rough from disuse. "They're not as terrifying as some things I've faced. But yeah, they wear you out fast."

Killian raises an eyebrow, clearly intrigued. "Oh, yeah? What kinds of things have you faced, then? Bigger than demons, huh?"

I almost laugh at the thought. "Bigger, faster, stronger... but they're not always as nimble as the demons."

"Like what?" he presses, leaning forward slightly, clearly fascinated. "You've got me curious now."

I glance at him out of the corner of my eye, but I don't feel the usual irritation. Instead, there's something about his persistence, his genuine curiosity, that's starting to draw me in. It's not something I'm used to. Most people leave me alone, too afraid to pry. Even Imran stops persisting after a bit of silence.

"I've fought in a dungeon," I say, my voice quieter now, more distant. I don't even know why I'm telling him this in the first place, but the words keep spilling out. "Huge, ancient places. Full of monsters you can't even imagine. Things that can tear you apart in seconds if you're not careful."

Killian seems to lean in a little closer, his eyes alight with interest. "What kind of monsters? I've been in dungeons myself, but never anything… like that. What's the worst you've fought?"

I hesitate. It's not something I talk about often. Not because I'm afraid, but because most people won't understand. But for some reason, with Killian sitting there, I feel like I can tell him. Maybe it's the fact that he's listening. Actually listening.

"Ever heard of the Maw?" I ask, the words slipping out before I can stop them.

"The Maw?" Killian repeats, his voice low, as if testing the word. "Never heard of it. What is it?"

I take a deep breath, gathering my thoughts. "It's a thing. A creature. It's got eyes everywhere. And I mean everywhere. Its whole body is covered in eyes, on the skin, in its mouth, and under its limbs. And it doesn't move the way you'd think. It doesn't walk or crawl. It just… shifts. Like it's part of the walls, part of the dungeon itself. And when it comes for you… you can't run. You can't hide."

"Shit," Killian mutters under his breath. "That sounds... terrifying."

"It was," I say, the memory still fresh. "I had to fight it for hours, just trying to figure out how to kill it. I couldn't just brute force it. It's too fast, too elusive. Every time I thought we had a hit, it was already gone."

"That's insane," he says, his voice full of disbelief. "You really fought something like that and lived?"

I nod, the ghost of a smile pulling at the corner of my mouth. "Barely."

Killian whistles low, clearly impressed. "Damn, Crilt. You've got some stories, huh? I wouldn't mind hearing more."

I shake my head, trying to brush off the feeling of being unsettled. "It's not worth hearing. That's not why I'm here."

"Fair enough," he says, not looking disappointed. "But hey, you've got my respect. You're tougher than I thought."

There's a strange silence between us for a moment, not uncomfortable, just…quiet. And for the first time tonight, I feel myself unwinding just a little.

"So," Killian continues after a while, "you've been through all that and you're still standing. Why join a group like this, then? I mean, I get it—Hurin's in danger, but you don't strike me as someone who needs to prove anything."

I'm caught off guard by the question. "I don't need to prove anything to anyone," I finally say. "But...I've done a lot of thinking within myself, and I've decided to help in whatever way I can,"

There's a long pause, and I can feel Killian's gaze on me, studying me carefully. He's waiting for more, but I don't know if I'm ready to say more. Not yet.

"Well, I'm glad you're with us," he says finally, breaking the silence. "Even if you don't talk much. It's nice to know there's someone out there who knows what they're doing."

I don't respond at first, but I feel something shift inside me. It's strange. I'm not used to this feeling—this connection, this sense of camaraderie. Maybe I've spent too long being alone, keeping everyone at arm's length. But right now, I realize, I'm not as alone as I thought.

I let out a quiet sigh, feeling the tension in my body begin to ease just a little. "Yeah, well. Maybe it's nice not to be alone for once."

"Yeah," Killian says with a grin, his voice warm. "Maybe it is."

We fall into a comfortable silence after that, the fire crackling in the background, the night air cool against my skin. Eventually, I feel my eyelids growing heavy, the pull of sleep finally taking over.

But just before I drift off, I realize something.

I've made an attempt to make friends. And for the first time in a long while, I think I might actually want to try again.

***

The morning comes too soon, and as we pack up camp, each of us grim, knowing what's to come. Even Risa isn't as talkative as she was yesterday, and I don't know whether to be worried or thankful for that. There's a stiffness in the air that I can feel, an unease that lingers even after we mount our horses. We ride in silence, the clopping of hooves the only sound breaking the morning stillness. It's as though the calm before the storm has settled around us, waiting for the inevitable chaos.

As we ride, I catch Killian's eye briefly. We don't speak. It's a silent understanding, one that doesn't need words. We know what's coming, but neither of us is in a hurry to voice it. The tension from yesterday still hangs in the air between us. The demons are near. They're coming for the village, and we'll be in the thick of it.

It's not until we crest a hill that the sight hits us: Hurin, the village we've been sent to protect, is already burning. Thick plumes of smoke rise into the sky, dark and foreboding. From this distance, we can already hear the chaos. Screams and cries of agony pierce the air, mingling with the sounds of destruction. My gut twists.

"They're here," Imran says, his voice low and grim. His face is set, with no sign of fear—only resolve. "We need to move quickly. We can't afford to waste any more time."

Kamea doesn't say a word, but his hand tightens on his reins, his knuckles turning white. His eyes narrow, scanning the horizon. I'm not sure if he's calculating the best way to approach or if he's already made up his mind about what's to come. There's this air of resignation that he carries; a man not afraid to die. Either way, there's a stillness to him that I've come to associate with acceptance. He's seen too much.

Risa is the first to break the silence, her voice filled with urgency. "What now, Imran?"

Imran exhales slowly. "We ambush them. Quietly, without being seen. We approach from the side and take them out one by one."

Bran, ever the aggressive one, grunts. "Ambush? Why not just charge in and end it fast?"

Imran doesn't even look at him. "Because charging in will get us all killed, Bran. We move quietly, hit them hard, and get out before they know what hit them."

The plan is clear, but I don't trust it. The demons have a way of being too unpredictable. Still, we have no other choice but to follow Imran's lead. We ride in silence for a little while longer, the urgency of our mission weighing heavily on all of us. As we draw closer to the village, the heat of the flames presses against us, and the sounds of the demons' rampage grow louder.

We split up into two groups. Kamea leads one, and Imran takes the other. I'm in Imran's group, and I find myself side by side with Killian once again. For some reason, I'm not as bothered by his presence today. Maybe it's because the situation demands focus, and right now, talking seems futile. We need to make this work.

We crouch low behind a line of trees as we near the edge of the village. I can see figures darting between the burning buildings—demonic shapes, grotesque and dangerous. Their agility makes them far more deadly than any brute force. They move with inhuman speed, cutting down anyone in their path without hesitation.

These demons are different from the ones we've fought before. They look organized, calculated, and smart. That's not a very good sign. No wonder they called it an urgent mission. My grip tightens on my weapon, and I glance at Killian, who is staring ahead, his jaw clenched.

Suddenly, the air splits with the sound of a high-pitched whistle, and then… a sharp, wet sound. Did…did they just throw an arrow? Risa's voice echoes in the air, but it's not one of triumph or victory. It's a strangled gasp.

I turn just in time to see an arrow—the one that has pierced right through Risa's neck. Blood pours from the wound, soaking into the dirt beneath her. She stumbles backward, her hands grasping at her throat in a futile attempt to stop the flow. But it's no use. The whites in her eyes become more prominent, and she collapses, dead before she hits the ground.

A chill runs through me. For a moment, everything freezes. The plan is shattered, and the suddenness of Risa's death paralyzes us all. The demons turn in our direction, watching us through the bushes with a grin like they've predicted our movement from the start. Another wave of chills goes through me. Bran is the first to move, his rage consuming him. He charges, his massive body plowing through the demons as he swings his great axe. His roar fills the air, a battle cry that seems to shake the very ground beneath us.

"NO!" Bran screams, swinging his axe with brutal force, taking down two demons in one fell swoop. "I'll make them pay for this!"

But Kamea, the realist, sighs. I can see the weariness in his eyes as he watches Bran's reckless charge. He's seen this before—the reckless, desperate attacks that end in more bloodshed. There's no winning this battle with blind rage.

"Bran," Kamea says, his voice calm but heavy, knowing the inevitability of this situation. "There's no point in trying to sneak attack again. They're just toying with us now. We're not going to win this way."

Bran doesn't listen. He doesn't even hear Kamea. He charges forward again, knocking over demons with a single swipe of his axe. But Kamea's words hit me hard. They're true. The demons are playing with us. And we're too outnumbered to keep up the fight for long.

Kamea turns to me, his eyes meeting mine with an almost unnatural calm. "Stay safe," he says quietly. His voice is low enough that only I can hear him. "We don't know how this will end, but don't do anything reckless. Just get out if you can."

I nod; my throat tight. He's asking me to live, or at least try to, and I'll do my best, but I know that survival is never guaranteed in these situations.

The air is filled with chaos as the battle begins. Bran is locked in combat with two demons, his axe a blur of deadly movement, while Imran orders the rest of us to stay low and take out as many as we can without being seen. But it's a losing battle.

I grip my weapon tighter, ready to fight, but I can't help the feeling that we're already too late.

In the chaos, I spot Killian out of the corner of my eye. He's fighting too, but his gaze is darting back toward me. His expression is unreadable, but I can see the way his muscles tense with each swing of his blade. I don't know what he's thinking. I don't know if he's feeling the same dread that's creeping up my spine, but I can't focus on that right now.

All I can focus on is the fight, the blood, the screams. And as Kamea's words echo in my mind, I realize something I've never fully accepted before: this is war. And there's no way to control it.

I'm moving with Killian at my side, my heart hammering in my chest. The clash of steel against demonic flesh rings in my ears, the shouts of battle mingling with the screams of the village burning behind us. The air is thick with smoke, and the heat from the flames licks at my face, but I push it all aside as I focus on the fight. There's no room for hesitation now.

Killian is beside me, his movements smooth and deadly as he slashes through the demons with his sword. His blue eyes are intense, a fire burning behind them as he cuts down one demon after another. I keep up, taking down my own share of foes, but I'm not as fast as him. I'm not as agile. What I have is brute strength, the ability to take down anything that stands in my way, and I rely on it to plow through the demons.

One demon lunges toward me, claws outstretched, and I don't hesitate. My weapon swings through the air, connecting with its torso and splitting it open in a spray of dark blood. I don't even pause to see if it's fully dead; another demon is already rushing me. I duck under its swipe and slice upward, taking it in the belly. Its screech pierces the air before it crumples to the ground.

I look around for a moment, scanning the battle as we push forward. The others are still fighting, but there's no sign of the demons slowing down. Bran is charging through the front lines, his massive frame sending demons flying with each swing of his axe.

Imran is at his side, taking out demons with precision, his eyes constantly scanning for weaknesses, for any openings. Kamea is quieter, his arrows a blur as he moves in and out of combat, cutting down demons with deadly accuracy.

But then there's a scream—a horrifying, gut-wrenching scream that cuts through the chaos, and I know immediately that something is wrong. I look toward the sound and see Falin, clutching her side, blood pouring between her fingers. She stumbles backward, her face twisted in pain, but before anyone can reach her, a demon lunges, sinking its fangs deep into her throat. She dies with a gurgling cry.

I don't have time to process it. I don't have time to mourn. Bran is already roaring in fury, charging toward the demon who killed Falin, but as he swings his axe, the demon sidesteps, laughing, before it slashes across Bran's chest, tearing through the armor as if it were nothing. Bran stumbles back, blood pouring from the wound.

"No!" I shout, rushing toward him, but the demons press in on all sides, forcing me to turn and fight them off. My muscles ache, my breath comes in ragged gasps, but I keep swinging, keep cutting through the demons like they're nothing.

Behind me, I hear Seni cry out, but by the time I turn around, it's too late. One of the demons has pierced his chest with its claws, and the elderly mage collapses to the ground, his staff falling beside him. His life drains away before my eyes.

The weight of the losses is heavy. Falin, Bran, Seni—all gone in the span of minutes. The realization hits hard, like a blow to the gut, but there's no time to stop. No time. We can't afford it. The demons are still here, and they're not going anywhere.

"Fall back!" Imran orders, his voice a growl of authority. His face is grim, his eyes cold with the knowledge that we're losing. But we can't stop fighting.

Kamea nods, his expression unreadable. He doesn't speak, but he moves with the calm efficiency that I've come to know. He's already in motion, directing us toward a more defensible position. We're outnumbered. We're losing, and we all know it.

I push forward, my body protesting the movement as I fight my way to the rear of the group, where Imran and Kamea are rallying us. Killian follows close behind, his face hard with determination, but I see the sorrow in his eyes. After all, those were his friends. His teammates.

We're down to four now. Four against a horde of demons. The odds aren't good, and I can feel the tension building, the sense of doom in the air.

Then, suddenly, in the midst of the battle, something changes. The demons begin to retreat, one by one, pulling back from the fight. It's almost like a signal has gone out, and they all know it's time to leave. The retreat is swift, coordinated, and terrifyingly orderly. The demons who had been charging at us just moments before now seem to disappear into the smoke and shadows, melting away like ghosts. The battlefield goes quiet for a moment, the screams of the villagers and the sound of battle fading into the distance.

"What the hell's going on?" I mutter, glancing at Killian.

He shakes his head. "I don't know, but it doesn't feel right."

Imran looks around, his eyes scanning the retreating demons. "Don't trust it. Stay on guard."

And then, through the haze of smoke, we see it. A figure, clad in pitch black armor, riding a dark, imposing horse. The rider's silhouette cuts through the smoke like a nightmare come to life. It's a sight that sends a chill down my spine, and my instincts scream at me, urging me to either run or die fighting.

The figure rides forward, slowly and deliberately, as if the retreat of the demons was a prelude to something much worse. The horse's hooves strike the ground with a heavy, ominous sound, and the air seems to thicken around us, charged with an unnatural energy.

I glance at Imran, who is already reaching for his weapon. Killian does the same, his sword steady in his hand.

"What is that?" I ask, my voice low.

"I don't know," Kamea says, his tone grim, "But if I should take a guess, it's an underling of one of the demon generals. Which means that everyone should take caution."

The figure on the horse stops just a few dozen yards away from us, the flames of the burning village casting long shadows. The rider remains still for a moment, as though assessing us before they speak, their voice cold and commanding.

"You are the ones who have dared to stand in my way?" The voice is deep, layered with an unnatural power that vibrates through the air.

There's a moment of silence as we all take in the figure before us. It's no ordinary demon. The air around it crackles with dark magic, and its presence alone feels like a weight pressing down on our very souls.

"I am Sirath," the rider continues, his voice dripping with disdain. "You are the ones who will die today."

The world seems to hold its breath. The demons, now retreating fully into the shadows, have left us alone with this new foe. And in that moment, I realize just how outmatched we truly are, even with us outnumbering it.

Imran steps forward, his eyes never leaving Sirath. "We've already lost enough today. If we die here, it will be with the blood of our enemies staining the ground."

Sirath laughs a sound that seems to chill the very air. "Foolish mortal. You are already dead."

Before any of us can react, Sirath raises one gloved hand, and the ground beneath us shudders. The air is thick with a surge of dark energy, and the ground begins to crack as if the earth itself is protesting the presence of the rider. The flames of the village flicker and twist unnaturally, turning an even darker hue.

I grip my weapon tighter, my knuckles white. This is not something we can win with brute force alone. The battle has escalated into something far more dangerous than I had ever anticipated. The demon forces have pulled back, not because they are afraid, but because their master has arrived.

"We survive this," Imran mutters under his breath, "or we die trying."

Sirath hops down from his horse with a terrifying, almost predatory grace. His heavy boots make a deep thud as they meet the ground, each step mirroring the beat of my own frantic heartbeat. The sound is unnervingly rhythmic, like the ticking of a clock, counting down to something inevitable. A slow, creeping dread settles in my chest, and the rest of the group seems to freeze. Even Imran, who is always the first to act, stands rigid, his eyes locked on the new threat before us.

I want to move, but I can't. My body is paralyzed, my muscles stiff, as the demon approaches, its eyes fixed solely on me. There's something in his gaze—something cold, calculating. He doesn't acknowledge the others, doesn't spare a glance at Killian or Kamea or Imran. His focus is entirely on me.

"You," the demon growls, his voice a low, gravelly rumble that seems to vibrate through the air. "Hm. Interesting. You seemed to have slipped out of my Lord's grasp. He'll be pleased when I bring him your head."

I stiffen, my stomach sinking. What is he talking about? Escape? His lord?

"Who are you?" I manage to choke out, my voice hoarse despite my best efforts to sound confident. "What do you want from me?"

The demon grins, a grin so wide and filled with malice that it makes my blood run cold. His teeth are sharp, his face angular and twisted in a way that only demons can be. "I am Sirath," he repeats as if his name alone should be enough to explain everything. "And we've been looking for you, Hybrid. For a long time."

Before I can react, a sharp pain sears through my head—like a thousand knives stabbing into my skull at once. I stagger back, my hands gripping my temples as the pain intensifies, blurring everything around me. The world spins as my vision distorts, shifting to something else entirely.

***

The new vision is vivid and overwhelming. I see a man—tall, with sharp features and strong, defined muscles. He's wearing the armor of a warrior, his sword gleaming in the sunlight. His name comes to me even before I can fully recognize him: Arius.

Arius. A legend. A hero.

But the Arius I see now is not the man I remember from stories. He's different—cold, distant, mocking. His eyes lock onto mine, and I can feel the weight of his gaze pressing down on me, like an anchor sinking into my soul.

"You're still clinging to that naive idealism of yours," Arius sneers. His voice is filled with contempt, but there's something else there too—something... darker. "You think humanity is worth saving? You think you're some kind of hero, fighting for a cause that's already lost?"

I open my mouth to respond, but the words catch in my throat. The pain in my head is unbearable, and I can barely concentrate enough to understand what he's saying. His words keep coming, relentless, a constant stream of mockery.

"Look at what we're up against, Crilt. The Demon King is right. His conquest is inevitable. You'll never win. And what's worse—" He pauses, a wicked grin spreading across his face. "—you'll never even realize how much of a fool you've been until the very end."

A deep chill runs down my spine, and for a moment, the pain is replaced with a sense of helplessness. The vision is so real, so vivid, that I can almost feel Arius's presence beside me. I want to scream, to shake off the vision, but it's as if it has a hold on me—gripping me tightly, refusing to let go.

***

I snap back to reality with a gasp, the vision fading like smoke in the wind. My breath is shallow, my hands trembling. For a moment, I just stand there, blinking in confusion, my thoughts swirling around in a tangled mess. What was that? It looked and sounded so real. The words Arius spoke—the conviction in his voice—linger in my mind, gnawing at me.

Could he be right? Could the Demon King's conquest be the only way forward? My heart aches with the thought, the sheer idea of betraying everything I've believed in.

"Crilt!" Killian's voice shatters the confusion in my mind, and I turn to see him lunging forward, his sword raised, eyes burning with fury. He's trying to fight Sirath.

But the moment he moves, it's clear that the fight has already been decided.

With inhuman speed, Sirath raises one of his long, jagged arms, and a tendril—black, slick, and twisted—shoots out from it like a whip. The tendril strikes Killian's chest, impaling him in an instant. The force of the blow lifts him off his feet, and he's thrown backward like a rag doll, crashing into the ground with a sickening thud.

"Killian!" I scream, my heart leaping into my throat. He's not moving, his body limp and crumpled, blood spilling out onto the dirt.

I feel a flash of white-hot anger—a fire so intense that it consumes everything in me. My vision blurs and all I can see is red. The pain, the loss, the overwhelming helplessness—it all merges into a single, uncontrollable rage.

At that moment, something inside me snaps. The white-hot flash grows brighter, and sharper, consuming every thought, every ounce of hesitation. My body is flooded with power, a surge of strength that I've never felt before, but it's not like before. It's not just physical strength—it's something more primal. Darker.

I turn to face Sirath, my teeth gritted, my breath ragged. The pain in my head, the doubts, the fears—they all disappear in that moment. All that matters is the fight. All that matters is taking down the demon who's killed my friends.

"YOU WILL PAY!" I roar, my voice an animalistic growl.

The ground beneath me trembles as I surge forward, my movements wild, fueled by a bloodlust I can't control. I swing my weapon at Sirath, the blow so powerful it cleaves the air in half. The demon grins, clearly amused by my fury, but he's not ready for the force behind my strike.

I catch him off guard, the edge of my weapon striking his side, leaving a deep gash across his armored form. Sirath stumbles back, his grin faltering for a split second as he assesses me with new interest. His black eyes narrow.

"You're stronger than I expected," Sirath murmurs, his voice filled with a mix of admiration and disdain. "But it won't be enough."

I charge again, faster this time, my muscles screaming as I push past my limits. My weapon swings in a wide arc, and Sirath barely manages to dodge, the tip of my blade grazing his shoulder. But he's still grinning. Always grinning.

"You're a fool," Sirath says, his voice full of mocking amusement. "You think your rage will save you? You think it will save them?"

I don't care. I don't care what he says. I don't care about anything but making him pay for what he's done.

I charge again, but this time, Sirath is ready. He flicks his wrist, and a tendril shoots out, wrapping around my arm with the speed of a striking serpent. It tightens, pulling me off balance, and I stumble, my weapon falling from my grasp.

Before I can recover, Sirath slams a fist into my chest, sending me flying backward. I crash into the ground, the wind knocked from my lungs, but I barely register the pain. All I can feel is the fury—raging, uncontrollable, like a storm inside me. I push myself up, my hands shaking, but I don't stop. I can't stop.

The vision of Arius flashes through my mind again, and for a moment, doubt creeps in. Is this what I've been fighting for? A cause that's already lost? But then I remember my friends— Killian, Kamea, Imran. I remember what they're fighting for. What we're all fighting for.

And I know—*this is worth it*. Whatever the cost.

With a roar, I surge forward once more, fueled by the white-hot rage that has taken over me.

The ground shakes beneath me, the air itself quivering with the ferocity of our clash. Sirath and I are locked in a fury, a savage whirlwind of steel and blood, and it feels as if the entire world has bent around us, awaiting some violent conclusion. The shrieks of our blades cutting through the air, the thuds of our strikes, the crashing of bodies into the earth — all of it drowns out everything else. Every sound I hear, every movement, is a part of the storm that's consuming me. It's as if I'm being pulled into a vortex, a vortex that feeds only on destruction, on death.

All I can think, all I want, is to *kill*. To tear him apart, to rip him from existence, to extinguish every breath he's ever taken. He's laughing, grinning that sickening grin of his, the one that mocks me, mocks my rage, mocks my very existence. *I can't stand it.* The sound of his laughter drives me further into madness. His smug, self-satisfied expression makes my blood boil. His arrogant, goddamn grin makes me want to *crush him*, to *break every bone in his body* until he stops looking at me like that.

The rage is primal, raw, untamed, a beast that surges through me, growing stronger with each swing of my sword. The heat of my fury blurs everything. I can't think, can't feel anything but the need to *kill*. My hands are slick with blood, my muscles burning with the force of each blow, but I don't care. The pain, the exhaustion — it's all irrelevant. I keep moving, keep striking, because the beast inside me demands it.

Sirath staggers back, barely keeping his footing, but that damn grin never leaves his face. His eyes glint with madness, with something that isn't fear. He doesn't fear me. He never has. And that just makes me angrier. He wants me to lose control. He wants to see me snap. But I won't let him have that. *I won't let him win.*

I roar as I lunge forward, my sword slicing through the air. Sirath barely manages to parry, but I'm relentless, my rage propelling me forward. I feel my blade connect with his side, feel the satisfying resistance as it cuts through flesh. He hisses in pain, but still, that grin remains. *That damn grin.*

"You're nothing but a rabid animal, Hybrid," he sneers, his voice rasping through gritted teeth. "Just a beast with a blade."

I don't hear his words. All I hear is the pounding of my own heart, the roar of blood in my ears, the fury inside me growing until it's all-consuming, overwhelming. The part of me that knows the reason, that understands the consequences, that feels human — it's fading, swallowed by the madness. The desire to kill is all that remains. My movements are faster now, erratic, uncontrolled, but I don't care. It feels good. The power surging through me feels like fire like it's igniting my very soul.

Sirath stumbles again, and I see the glint of desperation in his eyes. I'm finally getting the upper hand. I'm winning. But he doesn't seem afraid. No, he's still grinning, even as I strike him again and again. He's staggering, his blood pouring from his wounds, staining the earth beneath us, but that damn grin never fades. It makes my skin crawl. *I want to rip it off his face.*

I strike again, and again, my sword meeting his flesh with each blow, but it's not enough. *It's never enough. I want to hear him scream. I want to break him, to make him feel every ounce of pain that I've ever felt. I want him to suffer.*

I see it — the opening I've been waiting for. He's weak, too weak to defend himself. His body is broken, his movements sluggish, but his smile... that damn smile. It only fuels my fury, making me lose myself even further in the bloodlust. *I can't stop. I won't stop.* The blood is flowing now, flooding the ground beneath us, but I keep stabbing, keep tearing into him, feeling the satisfaction surge through me with each thrust. Each time my blade sinks into his flesh, I feel a sick, twisted pleasure spike in my chest. *I want more. I need more. I need to feel him die.* The beast inside me screams for more, and I answer, blindly, recklessly, lost in the frenzy.

The world is a blur. Sirath's body is barely recognizable now, a mangled mess of blood and shredded flesh, but *I can't stop.*

I won't stop. His life is slipping away, but it doesn't matter. I need to finish it. *I need to make him suffer.*

Then, suddenly, there's a sharp yank on my arm. I barely register it, too lost in the bloodlust to comprehend what's happening, but then I feel another pair of hands grip my shoulders. Someone is pulling me away. Someone is stopping me.

"No!" I roar, trying to break free, trying to keep going. But my sword is pulled from my hands, and I'm spun around, my body violently shoved backward.

"Crilt!" Imran's voice breaks through the haze in my mind. "Crilt, stop!"

I turn, wild-eyed, frantic, my chest heaving with every breath. I lash out, swinging my fists, my body still trembling with the aftershocks of the frenzy. But they're faster. They dodge, grabbing my arms, holding my wrists, and pinning me down to the ground.

"Get a hold of yourself! He's dead already!"

Kamea's words immediately snap me out of my trance, and the red instantly clears from my vision. I look down to see that

Sirath is indeed dead and disemboweled, thanks to my rage. The blood around me is a puddle, spreading all over my hands and armor.

Panting, my breath comes in jagged bursts, each inhales filling my chest with more fire and frustration. I don't understand what came over me. I don't understand why I reacted like that, why the violence tore through me like some primal instinct I couldn't control. The adrenaline is still pumping through my veins, a pulsing, almost uncontrollable force that makes my hands shake and my chest tighten.

Everything from the fight feels like it's still buzzing in the air around me. The shrieks, the blood, the sounds of steel meeting flesh—they echo in my mind, and I can't push them away. I don't even know how it all happened. One second, I was barely surviving against Sirath, and the next—everything snapped. I lost it. I became an animal.

I killed him.

My eyes move over to the body of Sirath. His mangled form, his blood soaking the ground beneath him—this is the result of my rage. I killed him with the same brutality that I barely recognized in myself. My sword, slick with blood, is now lying at my feet, discarded. I didn't even think about it. It was instinct. But now, standing over his lifeless body, there's no satisfaction. Only a heavy, gnawing emptiness.

I never wanted to be that kind of person. I never wanted to lose control. And yet here I am, surrounded by the aftermath of it, wondering if I've gone too far. But before I can dwell on that, a different sound breaks through my thoughts. A gurgling.

I freeze, turning my head slowly.

On the ground, a pale form struggles for breath, blood pouring from his mouth. Killian. He's on his back, gasping, clutching at his chest as if he's trying to keep himself from falling apart. I move before my mind fully registers what's happening, my heart pounding in my ears as I rush to his side.

"Killian..." The name is a whisper, almost foreign in my mouth, but I can't think of anything else to say. I pull away from Imran and Kamea, crawling over to him. My hands are shaking as I lean down, pulling him into my lap, trying to support him. Blood bubbles from his lips, and he struggles for air like a man drowning in a sea of his own life.

His pale face is distorted with pain, but he somehow manages to lift his eyes to mine, a weak smile tugging at his cracked lips.

"If I had lived longer..." His voice is a rasp, barely audible over the sound of his wheezing. "I'd have made you my friend, Crilt. You're... not so bad, for a bastard."

I don't know what to say. The words sit heavy in my throat, tangled with something I can't quite grasp. But his words, despite everything, make me feel... something. A sharp twist in my gut. Guilt? Regret? Something I don't want to feel. It doesn't matter.

His head falls back, and his chest stills. The blood continues to pool around him, staining the earth beneath.

No.

This wasn't supposed to happen. He was supposed to live. He couldn't just... die like this. Not like this. Not after he said that. The guilt cuts through me in waves, suffocating me as I try to hold onto him as if somehow that could bring him back. But I know it can't. I can feel the life leaving him, slipping through my fingers like sand.

I close his eyes with trembling hands, feeling the weight of my own inadequacy. My chest is tight, a knot of emotion I can't untangle. I feel... hollow. Angry. What is this feeling? This isn't just grief. It's rage, something deeper and more dangerous.

I don't understand it, but it's there, burning hot in my chest.

I try to breathe through it, try to steady myself. But the anger, it keeps bubbling up. The frustration. The powerlessness. It feels like I could burn the world down with it, and it scares me.

"Crilt..."

I don't need to look up to know it's Imran's voice. I glance up at him and Kamea. They stand several feet away, their faces painted with concern, confusion, and a bit of fear. I see it in their eyes, though they try to hide it.

For a moment, we just stare at each other. The three of us, standing amidst the carnage of a battle that feels like it's never going to end. I want to scream at them, tell them to leave me alone. I want to push them away, but I don't.

They don't deserve that.

I look down at Killian again, the body growing cold in my arms. My throat tightens as I fight to swallow the lump that forms. But it's pointless. Nothing changes.

"Let's go," I manage, my voice hoarse and rough. I stand, my legs unsteady, but I force myself to move. I turn away from Killian's body. I don't want to be here anymore. I don't want to feel this. I just want to get out of here.

Imran and Kamea look at each other briefly as I walk past them, both speechless. I hear their footsteps follow behind me softly after a while.

***

The ride back to Ashroth is quiet—uncomfortably so. The only sounds that break the stillness are the rhythmic clop of hooves against the dirt and the occasional shift of our horses, but it feels like the very air around us is holding its breath, waiting for something. I can't quite place it, but there's this suffocating tension that presses down on me, making every movement feel heavy.

The wind whips through the trees, and I wonder how long it'll be before the forest gets swallowed up by the night. I can feel it—a presence lingering in the corners of my mind, a weight that has followed me from the battlefield. It gnaws at me, reminding me of what happened earlier, of the destruction I caused, of the death I dealt.

Why am I still here?

I thought I already had my goals figured out, so why am I still dwelling on it? I've killed hundreds of creatures back in the dungeon as a child till I became an adult. So why is this hard now? Why am I feeling this way? Shouldn't I be immune to death right now?

Three of us survived. That's what keeps playing in my head, over and over. Three. Not a single soul from the other party. And not just any party—those were seasoned warriors, mages. They should have been stronger than us. But somehow, here we are. Alive. I'm alive.

I don't get it. Was it luck? Or was it something more?

I glance at Imran, sitting stiffly on his horse in front of me, his back straight, his face hard as he gazes ahead. The quiet is just as unnerving to him as it is to me, though I can tell he's fighting it, trying to keep his focus sharp. It's the same with Kamea, who's riding just ahead of me. His usual quiet confidence is gone, replaced by an awkward tension that only makes the silence even more unbearable.

I've caught glimpses of their faces throughout the ride, glancing back at me with worried expressions, probably wondering the same things I am.

The battle.

The frenzy.

The kill.

I still don't understand how it happened. There's still this coldness inside me now, this... emptiness, this hollow feeling that's settled into my chest like a stone.

The moon is high in the sky by the time we make camp, and I'm thankful for the quiet that surrounds us. The crackling of the fire is the only sound breaking through the night air, casting flickering shadows on the ground. We dismount and make camp in the small clearing we find, the horses tethered nearby, munching on sparse grass. I don't have the energy to do anything beyond sit down next to the fire, my limbs heavy as if made of lead.

Imran and Kamea begin the usual routine of preparing for the night—setting up the fire, arranging blankets, and checking their weapons. But their movements are slow, and distracted. Neither of them speaks, but I can feel their eyes on me. Their questions, hovering just under the surface, hang between us, thick as smoke.

I don't blame them. I can feel the questions pressing on my own mind, too. But I'm not ready to face them. Not yet.

The night is cold, but the fire offers some warmth, though it doesn't touch the cold inside me. The hunger I felt earlier, that bloodlust, has faded, but now there's this... unease, a lingering discomfort that refuses to let go.

It isn't until we've all settled down that Kamea finally breaks the silence, his voice low but insistent.

"Crilt... I have to ask," he begins, not looking directly at me but instead poking at the fire with a stick. "How did you do it? How did you manage to take down a demon underling so easily? I know you're strong, but that was... something else. And..." He pauses, his voice dropping even lower. "That frenzy you were in. What was that? I've never seen anything like it."

I stare at the flames, their flickering glow reflecting off my dark eyes, and for a moment, I can't speak. His words ring in my ears, but I can't find the answers I need. I don't understand it myself. I don't know how I killed Sirath. I don't know how I went from fighting to that mindless rage, stabbing, and stabbing until the world turned red.

I can still feel it—his blood on my hands, his body beneath my sword. It wasn't just the physical act of killing. No, it was something deeper. Something... more instinctive. Something that felt like it came from somewhere *inside* me, somewhere buried deep, but all the while it felt so *right*. The violence. The rage. The satisfaction of watching him crumble under my strikes.

I rub my face, trying to shake off the images. The memories. But they cling to me, like a shadow that won't let go.

"I don't know," I shrug tiredly. And that's the truth. I don't know where that came from. I don't know how it happened. And never have I experienced it before. All I know is that an overwhelming anger took over both my body and my mind and that's it.

The fire crackles one last time before silence takes over again. No more questions, no more answers. Just the nocturnal animals singing their merry tunes in the night air.

Tomorrow, we'll head back to Ashroth. The raid, the battle, the deaths, the struggles—it's all over now. But something inside me has changed, and I'm not sure how I'll ever be able to face it.

CHAPTER 6

A month has passed since the raid, and I've gotten used to life in Ashroth. Well, as much as one can get used to a life like this. I still think about the raid. A lot, actually. More times than I can count. But I try to drown all my thoughts about it by training.

I spend most of my days wandering the castle grounds, training, and helping Imran with whatever task needs doing. I've learned to keep my head down and avoid unnecessary attention, even though I don't think I should. But people are different, and I'm still trying to figure out how to act around them. But I'm not alone, I keep having to remind myself that. Kamea sticks close by, and though he doesn't say much, he's a silent comfort. Imran always bursts with energy for the two of us, and I appreciate that.

Today, though, the city feels different. There's an unsettling energy in the air, like a storm brewing just on the horizon. Imran and Kamea are with me, as usual, and we're making our way toward the castle for a meeting with some of the higher-ups. I've learned not to ask too many questions about what exactly they do, but I know it's important. They don't involve me much in their politics, which suits me just fine.

The streets are crowded as we walk through the market district. People hustle about, merchants calling out their wares, children running between the legs of adults, their laughter filling the air. It's a stark contrast to the tense quiet that has been hanging over Ashroth ever since the raid. The people here can feel it too, I'm sure. The city isn't the same as it once was. There's something lurking in the background, something dark that none of us can escape.

We pass by an alleyway, and a whisper catches my ear. I glance toward the source, a group of soldiers huddled together, speaking in hushed tones. The words are barely audible over the noise of the market, but one phrase stands out: *Arius*.

I stop in my tracks, and Kamea almost bumps into me. I look back at him, then at Imran, and see that he's already paying attention. He's always been quick to catch onto these things, his instincts sharp. I know that look on his face. He's heard it too.

Imran motions for us to follow, and we veer off into a side street. The soldiers don't seem to notice us as we approach, and we slow our pace, trying to blend in with the crowd. The conversation drifts to us, and I can make out more of the words now.

"Did you hear? Arius was captured."

"Not just captured. Turned. He's one of them now, a demon general."

"Impossible. He was one of the strongest knights. How could he fall so low?"

"The whispers say it was a betrayal. Someone close to him turned on him, gave him up to the demons."

I feel my heart tighten at the name. Arius. I still think about him, despite myself.

"Who betrayed him?" I ask softly, stepping closer to Imran and Kamea.

Imran's eyes flicker with uncertainty, but Kamea is already shaking his head. "We don't know yet. But more rumors are popping up about it, that it's hard to ignore. If Arius has truly fallen... it means this war is much worse than we thought."

I can feel a sense of dread creep over me, a gnawing suspicion that things have gotten too dire to the point that we can't handle it.

The soldiers continue their conversation, oblivious to the three of us eavesdropping from the shadows.

"They say it happened during a raid on one of the southern towns, years ago. Arius was leading the charge, but something went wrong. He disappeared, and when they found him again... it was already too late."

"The rumors are that he's been reprogrammed, turned into one of those demon generals that are impossible to kill. It's like they broke him, molded him into something else."

Imran straightens, his expression darkening. He motions for us to leave, and we move quickly, ducking around corners and away from prying eyes. The castle looms ahead now, but there's no sense of peace in its shadow. I can't stop thinking about Arius. Who betrayed him?

As we enter the castle gates, the weight of what I've just learned settles heavily on my chest. I've always known war was a thing of darkness, but this... this is something else. If they can take someone like Arius and twist him into a demon general, what hope do we have?

We head into the castle courtyard, and I feel a mixture of anger and fear building inside me. I need to know more. I need to understand how deep this betrayal runs, who was behind it, and how it all ties back to the war we're fighting.

Imran must sense my frustration because he glances over at me, his expression unreadable. "You're thinking about Arius, aren't you?"

I nod, not trusting myself to speak. The thoughts are too jumbled in my head, too overwhelming to process all at once. The pieces don't fit yet, but they will. I know they will.

Kamea says nothing, but his presence is a silent comfort as we move toward the castle's inner chambers. We're supposed to meet with some of the higher-ups to discuss the state of the war, but my mind is elsewhere.

Imran looks at me, his expression serious. "It's not safe to dig too deep, Crilt. I understand your attachment to the hero, but we have other things to focus on."

"Agreed," Kamea mutters. "We can't afford to be sidetracked."

"But Arius is our business now. If he's part of the demon generals, we're more likely to encounter him during battle, aren't we?"

The two look at each other, conflicted. "Yes, but we can handle that when the time comes, not right now, okay? Let's drop it," Kamea says with an air of finality. We make our way to the castle in silence.

The idea of betrayal in our ranks unsettles me. If Arius could be turned, what does that mean for the rest of us?

For me?

The castle's towering walls seem to close in on me as we enter the hallways, suffocating me. Something dark is lurking beneath the surface, and I can't shake the feeling that I'm not ready for what's coming.

That's unsettling and all, but what truly gnaws at me is the news of the demon generals. The fact that they've taken notice of me after what happened with Sirath sends a chill through my spine.

The halls inside the castle are even grander, with polished marble floors and tapestries depicting legendary battles. There's history with every step I take. Imran walks ahead, his usual confident stride unchanged, but I can see the tension in his shoulders. Kamea, as quiet as ever, keeps his eyes forward, his expression unreadable.

We're ushered into a meeting chamber, its stone walls lined with bookshelves and glowing lanterns. The room feels like a vault, both secure and suffocating, and for a moment, I wonder if that's how the people of Ashroth feel every day. Trapped in the security of their own walls, yet constantly looking over their shoulders, wondering when the next blow will come.

At the far end of the chamber, seated at an imposing wooden table, are the rulers of Ashroth. They're a group of five, all dressed in fine robes and armored in gold and silver. Their eyes are hard, their faces stern, but beneath that, I sense something else—fear.

Imran bows his head in respect, and I follow suit, not quite doing it out of respect, but rather as an obligation. I stand there, shifting from foot to foot, my mind racing with the implications of what I've learned.

The room falls silent for a moment before one of the rulers speaks—Lord Belvar, a man known for his sharp tongue and even sharper instincts. His eyes narrow as they fall on me, and I can feel the weight of his gaze like a physical presence.

"You," he says, voice low and grave. "Crilt, isn't it?"

I nod. "Yes, my lord."

"You've caused quite a stir," he continues, his tone harder now. "The demons… they've taken notice of you."

The words hit me like a slap. I swallow hard, fighting to keep my composure. I know that I'm not just a simple soldier or a mercenary anymore. Ever since I killed Sirath, I've become popular. The demons know my name. They know what I can do. And now, it's clear that they're watching me.

"Yes, but I don't quite understand," I say, my voice rough. "Why would they care about me? I'm just... a soldier."

Lord Belvar's lips curl into a thin, humorless smile. "It's not just that you're a soldier. It's what you did. You killed Sirath, one of the demon generals' underlings. And in doing so, you've marked yourself. The demons do not forget such things. They never forgive. And only a handful are capable of making such a feat,"

The words sink in, the weight of them pressing against my chest. Sirath was an underling, yes, but I never imagined his death would have consequences like this.

"And now," another voice interjects, this one belonging to Lady Morganna, a woman whose presence fills the room despite her quiet nature, "the demons are preparing for war. We can already see the pressure building on all fronts. They're mobilizing their forces, and we don't have much time."

"War?" I ask, my voice a bit sharper than I intended. "But we've been at war with the demons for years. What's different now?"

Imran steps forward, his usual calm demeanor slipping a little as he speaks. "It's not just the usual raids. The demons have begun targeting key locations in the kingdom. They're becoming more organized, and more aggressive. And what's worse, they've started taking our people—turning them into Demi-humans."

I freeze. The words hit harder than I expected. "Turning them?"

"It's been a while since they've done that," Imran continues, his voice low and grim, "I'm as surprised as you are too. It seems like Demon King has begun to add more to his army,"

My stomach churns. How many others are to be sacrificed because of this war? How many more will fall if we can't stop it?

"Which is why we must prepare," Lady Morganna says, breaking my thoughts. "We can't afford to be caught off guard. The demons are planning something far more devastating this time. They know their strategy, and they're willing to sacrifice their own for the cause. We need every able body, every weapon we have. And Crilt," she turns her gaze on me, "we need you."

I blink, confused. "Me?"

"Yes," she says, her voice firm. "What you did—killing Sirath—has made you a target, but it's also given you something valuable. Experience. And the demons, as much as they hate you for it, know that you're a threat. They won't underestimate you again."

I don't know how to respond to that. My mind is still reeling from the shock of hearing that more Demi-humans are to be created, and I can't help but feel responsible for it, even though I did nothing wrong.

Imran places a hand on my shoulder, his grip firm. "What Lady Morganna means to say is that your strength—your skills—will be crucial in the battles to come. You've proven yourself on the battlefield, and that's something we need right now. The war is escalating, Crilt. And we need everyone to be prepared. Including you."

I look around the room at the other rulers, their faces hard, but determined. They're all waiting for me to make a choice, to decide whether or not I'll stand with them in the fight to come. The weight of the decision presses down on me.

I think back to everything that's led me here: the raid, the demons, Sirath, and now Arius, twisted into something unrecognizable. And I realize that there's no choice for me but to fight. Not just for Ashroth, but for myself, for the people I care about, and for the countless others who will be caught in the crossfire of this war.

"I'll fight," I say, my voice steady despite the uncertainty gnawing at me.

The rulers exchange looks, and then, slowly, they nod. Lady Morganna's lips curve into a small smile, though it's not one of joy. It's a dark, understanding smile.

"Then it's settled," Lord Belvar says. "Prepare yourself, Crilt. The demons are coming, and we'll need all the strength we can muster. This war is far from over."

***

The castle is far too grand, too suffocating. Even though it's filled with corridors and chambers that seem to go on for miles, I still feel like there's nowhere to hide. Imran and Kamea are engaged in discussions with the rulers, no doubt about strategies, logistics, and preparing for the inevitable war with the demons. I know they're right to be focused, but I can't shake this feeling that something is wrong. I need space. I need to clear my head.

I've agreed to fight, but I'm overwhelmed, too overwhelmed by everything.

I slip away from the meeting chamber unnoticed, the marble floors echoing under my boots as I make my way down unfamiliar hallways. I'm not sure where I'm headed, just walking to put distance between myself and the suffocating weight of the rulers' decisions. The grand tapestries and polished wood doors seem to blur into one as my thoughts spiral.

The vision I saw in Hurin still lingers in my mind. The blackened remnants of what was once a proud man, a hero. Arius, standing in the midst of it all, his body twisted and broken by the very darkness he sought to control. I saw that, felt it, and the memory of it churns my stomach every time I think of it. It's hard to reconcile the man I remember—strong, unyielding—with the figure I saw in that brief flash of vision, corrupted and consumed.

I keep walking, my steps becoming heavier with each passing moment, until I turn a corner and nearly bump into an older man. He's dressed in the faded tunic of an old soldier, his back hunched slightly as if age has caught up to him in ways he didn't anticipate. His face is lined with scars and age, his eyes tired, but when they meet mine, there's a sharpness there—a knowing glint that immediately catches my attention.

"I haven't seen you before," the soldier says, his voice low and gravelly, but there's a faint warmth to it. "You new around here?"

I nod, unsure of what to say. I don't exactly feel like explaining myself to some random soldier.

The man looks me over for a moment, then sighs and glances down the hallway as if making sure no one else is around. "You're one of the ones who fought in the raid, aren't you? Crilt, I think they call you."

I stiffen. "Yeah, that's me."

He nods as if he already knows. "Good fight you put up. Too bad you had to face Sirath."

My stomach churns at the mention of Sirath's name, but I don't show it. I haven't thought about Sirath much lately, though the demon's death still weighs on me like a stone in my chest.

"Listen," the soldier says, his voice softening as he steps closer, "if you've got time, maybe I can tell you something you ought to hear. It's about Arius."

The name makes my heart skip a beat, and I can't stop myself from looking at him, eyes wide, as I search the soldier's face for any hint of what he knows. "Arius?" I ask, my voice barely above a whisper. "What about him?"

The soldier gives me a knowing look. "I was there. In the old days. I fought beside Arius. We were brothers in arms, long before any of this mess with the demons started."

I don't know what to say, so I just gesture for him to continue.

"Arius was... different," he starts, his eyes clouding with distant memories. "He was the best knight Ashroth ever had. Fierce in battle, loyal to his comrades, a man of honor. People looked up to him—hell, I looked up to him. We all thought he was untouchable, that nothing could ever break him. But the war with the demons... it changed everything."

I swallow, trying to digest his words, but my stomach twists painfully. "What happened?" I ask, even though I already have a sinking feeling in my gut.

The soldier sighs a long, deep breath. "The Demon King had his sights set on Arius. He knew what Arius stood for—what he represented. And the Demon King, well, he knows how to manipulate men like Arius. He didn't offer Arius a deal at first. He simply wore him down. And then, when Arius was at his breaking point when the pain of watching his comrades fall became too much... that's when the Demon King swooped in."

I can feel my fists clenching as the soldier's words hit me like a battering ram. "He made Arius an offer, didn't he?"

The soldier nods grimly. "Power. Revenge. The chance to bring his enemies to their knees. The Demon King offered him everything Arius had lost, everything he wanted, in exchange for his loyalty. He was promised unimaginable strength in return for becoming a servant of darkness."

I can feel my mind racing, thoughts tumbling over each other. Power. Revenge. It sounds like something Arius would have wanted in his darkest moments, but I refuse to believe that. Arius wouldn't just turn on his own people. He couldn't.

"Did he accept?" I ask the words like gravel in my mouth.

The soldier's face softens. "He did. But not because he wanted to become a demon, not because he wanted to betray anyone. Arius was broken, Crilt. The Demon King gave him a way out. And in his grief, in his rage, Arius chose it. But even after that, even after everything, he never lost the man he was. I knew him,

Crilt. He was still a hero, deep down, even if the world turned its back on him."

I shake my head, the words conflicting with everything I know. "A hero?" I scoff, though there's a bitter twist in my chest. "The Arius I saw in my vision—he was nothing but a weapon. A monster."

The soldier looks at me with a pained expression. "Arius never wanted to become what he did, Crilt. But the Demon King took everything from him—his comrades, his honor, his hope. The man you saw in that vision was a man who had already lost everything. What he became after that was not entirely his choice. It was the result of the manipulation, the darkness that consumed him. But somewhere in him, there was still a piece of the Arius we all knew. And that's the truth. The man you saw was a casualty of war, not a villain."

I stare at the soldier, disbelief clouding my thoughts. This is hard to accept, harder still to believe. But I can't help the nagging doubt that starts to form in the pit of my stomach.

I can't forget the vision. I can't forget the twisted, broken form of Arius. He was a hero, once. But now? I don't know anymore.

"I don't know what to believe," I mutter, more to myself than to him. "What about the betrayal? I've heard rumors go by saying that he was betrayed,"

The soldier places a hand on my shoulder, his touch rough but understanding. "I know. That's why rumors are dangerous. Nothing of the sort happened, they are all lies. But sometimes, Crilt, the truth is a lot messier than we'd like it to be. Arius was a hero. And maybe, just maybe, he deserves a chance to be remembered as one."

I stand there for a long moment, digesting his words. My thoughts whirl around, but I can't settle on anything. It's too much, too confusing. And deep down, I can't shake the feeling that this war—this whole damn war—has changed me, too.

"I'll think about it," I say, though I'm not sure what I'll find when I do. The soldier nods once, then turns and walks away, disappearing into the shadows of the castle halls.

But I don't feel any clearer. The truth of Arius, the demons, this war—it all feels like too much.

***

The hallway stretches ahead, its stone walls cold and silent. I feel the weight of the soldier's words pressing down on me, like a stone lodged deep in my chest. *Arius was a hero*, the soldier had said. But that statement feels more like a ghost than a truth, slipping through my fingers as I try to hold onto it.

I stop walking, my boots clicking against the polished floor as I stare at nothing, lost in thought. I can't wrap my mind around it. Arius, the man I once admired—hell, the man who taught me what it meant to fight for something greater than myself—had given it all up. Not for power or greed, but for something darker. Something broken. *Revenge*. And with that, he had lost everything he once stood for. His humanity, his honor, his very soul.

But even then, the soldier had claimed that Arius was still a hero deep down, that the darkness that consumed him wasn't entirely of his own making. That's the part I can't understand. I can't reconcile this image of Arius with the man I saw in my vision—the twisted figure, so far gone that he was barely recognizable. The man who stood, broken, surrounded by death and destruction, a puppet of the very force he had once fought against.

How could someone who was once so noble become something so monstrous? I thought I knew what good and evil were. I thought the lines were clear, etched in stone. But now? Now, those lines feel... blurry. Fading. I question everything I once believed in.

Is there such a thing as true evil?

I feel sick to my stomach, the nausea creeping up as the thought lingers in my mind. Maybe I've been naive, assuming that the world was divided into clear-cut sides: good and evil, right and wrong. But now, with everything that's happened—the war with the demons, Sirath's death, Arius's fall—those lines seem to dissolve like smoke drifting in the wind.

I lean against the cold stone wall, pressing my palms flat against it as my mind spins, desperately trying to make sense of it all. My breath comes in shallow gasps, the weight of everything threatening to crush me. *If Arius could fall like this... what does that mean for me?* What does it mean for anyone? If even the strongest, most honorable man can be consumed by his own desires for revenge and anger, then who am I to think I'm immune?

I shake my head, trying to banish the thought.

I never asked for this. I never asked to be part of this war. The demons, the humans... everything about this fight feels so... pointless. In the end, aren't we all just fighting for the same thing? Power? Survival? A chance to hold onto something, anything, that gives us meaning in this godforsaken world?

But the more I think about it, the more I realize that it's *not just about power*. It's not just about revenge. There's something deeper, something darker in all of this. *Is that what Arius was after?* Was he driven by a need to reclaim what was taken from him—his comrades, his honor, his humanity? Or was he simply consumed by the pain, by the emptiness that comes when you lose everything?

I press my forehead against the cold stone, trying to clear my mind.

But I can't stop thinking about what the soldier said. That Arius was a hero, even after all that had happened. That, deep down, somewhere in him, there was still a part of the man he once was. A part of the hero. I don't know if I can believe that. I don't know if I *want* to believe that.

What if this is just the way things are? What if the world is just a place where good men are slowly turned into monsters by the weight of their choices, by the darkness that seeps into everything they touch? *Maybe there's no such thing as a hero. Maybe we're all just one bad decision away from becoming something we never thought possible.*

The thought hits me like a punch to the gut.

But there's another part of me that refuses to let go of the idea that there has to be more to it. That maybe, just maybe, Arius didn't want to become what he did. That perhaps there was a flicker of the man he once was, a spark of the hero he had been, still fighting against the darkness that consumed him. And if that's true—if Arius was still a hero at his core—then maybe, just maybe, there's still hope for me, too.

I straighten up, wiping a hand across my face.

I don't know if I can forgive Arius. But I don't think I have to. Not yet, anyway. I don't even know why I feel the need to forgive him anyway. He doesn't owe me anything. But the two thoughts in my head continue to clash, leaving only a dissatisfying outcome.

What matters now is that I have to find a way to make sense of all this. To find out who I am in the midst of all this chaos before I lose myself completely. If I lose my humanity the way Arius did, then what was it all for? What will I have left?

I turn back toward the hallway, my thoughts a whirlwind of questions and confusion. I feel like I'm standing on the edge of something I can't fully understand. Something I'm not sure I want to understand. But I know one thing for certain: I can't keep going down this path of uncertainty forever.

I don't know what's ahead, but I can't ignore the burning question in the back of my mind: *Can I still be a hero, or is it too late for me?*

My thoughts are interrupted when I hear footsteps approaching. I glance up to see Imran and Kamea rounding the corner, their expressions unreadable but wary. They've probably been looking for me, no doubt concerned about where I've gone off to. I can feel the tension in the air as they stop a few feet away, waiting for me to speak.

I hesitate, unsure of how to explain the whirlwind of emotions tearing through me. But before I can say anything, Imran speaks.

"Crilt... You, okay?" His voice is low, but there's a note of concern in it, one I can't ignore.

I give a small nod, trying to shake off the weight of my thoughts. "Yeah, I'm fine. Just... needed some time alone."

Kamea steps forward, his brow furrowed. "You sure? You've been gone a while, and we thought you might've—"

"I'm fine," I interrupt, a little more forcefully than I intended. I don't want to talk about it. Not now. Not with them. "We need to prepare for what's coming next. Let's focus on that."

They exchange a glance, then nod in silent agreement. But I can tell they're still worried. Still, I don't have the energy to explain myself, to talk about the thoughts that are churning in my mind like a storm.

"Right," Imran says, his voice more serious now. "We'll need to be ready. The demons aren't waiting."

"Yeah," I mutter, glancing back down the hallway toward the looming darkness of the castle's depths. "The demons aren't waiting."

And neither am I.

CHAPTER 7

I can feel it rising inside me, like a fire, and it's burning hotter with each mile we ride. The air is thick with the scent of smoke and ash, and the landscape stretching before us is barren and desolate. The wind howls, but it's drowned out by the pounding of my heart in my ears, a constant, angry beat that drives me forward. I've got my sword at my side, my hand resting on the hilt, fingers twitching with the urge to unsheathe it, to feel the weight of it, to cut something—anything.

I don't look at the others. I can feel their eyes on me, the way they're watching me, curious, but I don't want to talk. They chatter, excited about the raid to come. Naïve fools. But I don't blame them, they're newly made adventurers, who don't understand the gravity of the situation. They're about six of them, but I don't care to know any of them at all. What's the point? I can barely hear their voices over the roar in my head—the relentless voice that screams at me to fight, to *kill*. My jaw tightens as I grip the reins, knuckles turning white. I'm not even sure what's driving me anymore. It's like something is waking up inside me, something that I can't control.

It's Killian's face I keep seeing, over and over again. That last, bloody grin of his. That damn forced smile. It's like it's burned into my brain, and every time I close my eyes, it's there. His words echo in my head, and they stab at me like a dagger. *If I had lived longer, I would have forced you to be my friend.*

I want to scream at him to shut up, to stop torturing me. But there's no point. I can't stop the memory, can't erase it. It haunts me. I don't know why. I barely know him, yet it does. The blood. The way it soaked my hands. And I can't stop feeling like it's my fault like I failed him. Like I failed myself.

My hand tightens on the reins, the leather digging into my palms. I can feel the tension in my body, the fight rising in me again, but I don't want to lose control. Not again. Not like I did with Sirath. I don't want to hurt anyone else. But the bloodlust, the hunger, is still there, crawling under my skin, humming, buzzing, trying to get up to the surface.

We ride for hours, and the landscape doesn't change. The silence presses in on me, and I feel like I'm suffocating under the weight of my thoughts. Imran and Kamea are ahead of me, talking quietly, planning, and strategizing for the raid ahead. They're so focused on the mission.

I think of Arius. I think of what I learned about him—the hero who fell. The man who was manipulated, twisted by promises of power and revenge until he became a demon himself. He was supposed to be someone I looked up to, someone I admired. But now? Now I don't know what to think. I don't know what's true anymore.

The lines between good and evil are so blurred. I used to think it was simple, that the world had its heroes and its villains, but now I see that it's not that simple. I've seen too much, and done too much, to believe in that anymore. Maybe we're all just monsters, waiting for the right moment to show our true faces.

I look at the others again, and I can't bring myself to care. They're trying to stay positive, trying to hold things together. Imran is discussing strategy with Kamea, but I can tell they're both worried. They've been noticing the change in me, I know they have. They keep glancing back at me like they're afraid I'll snap. They're right to be afraid. I feel like I'm already slipping.

I hate it. I hate how out of control I feel. How my hand itches for my sword. How my heart races when I think about the upcoming battle, how the idea of killing again almost excites me. I don't want to be like this.

I ride on, the weight of my thoughts dragging me down, the bloodlust clawing at my insides, threatening to take over. The others keep talking, but their words feel distant like they're coming from far away. I'm not really listening anymore.

I have to focus. I have to keep control.

The more I try to fight it, the worse it gets. My vision starts to narrow, and the ground beneath me seems to vibrate with the tension building inside me. I can hear the sound of hooves in my ears, but it's not the sound of our horses. It's the sound of battle, the sound of violence, of death.

I feel like I'm choking.

And then, it happens. A flash—Killian's face again. That smile. That damn smile. I see him, lying there, dying in my arms, and I feel the rage come crashing over me, drowning everything else.

Without thinking, my hand is on the hilt of my sword, and I'm pulling it out, the blade singing as it slices the air. I want to feel it. I want to cut through something, anything.

"Crilt." Imran's voice, sharp now, cuts through the fog in my mind. "Stop. What are you doing?"

But I can't stop. The blood is rushing in my ears now, my vision narrowing as the beast inside me wakes up, hungry. My breath comes faster, and I can feel the power building in my body, rising from deep within me. It's like a flood, a tide of destruction, and it's all I can do to hold it back.

I feel something in my chest crack, and I lose it. My sword swings forward, almost of its own accord, but before it can connect with anything, I hear Kamea shout, "Crilt, *no!*"

I blink, and for a moment, everything is clear again. The haze lifts, and I see Kamea and Imran, both on their horses, looking at me with wide, terrified eyes.

"What the hell are you doing?" Kamea demands, her voice trembling with fear.

I'm shaking. I didn't even realize I was trembling, but I can feel the tremors in my arms, in my legs, in every part of me. I look down at my sword, at the energy that's still thrumming in my chest. I can taste it, that raw, primal need to kill.

"I... I don't know," I mutter, my voice barely a whisper. I don't even recognize it. "I can't stop it. I can't stop myself."

Imran's expression softens, and for a moment, I think I see pity in his eyes. But then he reaches for my arm, gripping it tightly. "Crilt, listen to me," he says, his voice steady. "You're not alone in this. We're here. But you have to control it. You have to fight it."

The words are hard to swallow. I want to tell him he's wrong, that he doesn't understand. But I can't. I just stand there, panting, trying to rein in the fury inside me, the violence that's waiting to break free. I can see the young adventurers in the carriage behind me, staring at me in pure shock and horror. I almost forgot they were there in the first place.

For a long moment, there's nothing but silence, the tension crackling in the air around us. And then, slowly, I lower my sword.

I'm not sure if the urge has completely disappeared, but for now, I can hold it back. For now, I can still fight it.

But I know it's not over. Not by a long shot. The beast inside me is still there, waiting. And the next time I lose control; I might not be able to stop it.

The wind howls as we approach our destination—the Endzone. The sky is a sickly, ashen gray, thick with clouds that obscure any hint of sunlight. The land stretches out before us in a barren, lifeless expanse, littered with the remains of what must have once been a thriving settlement. Bones are scattered across the ground, mingled with torn scraps of fabric, the remains of what might have been clothing or tents. The structures that were once homes or buildings have been reduced to nothing more than charred skeletons of wood and stone.

The air smells like decay—like death—and the silence is deafening. There's no chirping of birds, no rustling of leaves, no signs of life at all, save for the wind that tears at our clothes and stings our eyes. I can feel the chill in the air, and it digs deep into my bones.

My hand grips the hilt of my sword, and my muscles tense instinctively. The hairs on the back of my neck stand up, a gut feeling telling me something's wrong, something is off about this place. It doesn't feel like a battleground—it feels like a tomb.

I glance at the others, at Imran and Kamea. They look just as uneasy as I feel, their faces tight with grim determination, but I can see the flickers of doubt in their eyes. They feel it too—the unease, the dread that hangs heavy in the air. Imran's normally composed expression falters for a split second, and Kamea's grip on his bow tightens.

"We need to be careful," Imran says, his voice low but firm, as if he's trying to convince himself more than us. "Something's not right here."

Before any of us can respond, the wind picks up again. It's sudden, a massive gust that seems to come from nowhere, rushing through the land like a wild, untamed beast. The force of it is so strong that it nearly knocks us off our feet, the ground shaking under the pressure. Dust fills the air, and for a moment, we're blinded, unable to see through the haze. My chest constricts with a sudden surge of panic, but I force myself to stay calm, my body instinctively lowering to the ground as I fight to keep my balance.

I can hear Kamea cursing under his breath, and I feel Imran's presence beside me, his grip on his sword tight, ready for whatever comes next. We struggle to hold our ground, the wind pushing against us like a living force, trying to tear us apart.

And then, just as suddenly as it began, the wind dies down. The dust settles, and we're left in an eerie silence once again. But something is wrong. The air is thick with tension, a sense of foreboding hanging heavily over us. I can feel it in my gut—a knot that won't loosen, a warning, something telling me that we're not alone. The silence *now* is too heavy. Too unnatural.

Imran steps forward, his eyes scanning the horizon. His voice is barely a whisper as he mutters, "I can sense something,"

Before any of us can react, the ground beneath our feet seems to shift. The bones and fabric scattered across the dirt stir as if being disturbed by an invisible force. A soft, sickening noise echoes from the depths of the wreckage, and then, from the shadows, they emerge.

At first, they look like shadows themselves—dark, hulking figures that slither and crawl out from beneath the debris. But then I see them clearly—twisted, grotesque forms, with oozing, sickly flesh that drips with goo and pus. Their skin is a sickly, mottled color, stretched tight over jagged bones. Their eyes gleam with malice, sunken deep into their skulls, their faces twisted in unnatural grins that send a chill down my spine.

Demons.

My hand goes straight to my sword, but before I can unsheathe it, one of the creatures' lunges at me, its claws raking through the air with unnatural speed. I barely manage to dodge, the creature's claws grazing my arm and leaving a burning, acidic trail in its wake. I grimace and roll to the side, my heart pounding in my chest, my breath coming in ragged gasps.

"Behind you!" Kamea shouts, his voice sharp.

I turn just in time to see another one of the demons barreling toward me, its mouth wide open, revealing a twisted, jagged maw filled with teeth that are far too large for its mouth. It snarls, saliva dripping from its lips, and I can feel the rush of air as it lunges at me.

I don't think, I just react. My sword is in my hand before I even register it, and I swing it with everything I have, the steel slicing through the demon's body with a sickening squelch. It lets out a high-pitched screech, a horrible, shrill sound that cuts through the air like a knife, but it doesn't stop. It only staggers back, its sickly skin bubbling and shifting as though it's trying to heal itself.

I don't give it a chance to recover. I lunge forward, thrusting my sword through its chest with all the force I can muster, and the creature crumples, its body disintegrating into a puddle of black, viscous goo.

I don't pause to catch my breath. Another one is coming for me, this one crawling on all fours, its limbs bent at unnatural angles, its twisted body moving in jerky, twitching motions. It hisses as it approaches, but I'm already moving again, my sword arcing through the air and cutting deep into its throat. The creature sputters and screeches, but this time, it's too slow. It collapses in a heap of writhing flesh, and I quickly step back, my eyes scanning for the next threat.

Imran and Kamea are fighting alongside me, their weapons flashing as they carve through the demonic horde. Imran is fast, his sword strikes fluid and deadly. His focus is unwavering, and each of his blow's lands with precision. Kamea, though a bit further back, is no less lethal. His bow sings through the air, each arrow finding its mark with deadly accuracy, and he's always moving, never letting the demons get too close.

But the creatures just keep coming. For every one we kill, it feels like two more take its place. The air is thick with the smell of blood and rotting flesh, the ground slick with the remains of our enemies.

"We have to push forward!" Imran shouts, his voice strained but determined. "We need to clear a path!"

I nod, gritting my teeth, and together, we begin to carve our way through the oncoming swarm. My sword swings through the air, cutting down demon after demon, but they keep coming, relentless and insatiable. There's no end to them. No matter how many we kill, more rise from the ground, crawling out of the shadows.

It's like we're fighting against an unending tide of death.

"*Keep moving!*" Kamea orders, his voice fierce as he pushes forward, his bow firing arrow after arrow.

I nod, trying to ignore the unsettling feeling in my chest. I don't know why I feel an overwhelming sense of dread like something is coming after us.

The fight is chaos—absolute, unrelenting chaos. It's all I can do to keep my focus, to keep my sword swinging, to keep my feet planted on the blood-soaked earth beneath me. I can feel the ground shifting underfoot, the weight of the carnage that has settled into the soil, and I can hear the screams of those around me. But I don't have time for them. Not now.

A demon lunges at me with claws extended, its grotesque face twisted in an unnatural snarl. I meet it head-on, slashing my blade across its chest in a clean arc, blood splattering onto the ground and my hands. The creature lets out a horrible shriek as it crumples to the earth, but I don't even watch it die. I'm already moving on, my eyes searching for the next threat.

Another demon barrels toward me, this one much larger than the first. It's covered in boils and oozing pus that stains the ground beneath it as it charges. I don't hesitate, spinning to meet it and thrusting my sword deep into its stomach. The demon roars in fury, but I twist the blade, pulling it out in a flash, sending a torrent of blood spraying out as the creature stumbles back.

I'm not even sure how many I've killed by now; how many I've left behind in my wake. All I know is that it's never enough. There's always more of them. The demons keep coming, relentless and unforgiving, and with every fallen body, more rise in their place.

From the corner of my eye, I catch the death of one of our adventurers, a young man who had been charging with a large battle axe. A demon, smaller but quick, moves in from the shadows, its claws slashing across his exposed neck before he even has a chance to react. He crumples to the ground with a sickening thud, blood pouring from his wound, pooling around his body as the demon moves on.

I don't have time to stop, to even register his fall. Another demon is upon me, its jaw snapping as it lunges for my throat. I sidestep, feeling the heat of its breath as I swipe my blade upward, catching its neck in one swift motion. The demon's head falls to the side, its body twitching as it dies, but I'm already moving past it, searching for the next one.

I'm becoming numb to the death. It's not that I don't care. I care too much, more than I should, maybe. But if I think about each one, about each person who falls, I'll lose my focus, I'll lose myself. And I can't afford to do that. Not here. Not now.

Another roar breaks through the haze of battle, and I turn just in time to see a massive demon—more a beast than a creature of any recognizable form—charge toward us. Its muscles ripple beneath dark, thick skin, and its mouth is a cavern of jagged teeth, saliva dripping from its lips. It's an abomination, a disgusting form of life.

I know it's too strong for me to take on alone, and before I can react, Imran is there, his sword already in motion. He moves with the fluid grace of someone who's been fighting battles like this for years, his strikes are fast and precise, but the demon isn't slowing down. With a deafening growl, the creature swats at Imran, sending him flying through the air, his body crashing against the ground with a sickening crack.

"Kamea!" I shout, my voice cutting through the din. "Help him!"

Kamea doesn't hesitate. His bow is already drawn, an arrow nocked, and without even looking, he releases it. The shaft of the arrow catches the demon in its eye, but it doesn't even flinch. It roars in fury, its body lurching forward toward Imran's prone form.

Damn, that's not good. I can't let it attack. Not while Imran's still down.

I move with everything I have, my legs burning with exhaustion, my muscles aching from the endless fighting. But I reach Imran in time, stepping between him and the demon as it lunges again. My sword flashes, catching the creature in the side and driving it back. The demon lets out a howl of rage, but I don't wait. I don't give it a chance to recover. I strike again, and again, my blade cutting through the air with vicious precision.

The demon stumbles, its massive form lurching sideways as I force it back, but it's still standing. It's still dangerous. And I can feel that flicker of doubt creeping into my mind. What if I can't kill it? What if I'm not strong enough?

But that's not an option.

Imran groans behind me, struggling to get back to his feet, and I can see the pain on his face as he pushes himself up. But Kamea is there, pulling back another arrow and aiming it at the beast's head. The demon moves to strike at me again, but Kamea's shot is true. The arrow sinks deep into the creature's skull, and it lets out one final scream before it crumples to the ground, lifeless.

I let out a brief sigh of relief, but I don't relax. There are too many of them to do so.

The demons keep coming, each one more twisted and sickening than the last. They seem endless, pouring out from all directions. We're getting outnumbered with each wave of demons appearing. We lose more adventurers with each passing minute. I see another one fall, his throat torn out by a demon's claws. I hear the scream of another as a beast tears through her leg, leaving her crippled, helpless.

I look away, lunging toward a demon. The ground trembles beneath my feet as I swing my sword once more, cleaving through the demon's foul, oozing flesh. The creature crumples to the ground in a heap of putrid goo, but before I can catch my breath, another one jumps at me, jaws snapping.

I don't think. I just move. The blade in my hand becomes an extension of myself, an answer to the chaotic, bloodthirsty rage building up inside of me. I can feel the heat of battle, the adrenaline pumping through my veins. I see nothing but red. Nothing but the next demon to kill.

And yet, as I fight, something keeps tugging at the back of my mind, some nagging thought. Why does it feel so...natural? I don't have time to think about it. One of the demons gets too close, and I slice through its chest without hesitation. Its body crumples like paper.

The field is chaos. The air stinks of sulfur and blood. I barely register the screams of those around me, the shouts of my companions, the grinding of metal against flesh. We're losing people, but I can't bring myself to care.

Suddenly, the air stills. And a figure begins to erupt from the foggy air, making its presence known. I freeze. And I think the rest of us do too. Even the demons have a brief moment of quiet before attacking us again.

The sound of his heavy footsteps rumbles through the air, and despite the chaos, all eyes are drawn to him. He's tall—taller than any man I've seen before—and his build is monstrous, thick with muscle, scars etched into his skin like marks of a brutal life. His raven hair is cropped short, and his grey eyes glint with malicious delight as he surveys the battlefield.

He doesn't need to announce his presence. He just is, and the demons around us seem to part in deference to him. I feel an instinctive rush of terror in my chest. Who is he? Why is he here?

He grins. It's a sickening grin, one that promises pain, one that promises death. And then, with a sudden motion, he's right in front of me, his fist slamming into my gut with a force I didn't see coming.

I gasp for air as the blow knocks the wind out of me. The pain is instant—sharp, burning—and my vision blurs as I stumble back, my sword nearly slipping from my hand.

Before I can react, his large hand grips my throat, lifting me off the ground. My body goes rigid, and a rush of panic shoots through me. I claw at his hand, trying to pry it off, but it's useless. His strength is overwhelming, and I'm nothing more than a child in his grip.

"You're the one who killed Sirath?" Zaroth's voice is low and rumbling, full of mockery. "Pathetic. I know Sirath is a useless underling, but the fact that you killed him? What a laugh."

I try to kick, try to lash out with whatever strength I have left, but my body refuses to obey. The air is leaving me, my mind spinning as I feel my consciousness slipping.

"Such a waste of time. And I came all the way," Zaroth mutters, shaking his head, a cruel smirk spreading across his face. "Did you really think you could stand up to someone like me, Zaroth?"

Realization suddenly dawns on me, and pure horror seizes me immediately. Zaroth? Zaroth, one of the Demon Generals?

I force my head up, narrowing my eyes as I look at him. Despite the pain, despite the terror threatening to consume me, I refuse to let him see me break. I refuse to give him the satisfaction.

His smirk widens as if he's enjoying my struggle, savoring my weakness. "But, for your efforts, I'll reward you. I'll make your death…painless for the most part,"

I can't get a word out, can't even manage a growl of defiance. His grip tightens, cutting off the air. My vision begins to swim, the edges of my sight darkening. My body feels like it's shutting down.

But then, in the haze of impending unconsciousness, something inside me snaps. *I won't die here. Not like this.*

With a primal roar, I summon the last of my strength and kick out, my foot connecting with Zaroth's chest. He grunts in surprise, momentarily loosening his grip. It's not much, but it's enough.

I drop to the ground, gasping for air, every muscle in my body protesting. I don't know how much longer I can keep this up.

Zaroth, however, doesn't give me a chance to recover. He steps forward again, swinging his arm in a wide arc. The force of it catches me across the face, sending me crashing to the ground. My cheek burns with the impact, and I taste blood in my mouth. I spit it out, dragging myself back up despite the throbbing pain in my skull.

Zaroth is already on top of me, his boot slamming into my side. The breath leaves my lungs in a painful whoosh, and I crumple again, the air knocked out of me. I try to stand, but my body betrays me, trembling and weak from the punishment.

"Still not enough, huh?" Zaroth sneers, voice laced with cruel amusement. "I'm not even trying."

I clench my fists, teeth grinding, fighting against the overwhelming desire to collapse and give up. I can't. Not now. If I fall now, everything I've fought for, everything I've endured, will have been for nothing. I can't let this monster—this demon—take everything from me.

But my legs won't obey. My hands feel numb. My head spins as I stagger to my feet, struggling to stay upright. I can barely focus, barely see straight, but I force my eyes to meet Zaroth's again, and there's something burning deep inside me. Something... relentless.

He sees it too.

Zaroth grins wider, his grey eyes flashing with sadistic pleasure. "Ah, that's it. That fire in your eyes. It all makes sense now. Too bad it won't help you now."

I swing out, a desperate blow, my sword clumsy and slow. Zaroth doesn't even need to move. He just catches my arm mid-swing, twisting it violently. I feel my shoulder pop, a jolt of agony shooting down my arm as I cry out, but it's nothing compared to the pain in my chest.

Zaroth pulls me close, his hot breath on my face. His grip is still iron-tight, and I feel like I'm being crushed from the inside out. "You know what the difference is between you and me, human?" he says softly, almost condescendingly. "You fight with desperation. With anger. You're wild. But you'll never be able to control it. You'll always be a puppet, struggling against your strings."

He tightens his grip, and I gasp, trying to free myself, but it's useless. "I fight with purpose," he continues. "With discipline. I don't concern myself with weak, filthy humans. That's why I win. That's why I will always win."

His words burrow into my mind, and for a moment, doubt creeps in. I can feel it, the seed of fear. The realization that he's right. I'm nothing compared to him. He's a Demon General, a god of war, and I'm just a man—a broken, angry man who can barely hold onto his own life.

But then, something shifts.

It's a flicker, a spark of defiance that flares up in my chest. It doesn't matter what Zaroth says. It doesn't matter that I'm weak, that I'm struggling.

Yes, my limbs are heavy, and my breathing short. And yet, in the middle of the madness, I feel my focus sharpen. My sword feels lighter than it should in my hands, my grip weak as if my strength is being drained with each passing second. Every strike I land seems to have little effect.

I can feel the blood in my veins thundering in my ears as I swing my blade at him again, every movement a desperate attempt to gain ground. I'm exhausted, but I can't stop. I refuse to stop.

Zaroth grins wider. It's mocking, it's terrifying. It's like he's enjoying my struggle. He dodges my strike effortlessly, his massive form shifting with unnatural grace. His laughter echoes in my head, rattling me.

And then, in a move too fast for me to track, Zaroth slams his fist into my gut. The impact is like a hammer against a stone, a jolt of pain that knocks the wind out of me and sends me stumbling backward. My legs tremble, threatening to buckle beneath me, but I force myself to stay upright, fighting against the pain. My breath is ragged, my chest heaving.

Zaroth steps forward, his grin widening, the cruel amusement in his eyes unmistakable. I try to raise my sword again, but my muscles feel like lead, and my vision is starting to blur.

"You're quite the persistent one," he says, his voice deep and mocking. "I almost admire it. *Almost.*"

I'm not sure how I manage it, but I lunge forward, desperate, swinging my sword at him one more time. This time, something lands. I feel the blade sink into his side, and for a moment, I think I've finally struck a blow. But the smile on Zaroth's face doesn't fade. It only grows wider.

With a sudden, brutal motion, Zaroth grabs my sword with one hand, yanking it out of my grip and throwing it back at me with a force that sends me staggering.

"Pathetic," he sneers. "You can't even hold onto your weapon. You think you stand a chance against me?"

I reach out, catching my sword in mid-air, barely able to hold onto the hilt. I'm trembling, my body a mass of pain and exhaustion. I can't let go now. Not after everything.

But then, something strange happens. I look at Zaroth, and there's something off about him. He's not moving like a person anymore. He's twitching, jerking in an unnatural way. And then, slowly, with horrifying clarity, I realize what's going on. Zaroth's body...it's not real.

I freeze. My breath catches in my throat. The figure in front of me isn't Zaroth. It's a puppet.

My hands shake as I take a step back, the truth settling over me like a cold wave. This isn't the demon general. This isn't even a real fight. It's a lie. A decoy.

I look down, my stomach churning as I watch the puppet start to deteriorate before my eyes. The movements become more erratic, and the body begins to fall apart, crumbling into dust.

Zaroth's voice rings out, smooth and calm, as though he's just finished a pleasant conversation. "Well done, Hybrid," he says, and the mockery in his voice makes my blood run cold. "You actually managed to land a hit. *How cute.*"

I stand there, stunned. All this time, I thought I was fighting a real demon general, that I had a chance to prove myself, to grow stronger. But this—this was just a puppet. A lie.

A cold shiver runs down my spine, and I stagger backward, trying to comprehend what just happened. My heart pounds in my chest, the adrenaline of the battle giving way to the sickening realization that I'm out of my depth. I'm struggling to fight a puppet. What does that make me? What does that say about my abilities?

Zaroth's laughter echoes around me like a dark cloud suffocating my thoughts. The puppet before me continues to wither, falling apart until it's nothing but dust, and with it, my confidence.

"Arius is coming. And you are not ready for what he has in store," Zaroth continues, his voice now taunting. "But that's okay. You'll get a chance to see for yourself soon enough."

A chill runs through me, the unease settling deep in my bones. What's he talking about? What does he mean? Arius is coming?

Then he vanishes in a blur of shadows, the air around me growing colder in his absence. But before he disappears entirely, something drops from his wake, fluttering to the ground.

I don't know what it is at first. It's a flash of cloth, a glint of fabric against the blood-stained earth. I reach down, my fingers numb as I pick it up, the weight of it too significant to ignore.

It's a banner.

My throat tightens as I unroll it slowly, my hands trembling. The fabric is worn, the edges frayed, but it's unmistakable. The name "Arius" is emblazoned on it, bold and unyielding.

The breath leaves my chest in a rush, and for a moment, the world tilts. I blink rapidly, trying to process what I'm seeing. Arius. The name of the hero I once revered, the man I aspired to be. The man who fought valiantly, who led the charge against the Demon King's forces. The man whose stories I grew up hearing, whose legacy I clung to.

Arius is here. Or rather, he's coming. To bring destruction and chaos.

CHAPTER 8

The battlefield falls eerily silent after Zaroth's disappearance, the air thick with the stench of death and the quiet whispers of the wind. The demons—all of them—vanish into the ground, like they were never there in the first place. They melt away into the earth, leaving nothing but the hollow sound of their absence and the acrid smoke that lingers in the air. My body is still trembling from the clash, my muscles sore and my skin singed from the barrage of attacks I've just endured.

I slump to the ground, my knees buckling beneath me, the adrenaline that had been keeping me on my feet suddenly fading away. My sword slips from my grasp, hitting the dirt with a dull thud. I can barely focus my eyes on anything. The world around me feels distant, as though it's spinning too quickly for me to keep up. My breath comes in ragged gasps, each inhale and exhale punctuated by the dull throb of pain that reverberates through my body. Zaroth's strength had been overwhelming, like a storm crashing over me, and though my demon blood is healing me faster than a human would recover, it didn't change the fact that the impact of his blows still left me rattled, my senses scrambled.

I feel a hand on my shoulder, warm and firm, and then another beneath my arm, helping to lift me up. Imran's voice cuts through the fog in my head.

"Crilt, you're alive. Damn, we almost lost you there. We were trying to get to you, but we got bombarded by a lot of demons."

His grip is tight, and steady, grounding me. I blink up at him, trying to bring my focus back, but the battle and the exhaustion are too much to shake off in an instant. Kamea's face is grim as he kneels beside me, his usual cold expression now hardened with something deeper, more troubled. He says nothing but helps steady me, his presence as solid and unyielding as the stone beneath my feet.

I glance around, finally realizing just how much has been lost in the chaos. The remnants of our forces are scattered, blood-soaked bodies of fallen adventurers marking the ground like grim reminders of our failing. Their faces are twisted in pain, their eyes unseeing. The few who remain are battered and bruised, some of them already too far gone to be of any help. My stomach churns as I take in the sight, a wave of anger and frustration threatening to overwhelm me. How did we get here?

Imran helps me to my feet, but I can barely keep my balance. I feel like a shell of myself, hollowed out by all that has happened today. Arius's name still echoes in my mind, a poison that taints every thought. How could it be true? How could the man I once admired, the hero I looked up to, have fallen so far? Zaroth's words ring in my ears, and I can't shake the feeling that everything I've believed in has been nothing more than a lie.

"Crilt, we've lost too many," Imran says, his voice tight with frustration. "Our forces are decimated. And there's still no sign of Arius, no sign of when he'll show up. He's a wild card, and we have no idea when he's coming, or how powerful he's become."

I nod slowly, my teeth gritted together as I clench my fists, my nails digging into the palms of my hands. I know what he means. The raid, the demons, the constant struggle—none of it matters in the grand scheme of things. Not anymore. The threat of Arius, the possibility of facing him, is the true terror now. I can't even begin to fathom how strong he's become as a demon general. The very thought sends a shiver of dread down my spine.

I shake my head, my vision blurring as I try to steady myself. "We can't just…let him win. We have to prepare."

Imran looks at me, his expression unreadable. I can see the same flicker of fear in his eyes—the fear of what might come if Arius truly has turned against humanity, if he's become nothing more than a weapon for the Demon King. The man who once stood for hope, for the future of humanity, is now a general in the army of the very forces we've been fighting to destroy. It doesn't make sense. It can't make sense. But the evidence is mounting, and the reality of the situation is sinking in like a stone in my gut.

Kamea stands up, his sharp eyes scanning the battlefield. "We need to fall back," he says quietly, his tone as cold and calculated as ever. "We can't just stay out here in the open. We need to regroup, lick our wounds, and hold out for the night, hoping that he doesn't strike today."

I don't argue. Kamea's pragmatism is something I've come to respect, even if it grates against my own impulsiveness. There's no point in staying here, in risking more lives when we've already lost so much. I look at the bodies strewn across the ground—the friends, the comrades I've fought alongside—and I feel my heart harden. We owe it to them to survive. We owe it to everyone who's still counting on us.

I sigh, all optimism disappearing out of me in a flash. What good is fighting again if Arius is truly coming for us? What hope do we have left against a force like him? I don't know, and I'm not sure I want to find out.

Imran and Kamea exchange a brief look, an understanding passing between them. They know what I'm thinking—they've seen the doubts creeping into my eyes, the hesitation that's started to take root in my chest. But they don't say anything. They don't need to.

Kamea gives me a single nod. "Let's move, then."

We don't waste any time. With no words of encouragement, we begin to make our way back to our carriage. With Imran's help, we manage to make a small fire out of whatever materials we can find, while Kamea helps the injured ones back into the carriage, and helps to put aside what ever is left of the corpses. The faces of the fallen haunt me. Killian's face, that goofy smile flashes in my mind. Risa's red hair, Falin's seafoam eyes. Bran and Seni, too. All of them—gone. Now, more that I don't know are gone as well. Lost to battles that, in the end, didn't matter. The truth is staring me in the face, and I can't escape it. We've been playing into their hands all along, and the worst part is, I don't know if we can stop it.

Arius.

The name echoes in my head like a curse, and I can't shake the fear that now claws at me. Not only did we lose some today, but now we have to contend with the arrival of Arius—the man I thought was our salvation. The man I thought would lead us to victory. And now?

Now he's our enemy.

We ride in silence, the sound of hooves against dirt the only noise that accompanies us. Each of us is lost in our own thoughts, each of us fighting our own battles within. We don't speak as we're each consumed in our own work and I'm thankful for that. I don't know what I would say to them if they asked about Arius. If they asked me how we're supposed to fight against someone who was once our hero.

I don't know if we can win this war.

And I don't know if we can ever truly defeat Arius.

The campsite is quiet, too quiet. It's so silent, that you can even hear your heartbeat. There's no sound to distract us from it, no rustling of leaves, no birds chirping, no sign of life anywhere. Nothing. And no one is willing to talk, though I don't expect anyone to. The battle had drained us all, and the air around us was thick with exhaustion and fear. I could see it on everyone's face: the stress, the uncertainty. Each of us had lost comrades today. Friends who'd fought beside each other laughed with each other, and now lay scattered on the battlefield. All of them are gone. It's hard to even think about them.

The air is still thick with smoke and ash, the remnants of the fight we had just escaped. The smell of death still lingers, sharp and unrelenting.

Imran, Kamea, and I sit off to one side, while the others gather what little supplies, we have left, tending to the wounded. The sound of the campfire crackling is the only noise that fills the void.

I look over at Kamea, his face as unreadable as always, but even he can't hide the weight of what's to come. He hasn't said a word about Arius, but I can see it in his eyes. We all know the truth now. Zaroth has confirmed it.

I feel a deep anger stirring within me—an anger I can't ignore. A rage that wells up from deep inside my chest and burns through my veins, making my hands tremble with the need to do something, anything, to make this all stop. How could this be happening? How could he have fallen so far? What reason can there be to join the Demon King?

The others are silent, and I'm sure they're all stewing in their own thoughts. Imran's face is tight, his expression hard and cold. I can tell he's thinking about his family, about what this all means for the future of humanity. He has revenge on his mind, I know it. Kamea, too, is quiet. He always is, but tonight, there's something different about the way he's holding himself. I know he's processing everything too—the battle, the loss, the knowledge that Arius, is now the enemy.

And then there's me.

I can't sit still. My mind is racing, and my body feels like it's constantly on edge. I can't shake the vision of Arius I saw back in Hurin, mocking me, telling me that maybe the Demon King's cause isn't so wrong after all. I can't shake the thought that this might be our fault—that we might have pushed him to this point. That maybe, just maybe, there was a part of him that was always destined to fall.

The truth is, I don't know what to believe anymore.

But I do know this: Arius has to be stopped. Even if it means I have to kill the man I once revered.

I stand up, my legs shaking from exhaustion, but I push it aside. "We need to talk," I say, my voice louder than I intended. It's enough to get their attention, but neither Imran nor Kamea say anything. They just look at me, waiting for me to explain.

"I spoke to Zaroth," I continue, trying to steady my voice. "Before he left, he told me... he told me the truth about Arius."

There's a long pause, the silence pressing in on me like a physical force. I take a deep breath and let it out slowly. My heart is pounding, my thoughts scattered, but I know I have to say it.

"Arius is a general. A general for the Demon King. And he's coming for us soon,"

Imran's eyes harden. Kamea's expression doesn't change, but I can see the tension in his jaw, the way his fingers twitch as if itching for a weapon. We've all known that something had changed with Arius. The rumors we heard, the whispers about him being alive, had always been a nagging doubt in the back of our minds. But now, the truth was right in our faces, a head pill to swallow.

"He's coming," I continue, my voice low, barely above a whisper. "And when he does, we won't be ready. Not unless we prepare ourselves. Not unless we can come to terms with what he's become."

One of them grits his teeth. "I can't believe it," he mutters under his breath. "Arius, the man who gave us hope, who fought for humanity's future, now... now he's their general? He's leading their charge?"

I nod slowly. "That's what Zaroth said. The myths about him, about his power, they were all true. Arius, the hero who defeated countless demons, is now serving the very forces he once fought against."

Kamea stands up, his sharp eyes scanning the camp as though assessing every threat in the distance. He doesn't speak for a long time, and when he does, his voice is calm and controlled. "Then we have no choice. We'll face him when the time comes."

But there's an unspoken hesitation that ripples through everyone. No one wants to fight such a powerful hero. Each for their own reasons. Whether they're afraid of the strength Arius possesses, or because of the position the former hero has, it's hard to let go of the fact that many of them here have once put their faith in him.

And that's what stings the most.

The fact that we have to kill him. I haven't even been in this world for a long time, yet I can feel his impact all through. The man who once inspired us all. The man who once stood as a beacon of hope for humanity. Now, he's the enemy. And the hardest part is that there's no other way. We don't have a choice.

I pace back and forth, my frustration mounting with every step. "We can't just wait around," I mutter, more to myself than to anyone else. "We need to be ready. We need to find a way to stop him before he destroys everything we've worked for."

Imran steps closer, his hand resting on the hilt of his sword. "It's dangerous, I know. But we have no other option. We can't let him go through us, or else, Ashroth is doomed. Everyone we know, and everyone we care about will all be in danger. It's unfair, I know, but there's nothing we can do."

His words, though filled with determination, ring hollow in my ears. It's unfair, alright. No matter how we mentally prepare ourselves for Arius' coming, we'll never be ready for what he has in store.

We've lost so much already. What else can we sacrifice?

Kamea looks at me, his eyes piercing. "We'll stop him. One way or another." His words, though blunt, carry a conviction that cuts through the doubt in my chest. "But it won't be easy. And it won't be painless. We might die. We might be hurt terribly. But we don't have a choice. We're in this together."

Silence falls on us all, and revert back to thinking.

We might die.

***

The next day rolls on, though it's hard to tell in the Endzone, the ever-darkened, windswept wasteland. The sky is perpetually overcast, the air thick with the scent of damp earth and a foreboding chill that hovers over like a dark cloud. If there was ever a place that could reflect the mood of our situation, it was here. The sun never seems to shine in the Endzone. It feels like the sky is hiding, waiting for something terrible to happen. Perhaps it knows what's coming. Perhaps it's already mourning the inevitable loss.

The air is filled with the sounds of metal scraping against metal and the rhythmic pounding of hammers on weapons and armor. Imran and Kamea are already at work, sharpening their blades, checking their gear, and making sure every piece of armor is intact. They've been through countless battles, but today, it's different. The air of finality, of resignation, is too prominent within all of us. We all have no faith that we're going to survive this.

I mean, if Arius is on par with Zaroth's puppet in any way, then we're not wrong in accepting death.

I watch them work, absent-mindedly running my hand over the hilt of my own sword. It's still stained with blood. The blade feels cold and unfamiliar in my grip, as though it's not even mine.

My thoughts are interrupted by Kamea, who looks up from his armor maintenance and catches my eye. There's something in his expression—something unspoken, like a burden he's been carrying but hasn't shared with anyone. He sets his hammer down and strides over to me, his boots crunching the gravel beneath them.

"You alright?" he asks, his voice steady but tinged with concern. His gaze is sharp, always sharp, but there's something softer in his eyes right now. He's always been the practical one, the one who focuses on the task at hand, but today, I see a flicker of doubt in him. He knows what we're about to face. He knows how dangerous Arius is, and he's worried about me.

Imran walks up behind Kamea, clapping a hand on my shoulder in the way he does when he wants to ease the tension. His grip is firm, and I feel the warmth of his concern, even if it's wrapped in the usual boisterousness of his personality.

"We've got your back, Crilt," Imran says with a grin that doesn't quite reach his eyes. "Don't worry about a thing. We've all been through worse."

I nod, forcing a smile in return. The expression feels foreign on my face, but I manage it anyway. The first real smile I've given them in…well, honestly, this is the first time I'm smiling at them. It shocks both of them into stunned silence. I think they were expecting more of the same brooding, more of the same dark silence I've been carrying around as usual.

"You two better keep up with me," I joke, my voice a little shaky but loud enough to mask the unease in my chest. "I don't plan on slowing down just because we're up against an ancient hero."

Kamea huffs a little, a small, almost affectionate sound that makes me feel just the slightest bit lighter. "If you think you can outrun me, Crilt, you've got another thing coming," he mutters, though I can hear the fondness in his tone. He claps me on the back, and I feel the warmth of his support.

Imran laughs, slapping my shoulder with a force that nearly sends me stumbling forward. "Kids, they grow up too soon." He wipes a faux tear from his eye.

I can't help but chuckle at that, though there's an edge of bitterness to it. "I'll pull through, alright. But I don't plan on making this easy for Arius. Not this time."

The moment stretches on for a few seconds, and I can feel the weight of it—the knowing that this might be the last time I can joke around with them like this. There's a chance none of us are going to walk out of this fight alive.

But still, I find myself clinging to a shred of hope. Maybe, just maybe, there's still something in Arius that can be saved, and maybe we might just make it out, alive. There's just a slight chance; a tiny probability, but at least it's something to hold onto.

When Imran and Kamea leave me alone, heading back to the campfire to check on the others, the smile on my face drops instantly. I sit down on a large stone near the edge of the camp, rubbing my eyes with the heels of my palms. There's a pit in my stomach—a cold, gnawing feeling of dread. I hardly feel like this, so this is new.

I think briefly about Sokh, my mentor. I haven't thought about him much since all of this started. Too much has happened, and there hasn't been time to focus on anything other than survival.

Sokh was the one who taught me everything I know—everything that made me the man I am now. I'd hoped that I'd find him again, that I'd be able to track him down after all this mess after I had time to reflect on everything we've been through. But now, with Arius looming on the horizon, I'm not sure there's even a chance for me to fulfill my promise after all.

I've been so focused on this war, on stopping the Demon King and his forces, that I've lost sight of the reason I started this journey in the first place. To learn, to grow, to find Sokh. I've been running headlong into this chaos, chasing a future I'm not sure I'm ready for.

And this path has led me to my doom. Do I regret doing this? No. Do I want more time? Yes.

But now, as I sit alone with my thoughts, I find myself wondering: if I die in this fight, will Sokh be proud of me? I would like to think so. He always says that I should trust my instincts and allow them to lead me. I've learned so much—maybe more than I ever could have imagined. But none of it feels like it's been worth it if I can't stop Arius if I can't bring the truth to light, if I can't stop the devastation that's going to fall upon us when he arrives.

I shake my head. This isn't the time for regrets or bitter thoughts. I have to focus. I have to keep my mind clear.

Still, the thought lingers.

Would Sokh be proud of me?

I wish I could be certain. I wish I could know that if I die today or tomorrow, that it won't all be for nothing.

My hand tightens around the hilt of my sword. The blade feels cold against my skin, and I can't help but think back to the moment when I struck Zaroth, the demon puppet who nearly killed me. I couldn't believe it then—the shock of realizing that the creature I'd been fighting wasn't even the true threat.

Zaroth had taunted me with the truth, in telling me that Arius is coming. Though he was vague about it, the fact that it's Zaroth of all people telling me such news, confirms that Arius has indeed fallen so far from redemption.

The betrayal stings, sharp and deep, but there's no time to dwell on it. We have to prepare for what's coming. And whatever happens next—whether I win, whether I survive, or whether I fall alongside my comrades—I won't let Arius's fall be in vain. I will stop him.

For all of us.

I stand up, my legs steady beneath me, and look toward the horizon. It feels like the end is drawing near, the storm that's been brewing in the distance has finally caught up to us, and we have no choice but to face it head-on.

"Arius," I murmur under my breath, feeling a shiver run down my spine. "I don't know who you are now, but I'll stop you. No matter what it takes."

I take a deep breath, trying to steady myself. This is it. The battle is coming. And I will fight. I will fight for my fallen comrades, for Sokh, for humanity, for the Demi-humans, and for the chance to bring an end to the darkness that Arius has become.

Even if it costs me my life.

We are ready.

CHAPTER 9

The air shifts and a heavy gust of wind slams into us, a violent reminder that something is coming. It howls through the desolate Endzone, whipping sand into our faces, carrying the bitter sting of imminent doom. I can feel the shift in the atmosphere, the way the temperature drops just enough to make the hairs on the back of my neck stand on end.

Then it comes. A sudden, unnatural stillness follows the storm of wind, the silence almost deafening in its intensity. The sky above us, already gloomy and oppressive, seems to crack open. It's as though the heavens themselves are splitting apart, and from that tear, a blinding shaft of light erupts, cutting through the dark clouds like a blade through flesh. My heart lurches in my chest as I squint into the distance, watching the sky warp and churn.

And then he appears.

Arius.

I can barely breathe as I watch him materialize in the distance. His figure stands tall and menacing against the darkened backdrop, a silhouette that shimmers for a moment before it becomes real. His presence is almost overwhelming. The wind around him seems to bow in respect, swirling in tighter, violent patterns. His armor is minimal—a few plates of metal armor strapped to his legs and right arm, but his stance alone speaks of power. The rest of his body is left exposed, the dark, bloody red of his long, flowing hair catching the light in a way that seems unnatural. It's like fire trapped in the strands, yet it gives off no warmth. His face is stoic, unreadable. Green eyes with a ring of black sclera around them scan the landscape with an eerie calmness as if he finds the situation lacking in interest. His build is slender but undeniably muscular, toned with the strength that comes from both training and battle.

Arius doesn't move much. He stands there, staring down at us from his elevated position as if he's surveying the scene before deciding who will be the first to die. His mere presence feels like a cold weight pressing down on my chest. The others around me tense, the fear obvious on their faces, but none of them look away. I don't think we can even if we try.

I can hear the distant, muffled voices of Imran and Kamea, rallying the few remaining adventurers to form up, to prepare for what's coming, but it's all just noise against the sharp reality of Arius's arrival.

The wind howls again, stronger than before like it's been whipped into a frenzy by Arius's power, and for a moment, I wonder if we're even capable of standing against him. He's a force of nature, a storm incarnates, and we are but specks of dust beneath his gaze. A part of me wants to turn and run, but the larger part— the part that remembers what I'm here for. I can't run from this.

But before I can process any more, something shifts again, and in an instant, he's no longer standing there.

He's right in front of us.

I barely register the movement. One moment, Arius is standing a distance away, his figure silhouetted by the storm behind him, and the next, he's standing directly in front of us, his feet a mere whisper of distance from the ground, as though he's gliding over the earth without ever touching it. The speed with which he moves is enough to make my heart skip a beat. There's no time to react. No time to blink.

And then, with a casual flick of his wrist, one of the adventurers who had been standing beside me is gone. Disappearing into ash.

Just like that.

The adventurer, a man who had been brave enough to stand at the front of the group, collapses into nothingness as Arius's motion causes the air around him to crackle. The flick of Arius's wrist isn't even a full movement, just a lazy gesture. Yet, the adventurer disintegrates before my eyes, his body turning to ash in an instant, the fine particles scattering in the wind. There's no blood. No scream. Just a pile of dust that catches the wind and blows away, leaving nothing behind.

I stand frozen, watching the place where the man had been, where his existence had been wiped away as though it were nothing. The others are equally still, staring in horror at the empty space. The reality of what we're up against hits us all at once—he's a living embodiment of destruction.

I can feel my heart pounding in my chest, and for a moment, I question my resolve. How are we supposed to fight this? How are we supposed to stop someone so far beyond us?

"Pathetic," Arius's voice cuts through the silence, his words like a blade scraping across metal. His tone is low, almost bored.

His eyes slide over the remaining adventurers, sizing us up, as if we were nothing more than ants underfoot. His gaze flicks toward Kamea and Imran, who are standing just a few paces away from me, their hands gripping their weapons tightly.

"You still think you can stand against me?" Arius asks, his voice dull, as if it's tiring to speak to insignificant creatures like us. "You've seen what I can do. And yet, you still hold hope."

I can see the doubt in their eyes—the way their grips tighten on their swords, their shields, as they try to steady themselves. They know we're outclassed. I know it, too. But there's no turning back now. We've come this far. We can't let him win. Not after everything we've been through. Whether we live or die.

I step forward, though my legs feel like lead. My hand tightens around the hilt of my sword, and I force myself to meet Arius's gaze. Arius's lips curl into a cruel smile, but there's nothing warm in it. He takes my confidence lightly, like a suicidal wish.

He raises his hand again, and the air around him seems to bend, crackling with dark energy. I can feel it, this oppressive pressure that gathers around us. His very presence seems to warp the space around him, making it difficult to breathe, as if the weight of his power is too much for the world to hold.

Before anyone can react, Arius's arm snaps forward, and a blast of dark energy erupts from his fingertips. It's so fast, so blinding, that I don't even see it coming until it's almost too late. I instinctively leap to the side, feeling the heat of the blast as it rips through the air just inches from my shoulder. The explosion rips through the sand, tearing up the earth beneath us, and sending rocks and debris flying in every direction.

"Move!" Imran shouts, but it's too late. A few of the adventurers are caught in the blast, their cries of pain drowned out by the sheer force of the explosion. I can see their bodies being flung back; ragdolls caught in a storm they can't hope to survive.

The remaining adventurers scramble to find cover, but it's clear we're outmatched. Arius doesn't even need to try. His power alone is enough to level us.

He's far from human now. We're fighting against a god.

Arius stands there, unfazed by the destruction he's wrought. He doesn't even look winded. In fact, he looks…bored. Barely paying us any mind. Every movement, every flick of his wrist, every word he speaks drips with disdain. We're nothing to him.

I glance at Imran and Kamea, who are both staring at Arius with sweat dripping down their faces. They know what we're up against. But they also know that, as long as there's life left in us, we'll keep fighting.

The dust is thick in the air, swirling violently in the wake of Arius's earlier attack. The ground beneath my feet trembles slightly as if even the earth itself is recoiling from the presence of the man—no, the monster—standing before us. The wind continues to howl, carrying with it the lingering scent of scorched earth and the acrid sting of battle. The scene before me is so surreal that for a brief, fleeting moment, I wonder if it's all a nightmare. But the heat in my chest, the adrenaline coursing through my veins, the sweat on my brow—these are all too real. This is happening.

His gaze is heavy on me, his green eyes laced with black, boring into me with an intensity that almost makes my blood run cold. He's like a force of nature, unstoppable, inevitable. My fists clench around the hilt of my sword, and I take a step forward, moving alongside Imran and Kamea, who are already positioning themselves for what's to come. There's no turning back now. If we're going to die, we're going to die fighting.

"Stay focused," Imran says through gritted teeth, his eyes not leaving Arius for a moment. "We've got one chance at this. We'll die trying if we have to."

Kamea nods, his bow held tightly, ready to fire. His expression is set, his lips pressed into a thin line, but beneath the surface, I can tell that he's terrified. I am too. But there's no time for fear. Not now.

Arius watches us, standing tall and imposing, his face an unreadable mask. The winds swirl around him, kicking up dust and sand. The only sound that remains is the steady, pounding rhythm of my heart.

And then, without warning, he moves.

In an instant, Arius vanishes from sight, reappearing right before us with a speed that is almost impossible to follow. It's not even teleportation. He's moving so fast that it feels like time itself is bending around him. I react instinctively, raising my sword to block, but Arius's fist strikes out faster than I can comprehend.

His punch slams into my side and the force of it sends me crashing into the sand, air leaving my lungs in a painful rush. The impact feels like a mountain falling on me. I roll to the side, trying to recover, but before I can catch my breath, Arius is already on the move again. His movements are fluid, and effortless, as if he's dancing, dashing through the air like he's one with it.

Imran charges in, his axe swinging wide, but Arius sidesteps him with a casual grace as if the strike was nothing more than a mild inconvenience. He grabs Imran by the wrist, twisting his arm with a sickening snap. Imran cries out in pain, but Arius isn't finished. He throws Imran to the ground like a ragdoll, sending him tumbling across the sand. Kamea rushes forward to support him, but Arius merely extends his hand, unleashing a pulse of dark energy that sends him flying backward. He crashes into the sand, the wind knocked out of him.

I grit my teeth, my blood boiling with frustration, with rage, white-hot anger.

And yet, as I watch him easily dispatch Kamea and Imran with a wave of his hand, something inside me snaps. A surge of anger—raw, furious—erupts within me, drowning out the fear, the doubt. It's the same feeling I had when I fought Sirath, that rage that burns so hot it consumes everything in its path. It propels me forward, faster than I've ever moved before.

I charge.

The ground cracks beneath my feet as I sprint, my sword raised high, my mind set on one thing: to take Arius down. The wind howls in my ears, but I block it out. My focus is absolute. Arius is here, standing before me like a god, but I won't let that stop me.

Arius's eyes snap to me as I close the distance between us. There's no surprise in his gaze, no acknowledgment of the effort it takes for me to close in on him. To him, I'm just another ant trying to bite back against a giant.

But then, something shifts in his expression—a faint glimmer of recognition. His lips curl into the smallest of smiles, a cold, mocking gesture.

"Impressive," Arius murmurs, his voice low but clear, cutting through the chaos like a knife. "So, you're the one who got away. Very interesting."

The words hit me like a slap to the face. Zaroth said something similar earlier. The one who got away? What does that mean? I shake my head. No, he's trying to distract me, this tricky demon! I can feel the anger in me building, coiling tighter as if it might explode. But I won't let it control me. Not yet.

I swing my sword at him with all the speed I can muster, my muscles straining, my body pushed to its limits. The blade sings through the air, cutting through the space between us with deadly intent. But Arius doesn't move. He doesn't even flinch. His right hand comes up lazily, and with a flick of his wrist, the blade of my sword is sent flying out of my grip, skittering across the ground like a discarded toy.

I freeze.

It's like the world has stopped moving. My sword, my only weapon, is gone. The ground beneath me seems so far away now, like a distant memory. My heart pounds in my chest, the adrenaline still surging through me, but the reality of the situation crashes over me with the force of a tidal wave.

I'm powerless.

Arius steps forward, his green eyes locked onto mine, his gaze cold, calculating. He raises an eyebrow, amusement flickering behind the depths of his eyes.

"How quaint," he says, his voice almost pitying.

I try to move, to find something, anything to fight with, but my body is frozen, caught in the web of his presence. His power is suffocating. It's like a storm cloud hanging over us, ready to burst and crush everything in its path.

"You've embraced your demon blood," Arius continues, his tone almost conversational. "You think you can fight me with that? Cute," He leans closer, his voice dropping lower, almost a whisper. "I've embraced something far greater than your blood. Something far more powerful."

The air around us shifts, crackling with an unnatural energy. It pulses and ripples through the ground like a shockwave. My skin tingles with the power radiating off of him. I can feel it in my bones, the weight of the darkness he's embraced. He's no longer a man, not truly. He's something far worse.

"You're not strong enough," Arius murmurs, his gaze never leaving mine. "None of you are."

Before I can react, he moves again. His hand shoots out, grabbing me by the throat with frightening speed. I gasp for air, but his grip is unrelenting, crushing. His fingers feel like iron like they're closing around my windpipe, suffocating me with each passing second.

"And you, you're the most disappointing out of them all. I expected something better from you, Hybrid," His eyes narrow, and I can feel the life draining out of me as he slowly lifts me off the ground. The world spins. My vision blurs.

"I've surpassed everything that once held me back," Arius continues, his voice a low growl. "The human you knew is gone. There's nothing left but power. And soon, this world will belong to the demons."

I try to fight, to break free, but it's no use. His strength is overwhelming. There's nothing I can do to stop him. I'm drowning in his power, in his rage, in all his emotions.

The wind howls around us, whipping the sand into the air like a storm. His presence is a weight like the world itself is bending under his will. It's as if reality is warping in his favor.

"You still don't understand," Arius says, his voice chillingly calm, as though the destruction he's already caused is nothing more than an afterthought. He speaks with the certainty of someone who's already seen the world through a lens of inevitability. "I'm not the hero you once knew. I never was. I was always destined for something greater. The Demon King's vision, his new world order—it's the only truth. The strong will rule. The weak will fall. There is no room for redemption. There is no place for weakness."

His words cut through the air like a blade, and for a moment, the world seems to stop around me. His gaze is unwavering, burning into me like a brand. And suddenly, everything—the pain, the anger, the fight—seems too much to bear.

"You're wrong, Arius," I spit, as much as I can muster, my throat aching from his grip. The blood in my veins seems to burn hotter as I dig my fingers deep into his hand, but he barely acknowledges it. "The world isn't just about power. It's about balance. Compassion. Strength without heart is nothing but a curse." I wheeze.

Arius's lips curl into a mocking smile. "You've learned nothing. Do you think your so-called compassion will save you? It'll only make you weaker. That's why you're still standing here, fighting me, instead of accepting your place in the world."

I don't have time to respond. A blur of motion catches my eye. Imran, always the brave one, charges toward Arius, his eyes filled with rage. "Crilt!" He tosses something through the air toward me—a sword. It's his spare, and without thinking, I reach out and catch it mid-flight. With that momentary distraction, I manage to get out of his tight grasp. The second my fingers close around the hilt, I feel a gust of wind cut through the air, and before Imran can even get close to Arius, the air shifts with a violent force. A shockwave of demonic power bursts outward from Arius, and the gust knocks Imran off his feet, sending him flying through the air like a ragdoll. He crashes to the ground with a sickening thud.

My heart skips a beat as I watch him crumple and groan in pain. Rage pulses through me. I turn my gaze back to Arius, whose smile remains as cold as ever. His eyes lock on mine again, and in that moment, a flicker of something—something akin to amusement—passes over his face.

"Is that it?" Arius asks, his voice dripping with condescension. "Is this all you have left to fight with? A few weaklings and your human ideals?" His gaze flicks over to Imran, now struggling to get up, before returning to me. "Pathetic."

But I can feel the bloodlust creeping deeper into my bones. I can feel it taking hold, the familiar, dark surge of power threatening to overwhelm me. The taste of it is almost sweet, like poison on my tongue. My vision starts to swim, and a sharp, agonizing pain shoots through my skull. It feels like my brain is being cleaved in two, my body caught in the throes of a storm I can't control.

I fight against it, pushing it down, forcing myself to focus, but the pain is unrelenting. "Ah!" I scream, feeling my head split in two. Blood drips from my eyes like tears, staining my vision crimson, but I don't stop. I can't stop. My legs move on their own accord, my body driven by sheer will and the desperate desire to kill.

With a cry, I charge.

The world spins around me as I rush forward, faster than I've ever moved before. My sword flashes through the air, cutting through the space between us. I'm not thinking. I'm not calculating. I'm just acting, driven by the need to make him pay, to end this madness.

Arius doesn't move.

At the last possible moment, he raises his right arm, and my sword clangs off his armor with a violent screech. The impact sends a shockwave of pain through my arm, but I don't stop. I swing again, faster, pushing through the agony. The blood that drips from my eyes only seems to spur me on, my movements becoming more frantic, more desperate. Each swing feels like it could be my last, but I don't care.

I can feel the surge of power coursing through me, the bloodlust spreading through my veins like fire. Agony burns through me so sweet, setting my entire body aflame. The world seems to narrow, and I focus entirely on Arius—his movements, his expressions, the way his eyes flicker with something I can't quite understand. Surprise, maybe? Hesitation? It's fleeting, but it's there. For a moment, just a moment, I think I see him falter.

He's surprised by me.

The thought doesn't quite register until after I've already swung again, my blade cutting through the air toward his neck. But this time, he isn't as quick. This time, he's just a fraction of a second too slow.

The tip of my sword catches the edge of his armor, scraping against it. It's not a clean strike—far from it—but the glancing blow is enough to force Arius to stagger back. I can feel his surprise, the momentary hesitation. And I know—I know—that he wasn't expecting this.

For a fleeting moment, something deep inside me burns with hope.

But the pain in my skull becomes unbearable. I feel as if my entire head is being crushed under the weight of the bloodlust, under the weight of everything that's happened. My vision begins to blur again, the edges of reality distorting. The blood flows faster now, dripping freely from my eyes, making it almost impossible to see clearly.

Arius's expression hardens, and for a split second, I see the full force of his power ready to erupt. His eyes flash with fury, and before I can react, he steps forward, grabbing my wrist in a vice-like grip. The pressure is immense, and the pain in my head intensifies.

I gasp, but I won't stop fighting. I don't give in. With everything I have left, I twist my wrist, breaking free from his hold. I feel like I'm dying, I can barely see through the blood that clouds my vision, but I can feel the energy coursing through me, urging me on. Every instinct I have screams at me to push harder, to never give up, to fight with everything I have.

I swing again, harder this time, my body fueled by pain, rage, and sheer willpower. I strike out, aiming for his face, for his chest, anywhere that might bring me closer to ending this fight. And even though the pain in my skull is blinding, even though I can barely stand, I push myself forward.

Arius dodges, but just barely. My sword grazes his side, and this time, the wound is deeper. A thin trickle of blood runs down his armored side, staining the surface. For a moment, the sight of it—the sight of him, even just a little wounded—fills me with a sense of victory, however fleeting.

But Arius doesn't flinch. He doesn't scream in pain or rage. He doesn't show the slightest hint of weakness. Instead, his lips curl into a small, almost amused smile.

"Impressive," he murmurs, his voice low, almost admiring. "You've got the blood of a warrior. You could have been something more. But instead, you choose to fight for a cause that will fall."

The world is a blur of motion, pain, and fury as I move, a blur of flesh and blood on a collision course with Arius. His cold green eyes meet mine with that same unnerving composure, that angers me even more. I can feel the bloodlust pulsing through my veins, urging me onward with an intensity that burns like fire in my chest.

I'm not thinking anymore. I can't think. I don't even think I'm able to. There's only the fight, only the rhythm of the sword clashing against his, the sharp, metallic tang of blood in the air, the sound of our grunts, the agony that threatens to take over my body. The pain in my skull worsens with every blow, and each swing of my sword, but I push through it. I force myself to ignore it. It's a crushing weight like the very earth is trying to crush me into the dirt, but I keep pushing.

The impact of our swords ringing together sends tremors through my body, and I feel the muscles in my body burning from the effort. Arius's strikes are precise, and deadly, like a serpent's strike, but I meet them with a force that's born from desperation, from the frantic need to stop him before he can bring about the chaos he envisions. My strikes are fast, fueled by anger and desperation, but I know deep down that it's not enough to merely react to him. It's maddening.

The sound of our blades clashing rings in the air like the crash of thunder sparks flying with each strike. My movements are becoming more erratic, more wild, but they have a certain precision. I've pushed myself beyond what I thought I could do. My body feels like it's on the brink of collapse, but I won't stop.

The longer I fight, the more I realize: Arius is struggling. He's not used to being pushed back, not like this. There's something in the way his brows furrow, the tension in his shoulders, that tells me I've broken through his calm façade. I can see it in his eyes now—a flicker of something. Doubt? Hesitation? For a fraction of a second, I think I see a brief glimmer of recognition, but it's gone just as quickly as it came.

He's surprised.

And it satiates a sadistic part of my soul. Yes. I want more. I need more. I want to see him powerless, under my mercy. I want to see the fear in his eyes. The realization that he can never win.

I push forward with everything I have left. My legs move on their own, fueled by adrenaline, my sword swinging with deadly intent. Each strike lands with the force of a storm. His armor, made for deflecting blows, cracks slightly with each hit. His green eyes, normally so cold and calculating, flash with something new—something closer to frustration. He blocks my sword with his, the clang of metal reverberating in the air, but I see it now. The mask is slipping.

In the corner of my eye, I see Kamea helping Imran up on his feet, both watching with shock on their faces, their gazes locked on the fight, not sure if they should intervene—if they even can, or if I'm capable of winning.

I glance back to Arius, who stands unwavering in front of me, eyes gleaming with cold fury. He swings again, but I'm faster. I can feel the surge of strength in my limbs as I duck under his blade and spin to the side, narrowly avoiding the deadly arc of his sword. For a split second, I'm inside his guard.

I charge again, sword raised, and at that moment, everything seems to slow. My body moves on instinct now, reacting before I even know what I'm going to do. I shift my weight, moving in a half-circle around him, aiming for his side, his blind spot. He tries to react, to bring his sword down in an attempt to block, but I'm already there.

I feint.

I swing low, making it look like I'm aiming for his legs, but at the last possible second, I twist my wrist, and my sword flies upward, catching the hem of his armor.

Arius, for just a heartbeat, hesitates. It's enough.

In one fluid, almost graceful motion, I dart forward, twisting my sword into his exposed side. My heart pounds in my chest, and for the briefest moment, time stops. I can feel the resistance of his muscles, and then the sickening feeling of flesh and bone giving way beneath the pressure. My eyes lock onto his, and I see something there. It's not anger, not hatred—there's something else, something unexpected.

Shock.

Arius's breath catches in his throat, and his grip on his sword slackens. For the first time in this fight, he falters. His eyes widen in disbelief. His mouth opens, but no words come out. His knees buckle, and for a second, it seems as though the world has stopped spinning.

And then, a slow, inevitable collapse. Arius falls to his knees, blood pouring from the wound I've inflicted in his chest. There's no rush of victory, no feeling of relief. I simply watch as the blood begins to pool beneath his body, staining the sand with a dark, sickening red. His breath rattles in his chest, his once confident stance now broken, and for the briefest second, I almost believe it's over. But then, with that same cold, calculating gaze, Arius shakes his head.

"You're a waste of potential," he coughs out, blood spattering from his lips as he speaks. His voice is empty and hollow, but there's still something in it—a final, mocking clarity that makes my stomach churn.

I clench my teeth, holding the sword firmly as I watch him. "I have humanity in me. That's why I won," I reply. "You're the one who lost, Arius. Not me."

For a long moment, there's only the sound of wind sweeping through the desert, carrying the scent of blood and dust. Then Arius laughs. It's a low, hollow sound, a rasping laugh that echoes in the silence. It's not a laugh of amusement. It's something darker, something maddening.

"You think you've won?" he croaks, blood oozing from the corners of his mouth. "You don't understand. You're just as weak as they are. You're all the same."

I grit my teeth, my grip tightening on the hilt of my sword. The words stung, but it's the look in his eyes that bothers me more. The coldness. The lack of anything—remorse, empathy, or even shame. His eyes are empty. No sign of humanity or anything that can prove that Arius is still in there. Absolutely nothing.

"Humanity is a weakness," he says through clenched teeth, his voice growing faint. "You should embrace it, Crilt. Embrace the demon blood that's running through your veins before it's too late. It's inevitable. All of you are fooling yourselves if you think you're any different from me. You're already a part of this world. You just don't know it yet."

His words hit harder than any blow. He's gasping for breath now, his body jerking as his strength fades away. But the darkness in his eyes doesn't falter. The emptiness. It seeps into my heart like a slow poison, and I feel that same cold creeping in.

I don't want to believe it. I don't want to accept it.

But deep down, I can't deny it. For the first time in a long time, a part of me wonders if there's any truth to his words. If all this fighting, all this bloodshed, was just the prelude to something far worse.

No. I can't go down that path.

I blink, shaking my head. No. I won't go down that path. I'm not like him. I'm not a monster.

But that thought lingers, twisting like a shadow in my mind.

Arius takes a final, shuddering breath. His chest rises one last time, and then he slumps forward, his body going limp in the sand. His sword falls from his hand with a clatter. Silence reigns over the battlefield.

I stare down at his body, my heart heavy in my chest. My breathing is ragged, my arms sore and aching, but there's something else. Something that's gnawing at the edges of my mind. Something that I can't shake. The bloodlust, the fury, the anger that had driven me for so long—it slinks back in like a snake, hiding in the deepest, darkest crevices of my soul. The pain that had twisted in my skull, driving me forward with such reckless abandon—it vanishes, as though it never existed.

I breathe deeply, trying to steady myself. My body feels exhausted and drained. I lower my sword and take a step back. I don't know what to feel.

But then, my gaze falls to Arius's weapon—the sword that had been so effortlessly wielded by the demon general. It's still lying there on the sand, its hilt glinting in the dim light as if waiting for someone to take it.

I reach down and pick it up, feeling the weight of it in my hands. The hilt is cold, and slick with the blood of its previous wielder. The blade is blackened and made of a strange material that almost seems to shimmer with an unnatural light. The scales that line the hilt are jagged, scaly, and dragon-like in their design.

I run my thumb over the edge of the blade. It's incredibly sharp. If I had been struck with this weapon, I would have been dead before I even had a chance to react. My chest tightens at the thought.

But I can't deny its practicality.

I don't want to take it, but I know I need it. I'll be the one to take over from Arius and lead a better legacy than he did. I grip the sword's hilt tighter, feeling the cold iron bite into my palm. It's not the weapon that makes me dangerous. It's the choices I make with it.

For now, this sword will be mine. I turn away from Arius's body, looking toward my companions. They've all been standing in stunned silence, watching the battle unfold, unsure of what to say, unsure of how to react. They've seen the madness in my eyes, the fury that drove me to fight, and now they see the aftermath.

Imran's eyes flicker between me and the sword in my hand, but he doesn't speak. Kamea stands a little further back, his face pale, expression unreadable.

I can't stand the silence anymore.

I take a step toward them, my boots crunching in the sand. The weight of the sword feels heavy in my hand, but I don't let it slow me down. I approach Imran first, and when he looks at me, I nod toward the blade.

"We've won. We've secured victory over Arius," I declare, raising the sword high up.

CHAPTER 10

The journey back to Ashroth is quieter than I imagined. The adrenaline of battle has long since faded, and the silence that now envelops us feels heavier with each passing step. Imran and Kamea fall into their usual banter, trying to fill the space with lighthearted conversation, but it's clear they're both deeply affected by what's happened. Their words are hollow like they're speaking through a fog, each of them trying to come to terms with the victory.

For me, it feels different. There's no sense of triumph in my chest. I don't feel like I've accomplished anything. The battle is won, sure. Arius is dead. The demon general who had once been a hero, a man I had once admired, is gone. But I don't feel like a hero. I feel empty like there's a hole in my chest where all those emotions should have been.

My hand tightens around the hilt of the sword, the new weapon a constant reminder of everything I've lost. I never thought it would come to this—never imagined that my journey would lead me to a moment where victory feels like a hollow ache. I had hoped, once Arius was dead, that I would feel fulfilled. I imagined standing over the corpse of the man who had betrayed everything I believed in, feeling a sense of justice, of righteousness. But what I feel is something far different: a quiet sense of dread, a gnawing in the pit of my stomach that won't go away.

Arius's death hasn't solved anything. It hasn't undone the damage caused by his betrayal. It hasn't erased the fact that the world is still teetering on the edge of destruction. The Demon King's forces are still out there, waiting for the right moment to strike. My mind races as I try to sort through my feelings, but everything is tangled, a knot I can't unravel.

As we travel through the barren lands, the desert stretching endlessly in all directions, my thoughts turn inward. I remember everything—the first time I learned about Arius, the way Arius had once been the beacon of hope for humanity. It felt like the start of something great back then, like I finally had something to aspire to, to emulate, during my confusion of being an adventurer. I had mapped a plan out, a path I should follow, a journey to restore balance, to defeat the Demon King and his army, then find Sokh and live happily ever after. That was the dream. But now the journey feels like a shadow, a distant dream tainted by the harsh reality of what I had to do to get here.

Sure, I have gained some experience. I'm stronger, faster, more skilled with a sword than I ever was before. But at what cost?

What does it mean to gain strength when the price is the very thing that makes me human? What does it mean to win a battle when it feels like I've lost a part of myself along the way? I had thought, in my naïveté, that defeating Arius would make everything right again, that this feeling would lift. But instead, it feels like the burden has grown heavier. The bloodlust, the anger, the pain—these things are all still there, buried deep within me, waiting to burst out and claim me.

And it's not just the loss of Arius that haunts me. It's the realization that I've been changed by this war, by everything I've seen, everything I've done. There's a part of me that is no longer the same person who first set out on this journey. I've seen more deaths here than I have ever experienced in the dungeon. I have embraced my demon blood in ways I never thought I would. The bloodlust that surged through me during the fight with Arius, the raw power that came from tapping into my darker side—it's still there, like a sleeping beast, waiting for me to let it out again.

And it's terrifying.

As we draw closer to Ashroth, my thoughts shift to the people waiting for us there. I wonder what kind of reception we'll receive. Will we be celebrated as heroes for killing Arius? Or will we be treated like weapons, tools in a war that has consumed so many lives?

I'm not sure what I want anymore. I never expected this to be easy, but I didn't expect it to feel this… empty. The reality of war has settled in like a stone in my chest. I don't know how to navigate this new world I've found myself in.

Imran looks over at me, his eyes full of concern. He's noticed my silence. "You good, Crilt?" he asks, his voice soft and concerned.

I force a smile, though it feels fake, hollow. "Yeah. Just tired."

Imran doesn't look convinced, but he doesn't press further. Instead, he changes the subject, trying to lighten the mood with one of his usual jokes. Kamea offers a small smile, but I can see the same unease in his eyes. He, too, feels the suffocating tension, even if he doesn't say it out loud.

***

As the days pass, I become more and more consumed by my own thoughts. I remember the way Arius had looked at me before he died—the way the fallen hero had mocked me, telling me that humanity was a weakness and that I would eventually embrace my demon side.

I don't want to believe it. I don't want to admit that there might be some truth to Arius's words. But deep down, there's a part of me that can't help but wonder if Arius was right. If the line between man and demon is truly so thin, then what does that make me? What does it make anyone?

I look down at my hands, clenching and unclenching my fists. I've used them to kill, to survive, to protect. But at what cost? The blood of my enemies, the blood of my allies—it all mixes together in a way that makes me sick to my stomach. And yet, there's no going back now.

The war is far from over, and the battles ahead will only be harder. But for now, the quiet uncertainty in my chest is all-consuming. I've survived the battle, but what about my soul? What's left of it after all I've been through?

And as I look around at my companions, I wonder if they, too, are feeling the same way.

***

Ashroth is a city of celebration, the streets alive with joy and the sound of laughter, its cobbled paths a blur of bustling activity as the news of the demon general's death spreads like wildfire. The people of Ashroth pour into the streets, draped in banners and waving flags, as the city's defenders return home victorious. The cheers grow louder as we make our way through the throngs of people, though I barely hear them. My mind is far away, lost in thoughts that won't leave me in peace.

It's strange, I think, how easily it all comes. The praise, the recognition. It's funny how a few months ago, I received scorn and dirty looks for my appearance, now I'm adorned with praises and celebrations like a cloak that doesn't fit, too tight and uncomfortable around my shoulders. I've done what was expected of him. I've fought, I've bled, and I've killed. And yet, none of it feels worth it. Not even their acknowledgment is enough to make up for anything. Not after everything I've seen, everything I've been forced to do.

The cheers grow louder as we pass through the gates of Ashroth, the city now a festival of noise and color. People throw flowers at our feet, raising their arms in triumph, hailing us as heroes. Kamea smiles and waves, Imran grinning and pumping his fist in the air. But I remain here, unfazed and wishing for it all to be over.

Humanity is a weakness.

The words ring into my ears without warning, like a curse.

I briefly wonder if Arius has gone through this before. All these feelings that are wedged deep in me, has he had such a conflict before. Has he fought a battle before, feeling dissatisfied with himself and everything else? Has he questioned life after that? How did he cope? What was his struggle? There are too many questions to ask, and I have no answers now. He's dead.

I can't shake the thought. If Arius could fall so completely, do I think that I am immune to it?

The demons in me—his blood, the curse that runs through my veins—had given me power. It had made me stronger, faster, more deadly. But the humanity in me is what keeps me from losing control. Am I on the same path Arius had walked? Would I, too, lose myself to the very thing that makes me powerful?

Is this the price of strength?

My chest tightens, and for the first time I feel the bloodlust creeping into my chest, and instead of pushing it back, I welcome it into my soul, unafraid. The only thing keeping it from overtaking me is my need to find Sokh.

But…why?

Why this sudden feeling? Is it because I'm a Demi-human? Do Demi-humans face this horrific and constant battle?

There are also the words Arius and Zaroth said to me, back at the Endzone, saying that I slipped out of their grasp. I don't know what they're talking about, and how they even know me in the first place. Maybe they know why I keep going into a frenzy, but it's not like I can go up to the Demon Generals and ask them about my heritage.

I sigh. There are so many questions left unanswered, and it makes me feel so anxious and unsettled on the inside.

The question lingers in my mind. Why did I become an adventurer in the first place? I can't even remember what my goal was anymore. Was it because I wanted to protect people, to do good? Or have I been looking for something more—something like the thrill of battle, the power to change the world through force? I'm not sure anymore. I thought that being an adventurer would give me purpose, but now it feels like I'm stumbling through a fog, unsure of where I'm going or why.

Kaze catches up with us as we make our way through the city, her face lighting up when she sees me. The way she smiles at me, as though everything is right with the world, makes my stomach churn. She's waiting for me to celebrate, to join the others, but I don't know how to explain what's swirling inside me.

"Crilt!" Kaze calls out, her voice is full of excitement. "You're a hero now! We all are! You should come to celebrate with us. It's your time to shine!"

I force a smile, but it doesn't reach my eyes. "Maybe later," I say, my voice distant, almost absent.

Kaze doesn't seem to notice. She leans in, pulling me into a quick hug. I nearly flinch at the sudden contact. "You deserve it, Crilt. You fought for us. For all of us."

The words fall flat, leaving a hollow feeling in my chest. I'm not sure if I deserve it. I don't feel like a hero. And I don't even know if I want to be one anyway. Not after all the killing, the bloodshed, the lives lost. Not after everything I've seen and done.

I watch Kaze walk away, her eyes still filled with hope, unaware of the storm brewing in my chest. I stay behind, standing just inside the entrance of the inn as the sounds of the celebration grow louder, the city's pulse echoing around me. I could join them. I can go back to the others, pretend, and join in their revelry, let the happiness wash over me like it does for everyone else. But something inside me keeps me rooted in place.

The room is dark when I slip into it, the cool evening air flowing in through the open window, the faint hum of the city outside barely reaching my ears. I sit down on the bed, staring at the wall as I try to calm my thoughts.

What am I doing here?

The question echoes in his mind, louder this time. Why did I start this journey?

I wanted to find Sokh. I wanted to be more than just a nobody, to help my people, to act as a symbol of revolution. But now that he's here—now that I've killed, now that I've fought—and now that I've finally taken down Arius—all that I want to attain is at the top of a mountain, and I'm merely at the bottom.

What was the point of it all?

Who am I joking? Someone like me, being a revolutionary hero to help save Demi-humans? I'm so naïve.

That's one thing I've noticed as a pattern throughout my stay in this world. My naïvety. I think that I'm experienced, I'm old enough to know what path to follow, and what to choose, but each time, it all backfired on me.

I was naïve to idolize Arius.

I was naïve to still believe in him after clear evidence showed me that he was indeed an enemy.

I was naïve to think that I can navigate this world without being scarred.

I was naïve to compare the deaths of actual people, to the deaths of monsters in the dungeon. They're nothing alike, and look how it has affected me. Look how it has scarred me.

Look where my naïveté got me.

I could have been happy before. I could have been adamant and chosen to look for Sokh, to prevent all this from happening. But instead, I chose to follow a path that led me through blood, death, and destruction.

I know a lot of good came out of all this, I made two good friends, I've learned a lot in my time here, I've experienced great things, and I'm not as lonely as I was back then. And besides, if I had left, Arius would have destroyed Ashroth anyway. Thanks to my help, we defeated him.

But is all the trauma worth it?

I think back to the time before all this, when I was just a boy with a sword, training with Sokh, learning how to be strong. How times have changed.

I lie back on my bed, staring up at the ceiling. The blood of Arius on my sword, the cheers of the crowd, the knowledge that they had won. But all I can feel is emptiness.

I grip the sword, Arius's sword, in my hands. Its weight feels familiar now, I trace the markings on the hilt absentmindedly, feeling it pulse under the surface. I can slowly begin to feel the fatigue wash over me, and I allow it to consume me, to take me far away from this ache that I feel.

EPILOGUE

I stand at the edge of Ashroth's gates, watching the horizon. The sun is setting, casting an orange hue over the distant mountains. The air is cold, biting with the reminder of how unforgiving the world can be. My breath comes out in slow, steady clouds as I take in the scenery, the quiet aftermath of it all. I feel a little at peace here, I discover. Just a small, calming sense of peace that lasts for a few seconds, but I savor it.

My mind has been in such a turmoil, that I appreciate every little moment of it that I can get.

The Demon King is still out there. His generals remain, and I've only just begun to scratch the surface of what's truly happening. Arius's death might have been a small victory in the grand scheme of things, but it's only a fraction of the war that's unfolding in the shadows. The pieces are in motion, and we're all just players in a game far larger than any of us realized.

I turn away from the horizon, walking back into the town, the weight of my thoughts dragging at me. Ashroth's celebrations are still in full swing, but I'm not in the mood for their hollow cheers, faux smiles, and praises. They're celebrating a battle, not a war. I can't let myself get swept up in it. Not yet. Not until I know more until I understand the full extent of what we're up against.

Imran and Kamea are still in the tavern, no doubt basking in the praise they've earned. I don't blame them for doing so, they've put in the work and they've earned it, and I have no right to impose on them with my depression.

I push open the door to the tavern, just slightly, the warm air washing over me. It's a stark contrast to the cold outside, but it does nothing to settle the storm in my chest. I glance around, catching sight of Kamea and Imran at a table in the back, laughing and talking with the others. They're happy. They should be. I should be there, celebrating with them, but I can't bring myself to. I can't push all these thoughts down.

For now, though, I know I can't stop. I need to get stronger. The war isn't over, and the demons aren't done yet. The fight is far from finished, and I have no choice but to keep going.

But for now, I think I'm just going to try to relax and take it easy. I push open the tent of the tavern, finally summoning up enough courage to enter. The low murmur of conversation fills the room, the clink of mugs, the occasional laughter, and the soft crackle of the hearth. The scent of roasting meat and spilled ale hits me all at once, a sensation that both comforts and stirs something restless in my chest. Imran looks up at me and his face lights up when he sees me, and I can already hear the shift in the atmosphere, the way the chatter livens up a bit when the other patrons turn their heads.

I can't even stop the small smile breaking out on my face even if I wanted to. I make my way over, boots scraping against the wooden floor. Kamea's at the table too, his dark eyes catch mine as I approach, a small smile tugging at his lips.

"Crilt!" Imran booms, his voice carrying across the room as he straightens up, wiping his hands on his trousers. "There he is! The man himself!"

I sit with them, me and Kamea watching Imran and the rest of them go on with their silly shenanigans with amusement. Maybe this is all that I need. I might not be fully okay, but right now, I feel content with my friends by my side.